Praise for *House of Holes*

"Truly uproarious. . . . Fiendishly clever. . . . [one of] the most consistently enticing writers of our time. . . . [R]eaders with a taste for richly ridiculous diction, witty prov. . . . [p]rose that celebrates desire, frailty and the comedy of life will not be disappointed. . . . Hilarious and extremely dirty."

—Sam Lipsyte, front cover of the *New York Times Book Review*

"Wild and hallucinatory. . . . Every page offers something smart and amusing. . . . The book reads like good-natured, priapic, free-form performance art . . . full of fearlessness, cheerfulness, wit and brio."

—Meg Wolitzer, *The Washington Post*

"Baker is one of the most beautiful, original and ingenious prose stylists to have come along in decades. He has some of his idol Updike's visual acuity and some of Nabokov's gift for metaphor, but he is funnier than either and takes a kind of mad scientist's delight in the way things work and how the world is put together. . . . *House of Holes* is as funny as it is filthy and breathes new life into the tired, fossilized conventions of pornography in a way that suggests a deep, almost scholarly familiarity with the ancient tropes."

—Charles McGrath, *The New York Times Magazine*

"Awe-inducing. . . . A joyful, almost Chaucerian book. . . . How has the English language done without *fuckwizard, manslurp,* and *thundertube*? I am not sure, but Nicholson Baker's awe-inducingly smutty *House of Holes* contains these pleasing new coinages, along with many others. . . . Had Dr. Seuss been a slightly insane pornographer, he might have written a book like this."

—Tom Bissell, *GQ*

"Nicholson Baker, grand master of minutiae, famously elevates the trivial to the level of high art and the deeply personal; nowhere is this gift for the explicit more heralded than in his erotic novels—with *House of Holes,* 'a book of raunch,' he reaches new heights of perversity and humor."

—*Vanity Fair*

"A sexy, disturbing, funny book. . . . *House of Holes* will no doubt attract attention and a certain amount of stylish ridicule for its manic preoccupation with sex, its boundless, resourceful, outrageous, cartoonish pornography, but it is altogether a darker, stranger, funnier, and more complicated book than that attention will imply. . . . *House of Holes* takes on a culture entranced by pornography, a culture that sees and feels in fragments; it dwells on the twist and fetish, and investigates generalized emptiness and banal sexual searching and exhilarating trysts in a comic, alarming, celebratory, orgiastic portrait of Internet-inflected sexual desire. . . . Whether one loves or hates the book, it is the extravagant, bravura performance of a writer as truly, manically interested in craft as he is obsessed with sex. . . . It may also challenge the usual reader of literary novels with its sheer dazzling excess of imagination."

—Katie Roiphe, *Slate*

"A funny, frisky novel that brings sexy back in a way that Justin Timberlake never dreamed. . . . He reminds us that books can be fun and sexy, that literature can have just as much raw energy and liberating chaos as a good f*ck."

—Mark Haskell Smith, *Los Angeles Review of Books*

"The wit, the utopian vision, and the pornographic utility of *House of Holes* all arise from the same fact of its fictional universe: no one is ever really shocked. Obscene declarations of desire are met with unsurprised calm. Sex is never so far out of mind as to be startling or unwelcome. . . . A world of universal arousal is common enough in pornography, but Baker has fully realized its comic possibilities—specifically, the possibilities that a roomful of horndogs offers for the use of deadpan, comic understatement, and up-tempo romantic repartee. . . . Baker can conjure fantastical sexual scenarios and unspool yards of charmingly filthy dialogue."

—Elaine Blair, *The New York Review of Books*

"[Baker] may be the most profound and audacious literary extremist of our time. . . . Attention must be paid. And laughter must ensue—and rather a lot of it, too."

—Jeff Simon, *The Buffalo News*

NICHOLSON BAKER

HOUSE *of* HOLES

a book of raunch

SIMON & SCHUSTER PAPERBACKS

New York   London   Toronto   Sydney   New Delhi

Simon & Schuster Paperbacks
A Division of Simon & Schuster, Inc.
1230 Avenue of the Americas
New York, NY 10020

First Simon & Schuster trade paperback edition February 2012

SIMON & SCHUSTER PAPERBACKS and colophon are registered
trademarks of Simon & Schuster, Inc.

For information about special discounts for bulk purchases,
please contact Simon & Schuster Special Sales at
1-866-506-1949 or business@simonandschuster.com.

The Simon & Schuster Speakers Bureau can bring authors
to your live event. For more information or to book an event,
contact the Simon & Schuster Speakers Bureau at
1-866-248-3049 or visit our website at www.simonspeakers.com.

Designed by Joy O'Meara

Manufactured in the United States of America

1 3 5 7 9 10 8 6 4 2

TheLibrary of Congress has cataloged the hardcover edition as follows:
Baker, Nicholson.
House of holes : a book of raunch / Nicholson Baker.
p. cm.
I. Title.
PS3552.A4325H68 2011
813'.54—dc22   2010047433

ISBN 978-1-4391-8951-1
ISBN 978-1-4391-8952-8 (pbk)
ISBN 978-1-4391-8953-5 (ebook)

HOUSE
of
HOLES

Shandee Finds Dave's Arm

Shandee's sister gave her all her makeup because she was going off to Guatemala. That night Shandee spent about two hours trying on lipstick. Then, the next morning, she went to a quarry with her Geology 101 class. The quarry was called the "Rock of Ages." It was vast and they dug granite there, mostly for tombstones. The tour guide was kind of cute although his hair wasn't good—he was maybe twenty-seven. Pretty drastically cute, though, she thought. They were standing on the brink of a space that looked like something from another planet, and he said, "There's enough granite here to last us four thousand five hundred years." My gracious goodness, thought Shandee, that's a lot of tombstones. She turned away from the edge, and that's when she saw a hand poking out from behind a rock.

While the others listened to the tour guide, she went over to the hand. The hand was attached to its forearm, and there was a clean torn cloth wrapped around the end that would have been

1

attached to the rest of his arm. There was no blood on the cloth. Shandee picked it up and felt it. It was warm; the fingers moved a little. The hand pointed urgently at her bag, so she stuffed it inside and went back to the group and listened to the rest of the tour.

When she got home she pulled the forearm out and laid it on her bed. It was strong, with sensitive fingers and a blue vein traveling up along the muscle on the underside. She lifted it and whispered, "Arm, can you hear me?"

In answer the arm caressed her cheek with two fingers. It had a gentle touch.

Shandee said, "Are you comfortable? Do you need anything?" The arm made a handwriting gesture. Shandee found a pen and handed it over. The hand wrote, "Please unwrap the rag and feed me some mashed-up fish food in an electrolyte solution."

"Where?" Shandee asked.

"Funnel it into the little hole with the green rim," the arm wrote. And then: "I'm glad you found me."

She unwrapped the towel and saw that the arm was capped with a sort of power pack made of black rubber. There looked to be a place for a battery and a place for waste to be discharged, and a place for nutrients to enter.

She had an intuition. "Are you Italian?"

"Half Italian, half Welsh," the arm wrote. "I'm known as Dave's arm."

"Well, Dave's arm, I'm very pleased to meet you." They shook. Then she noticed the clock. "Oh dear. Can you sit tight here for an hour?" she said. "I promised someone I'd go to his party and I can't bear to hurt his feelings."

Dave's arm scribbled something rapidly. "Sure, but—let me put on the lipstick for you," he wrote.

"Okay, you can try." Shandee grasped the arm firmly and held him so that his hand was in front of her mouth. He touched all the way around her lips, feeling the exact shape, and then, with very fine almost vibrating movements, he applied the lipstick. It was extremely red, a color called Terranova.

"Good job," said Shandee. "You're good. And this color is great." Her lips looked really luscious. "Thank you, Dave's arm."

He made a little nod with his hand and then, lifting the pen, reminded her that he needed to have some of the fish-food mash and to be relieved of his chemical wastes. She took him to the toilet and popped open a little vent on his cap. A tiny trickle of gray water dripped out. Then she fed him some fish-food gruel, and he seemed quite revived. He asked her to place him on the windowsill, because he had a solar panel for energy. She did, and then she went to the party and danced and had a wonderful time, but she came home early because she felt she had a new friend that she had to take care of.

When she got back her roommate Rianne was there. Rianne's lips were very red—she'd been sampling the new lipsticks, probably—and she was holding on to Dave's arm. The hand end was in her shirt, obviously doing something tender with one of her breasts. Rianne hurriedly drew him out. There was a pad of paper with lots of hasty writing scrawled on it next to where she was lounging on her bed.

"So, you've discovered my arm," Shandee said, with an edge.

Rianne nodded. "He has a lovely touch."

"That he does," Shandee agreed.

Rianne said that she'd found out quite a bit about the arm and where it came from. "It belongs to someone named Dave," she said.

"I knew that," Shandee snapped.

"He went to a place called the House of Holes. There Dave had requested a larger thicker penis. Apparently you can do that. But at a price. The director, this woman named Lila, said to him: 'Would you be willing to give your right arm for a larger penis?' Dave said no at first, because his right arm was necessary for his work. But Lila said that it was only temporary—only till someone found the arm and took it back and stuck it on him. Dave said, 'Oh, if it's temporary, sure.' So he underwent a voluntary amputation right near the elbow, and his arm had the self-contained life-support pack grafted on."

"You sure did find out a lot," said Shandee.

"I must say his touch is extremely sensitive," Rianne went on. She threw herself back on the bed and laid the arm on her chest.

Shandee watched the hand push aside the sides of Rianne's shirt and find her breast again.

"Hmm," Shandee said. "I don't know about this. I found him, not you." She felt finger-snappings of jealousy.

Rianne's lips parted. "Oh my gosh, his fingers know what to do," she said, flushing. The hand was gently rolling her nipple like a tender round pea. And then it surrounded her whole breast and shook it once. After that it turned and began crawling over her belly toward her pajama pants.

"Are you just going to let that happen?" Shandee said, riveted.

"Um, yes," she said. "Could you dim the light?"

Shandee turned off the overhead light and watched the arm undo the knot of Rianne's pajama bottoms. It disappeared. Rianne went "Shooooo."

Shandee turned away. "He's found it," Rianne said, "and, boy, he's got the touch of a master." Then her voice changed and she said, "Oh my god, two fingers. Haw. Haw." Shandee glanced at her. Rianne's knees had fallen apart and her eyes were slitted closed. "He seems to want to make me come, oh god, oh shit." Then: "Ham, ham, oo, oo, oo, oo, oo, oo, ham, ham, HAW!"

She lay still and held up the arm. He made an O with his fingers, which glittered with her sex juices.

"You want me to go with you?" Rianne said. "Okay, I'll go. Bye, Shandee, I'm going!" With that, her face and body began to blur, and she swooshed into a long thin shape that went through the finger-O of Dave's hand.

She was gone. The hand lay on the bed. It began crawling toward Shandee. It reached her thigh.

Shandee handed it a pen and folded back the yellow pad to give it a fresh page. "Where did my roommate go off to?" she asked.

"The House of Holes," the arm wrote. "Would you like to come, too?"

"Maybe," said Shandee. "How?"

"If you let me touch you," he wrote.

"Touch where?" said Shandee.

"Where it aches."

"It aches in my head," she said. "Never enough sleep."

"Let me help," the arm scrawled.

She held it, and the hand surged through her hair, and when she steered it around to the back of her neck it massaged the stiffness away.

His fingers were mobile and trembly now. She gave him back the pen. "Isn't there another place that aches?" he wrote.

"Yes," she said, "there is."

He wrote: "TWAT?"

"Mhm," Shandee said. "But I really don't think I can let you do that until I know you better. You need to be more than an arm to me."

"Take me to class tomorrow," he wrote.

The next morning she fed him some fish paste and drained his waste and wrapped the cloth around his life-support addendum and put him in her bag. In the middle of her nineteenth-century novel class she felt his fingers very gently brushing her calf. She reached down and held his hand and loved how it felt.

When she got home that afternoon, she washed the hand carefully in the sink and then took him back to her room and dimmed the lights and put on Appleseed's "When Are We Going (to Do It)." She said, "I'm ready for you to hold me now, any way you want."

His hand brushed over her lips—she was wearing Terranova again—and she opened her mouth and tasted his fingers, and he circled her tongue and tweaked it, and then as she steadied him he crawled down. She put her feet together and let her knees fall open. His hand found her stash and she looked down and saw his fingers half buried in her folds, and then she felt a warm filling feeling as first one, then two of Dave's fingers slid inside.

She held his arm and helped him angle his fingers in and then pull them out. Then she pulled him up to her clitty and he circled it. "Oh, that's nice," she said. Just before she came, he stopped and held his hand up to her mouth.

"What is it, baby?" she asked.

His fingers made the O and then he pushed the O shape to her mouth. She put her tongue through it, and her mind and neck and body stretched until they were very long and flowed through his fingers, and then his fingers flowed with her. She was pulled in a whoosh of wispiness, and she landed and condensed. Before her was a sign in the grass: "Welcome to the House of Holes."

She looked down at her hands. They were still holding Dave's arm.

Ned Gets Sniffed

Ned tapped the ball on the seventh green, using his new teryllium putter. It made an odd tight circle around the hole and then dropped in. "Did you see that weirdness?" said Ned, looking around for his golfer friends. But they were talking and hadn't seen it. No matter. Ned leaned to pull out the ball and heard strange sounds coming from the hole. He got down on his stomach to listen better. A woman's voice said, "Hi, Ned, my name is Tendresse. Come talk to me at the House of Holes."

"All right," said Ned. Immediately his head was jerked and stretched and twisted and atomized, and he was sucked powerfully down into the seventh hole. And then, a minute later, he rematerialized on a hillside full of clover and Queen Anne's lace, still wearing his golf hat, still holding his teryllium putter, but now without any pants on, just his black Eddie Bauer sports briefs. A small discreet sign in the grass said "All Bets Are Off." In the distance was a yellow Cape house with a wraparound porch, surrounded by softly swaying pale-green trees. Other bulky, oddly shaped buildings were visible behind it—in fact there seemed to be a whole complex of structures, including some sort of amusement park. A ridge of mountains hung smokily in the distance.

Ned, standing in the fragrant vetch, heard steps nearby. "Hi, welcome to the House of Holes, I'm Tendresse," said a pleasant woman with a strong aquiline nose. She had short brown hair pinned with a plain clip, and she wore a white linen skirt tied at her waist with a scarf. She was holding hands with a small, confused-looking bodybuilder carrying a squash racket. She was topless with interesting pointy nipples. "How was your trip?" she asked.

"Quick," said Ned. "I was in the middle of a round of golf and here I am."

"I gather your Bermuda shorts didn't make it through the First Conundrum. That can happen. Is that your putter, sweet attractive man?"

"Yes, it's new."

"Is it lively?" said Tendresse.

"Yes, it's very lively," said Ned.

"Good. This is Woo Ha—he's a new arrival, too. He plays squash."

Ned nodded at Woo, and Woo nodded warily back. Woo was also in his underwear.

"What do we do here?" asked Ned.

"I'm going to sniff your crotches, and then we're going to go on down the path to the house, where you'll meet Lila. Lila's the director. She'll talk to you, and you can describe your desires to her in detail if you want." She took Ned's hand, and they began walking down the stone path. "But I warn you both—this place is very, very costly."

"I own a tire company," said Woo.

Ned gave a short laugh. "I doubt it's worse than golf—the fees are bleeding me dry."

"Oh, yes it is, darling, much worse. We do have scholarships and work-study programs, though. For instance, if your sperm has magical healing powers, then you get a full scholarship. Does it?"

Ned thought. "I don't know. Maybe."

"Let me check for you. I'll have to sniff and juggle your balls. It's just a formality. Takes half a second."

"Okay."

"Woo, I'll do you first. Do you mind?"

"I don't mind," said Woo.

"Good." Tendresse knelt and tied her scarf around her eyes. Woo scooted his waistband down and clenched his fists in readiness. "Just hold your penis up out of the way, Woo, please."

Ned watched Woo flip his cock up. Tendresse pulled his slouchy hairless satchel toward her face and jostled its contents. "Nice size, nice movement," she said. She closed her eyes and sniffed. "Mmmmm, yes. Rainy ruins. Frogs. Cement statuary. Gongs. Tractor tires. Mushrooms."

Pleased, Woo said, "So do I have magic sperm?"

"No, sorry, no," said Tendresse. "But your balls are well shaped. Very nice pair. Thank you so much. You can pull your boxers up now."

Woo seemed disappointed. "Sometimes I do kinky things," he said defensively. "Once I let a girlfriend place a cucumber in my back end. It was a long British cucumber. They have the plastic sheath, and we thought that was safer."

"And how was it for you?" asked Tendresse.

"Good, but I had to go to the bathroom afterward."

"Please," said Ned.

"Now it's your turn," said Tendresse, turning to Ned. Ned held his cock up against his abdomen and stood with his legs a little apart so that Tendresse, still blindfolded, could smell his balls. She made several long sniffing sounds. "Mmmm, warm granite, campfires, catcher's mitts, Play-Doh, padded mailers. Very subtle. I think I know a good woman for you. I've sniffed hundreds of crotches, men's and women's. One couple I sniffed and matched got married. May I taste?"

"What on earth?" said Woo, outraged.

"By all means," said Ned.

Tendresse flicked her tongue over Ned's crinkled scrotatiousness, and then she drew the entire left ball into her mouth like a new potato. "Yow!" Ned said. His cock responded enthusiastically, although he had had a nice orgasm in the shower that morning. She suckled his other ball. Then she threw her head back and opened her mouth wide. "Now both together," she said. "Fill my mouth with the manly warmth of your nutbag."

"Very well," said Ned. He fed his manly nutbag into her mouth, and she made muffled gobbling and gargling noises.

"Just plain disgusting," said Woo, bending to get a better look.

"Now drop the cock," she said. "Drop it on my face, Ned. I want it."

Ned, canting his hips forward, let his cock fall gently against her nose.

"Mmmmmmmmm," said Tendresse, inhaling. "You do not have magic sperm, but I know several women for you. Come, let's meet Lila."

Luna Goes to a Concert

Luna met a man named Chuck at the soup kitchen. He was manning the sink and she was unloading the dishwasher, which wasn't an easy job because the steam was hot. They developed a nice wordless rhythm together of unloading and drying and stacking. Then, wiping the edge of the sink with a clean dish towel, Chuck directed his restless blue eyes directly at her and asked her if she would like to go with him to the Masturboats.

Just like that, all of a sudden: "Would you like to go with me to the Masturboats?"

"I'm not sure I'm ready for that," Luna replied with a laugh, not knowing exactly what the Masturboats were. But inside she was saying, Why not? Because she knew that his kind of easy glancing manner was not all that common. Men turned thirty-eight, thirty-nine, and it was like someone dimmed the lights. When they're young, they're hilarious and bubbly and boyish. And bad. So bad. When they're old, they're flat and stupid and dull. She watched them in airports with their wives: brain-dead, mostly. And yet this man, Chuck, was probably forty-five at least. He still had some humor left in him. He was funny about how hot the plates were. Not funny in a poking kind of way, but in a cheerful way. He had a shock of Jimmy Stewart hair that he flung around. In some ways a beautiful man, with a rough grace to him. Why had she refused his polite offer? Of course she should have said yes to the Masturboats, whatever they were. But she just didn't want to.

Chuck was unfazed. "Then would you like to go with me to an intimate concert of Russian piano music and sit in the Velvet Room, and I'll toy with your hair?"

She took a breath, thinking. "I like Russian music," she said finally. "That sounds nice. Sure."

First, though, she needed to go to Tan Wizards. She didn't want to have white shoulders when she wore her black dress with the spaghetti straps. She didn't want to be some blinking creature coming out of her nocturnal burrow for a grand musical adventure. She wanted to be working from a position of strength, with cinnamon-colored shoulders that shrugged and moved alluringly.

So she went to Tan Wizards and signed up. The girl there asked her which room she wanted, Room 1, Room 2, or Room 3.

"Which do you recommend for very fast results?" Luna asked.

"The bulbs are best in Room 3," the girl said, and she winked. "And I recommend this bronzer. It's on special, only twenty-seven dollars tonight."

"Leo's Tanlord Bronzer?"

"Yes, it's fantastic, it makes you irresistible."

So Luna went into Room 3 and closed the door. The upright tanning booth, with its rounded blue door, filled most of the room. There was a stool with a towel and a pair of goggles on it, and a clothes hook on the doorjamb. The walls were a deep red, and taped to one wall was a gross-out picture of an eye with a tumor in the tear duct, there to scare people into using eye protection. Next to the tumor picture was a large poster of a minister with a Bible in his hand, wearing a full robe, but exceedingly bronzed. The poster quoted him as saying that going tanning helped him be a better minister. Luna stripped down in front of the eye tumor and the tanned minister. Three eyes stared at her as she slathered on the Tanlord Bronzer. She circled her nipples with it and they began speaking to her in an odd kind of Braille.

With her goggles on, she pressed the on button and went into the warm blue privacy of the booth. It was loud, because there was a powerful fan over her head, and it lifted her hair up. She felt like Botticelli's Venus. She was standing nakedly there, with both her nipples on stun, and she heard a low voice behind her—almost a metallic voice, but confiding—and she felt some localized warmth on her shoulder. She said, "Who are you?"

"I'm Leo, the Lord of Tan," the voice said.

She looked back, and there standing close behind her was an elongated kind of luminous being, made up of long ultraviolet lightbulbs. He resembled a balloon sculpture, except that he was almost impossible to look at because he was so blindingly bright.

"Why are you here in the booth with me?" she asked.

"I'm giving you an irresistible allover tan," Leo the Tan Lord said, "and when I've given you an allover tan, I'm going to take you to the House of Holes, so that you can go with your new friend Chuck to an intimate concert of Russian piano music."

"This House of Holes," she said. "Is it safe?"

"They scan you seventeen ways when you're going in. Chuck is a recruiter, and he likes you, so you're getting a scholarship. Oop, it's rather close quarters in here. I'm afraid you've given me a large fluorescence."

Luna, glancing, couldn't help but admire the blinding wattage of Leo's long, warm blue bulbs. She felt she needed to be enveloped in his endless warmth. So she closed her eyes and let Leo do what he did so well. The fan was wonderfully loud, and Leo's humming bulbs felt good on her skin, and then he murmured, "Open yourself for me, let me take you to the House of Holes." She felt a long steady pressure, and then he lit her up inside. All at once she was liquefying into pure blue.

When the light went away, she was standing in front of the House of Holes concert hall, wearing her black dress and black stockings, still out of breath from her recent exertions. She looked at her shoulders—they were perfectly tanned, not too dark, just right. Chuck came up wearing a rumpled blazer, carrying floppy tickets. His shock of hair excited her.

"Hello, hello," he said. "You look lovely. I got us the Velvet Room."

They went inside, past the bar, and up a wide red stairway to the balcony level. It was very warm, and there were gold sconces in the shape of mermaids.

"Where's the rest of the audience?" Luna asked.

"It's a special kind of concert," said Chuck. They came to room 28L. The door said "Velvet Room." They went inside. It was very quiet, very private, and there were two holes in the wall. A strangely shaped low chair was positioned in front of the two holes.

"This is nice, but I can't see the stage," said Luna.

"You can't see the stage in the Velvet Room. It's not about seeing." Chuck smiled and moved his hand lightly over her hair. His eyes had an inner level, through the irises—it felt as if she was looking down a spiral staircase. "Now you must take off your shoes and your black stockings, although they're very nice, and sit in the chair."

"Okay," said Luna. She slipped off her stockings and handed them to him. He folded them and put them on a little side table.

"Good," said Chuck.

"And now I sit?"

Chuck nodded. "Make yourself comfortable," he said.

She sat and looked up at him, taking another hit of his eyes. The chair was low, and her dress rode up. "Sorry, a little indelicate here," she said, hitching to cover the sight of her red panties.

"Don't worry. You're going to put your legs through the holes."

"Now?"

Chuck nodded.

She pointed her right foot and put it through the hole. Then her left foot.

"Good," said Chuck. "All the way now."

Luna scooted forward on the seat.

"A little further," said Chuck, taking a position behind her in the chair. Luna felt her legs dangling out in space, and then she felt a man's hand touch her and cradle her right heel. "I do believe someone is holding my foot," she said.

"That's Alexander," said Chuck.

The touch was gentle, and Luna sensed that Alexander

16

had a little French-style goatee, perhaps. She could hear him murmuring. Her main thought was: Boy am I glad I shaved my legs this morning.

"What's he saying?" she asked Chuck.

Chuck turned up a volume dial. "You can speak to him if you'd like," he said.

"May I ask who you are?" she asked politely.

The hands stopped. "I am Alexander Borodin, the very famous Russian composer," said the voice.

Luna looked back at Chuck, who had begun playing with her hair. "But Alex," she said, "didn't you write the *Polovetsian Dances* something like a hundred and twenty, hundred and thirty years ago?"

"Yes, but I'm here now to play your leg like the keys of a piano keyboard," he said.

Chuck kissed her forehead. "Just enjoy it."

"Okay, carry on," Luna said.

Alexander began to play. He was up and down her leg, her thigh, trilling away on her kneecap, glissandoing down her calf. She leaned back and sighed a soft, murfling sigh, allowing her head to fall into Chuck's lap. "Oh, sorry," she said, feeling a large lump there.

"May I unpin this bauble from your hair?" Chuck asked.

Luna's eyes were closed. She nodded. Chuck took out the barrette and leaned and kissed her on her ear. Then, when Luna was almost swept away by the music on her right leg—she could hear it perfectly—suddenly she felt another man's hands on her left leg.

"Wait, who are you?" she asked.

The hands held her leg very firmly and confidently. "I am Nikolai."

"Nikolai who?"

"Nikolai Rimsky-Korsakov, the very famous Russian composer," the voice said. "I will be playing a piano transcription of my very famous *Scheherazade*."

"Where?"

"On your nude left leg. Starting now."

The two composers began fingering and squeezing her legs with great intensity, and then, as if by mutual agreement, they both seized her legs and gave a strong but gentle pull, sliding her farther down in her chair. "Woopsie," said Luna.

"Don't worry," said Chuck softly. "They're just pulling you down so that you're fully seated in the pussy cradle."

"Of course, the pussy cradle," said Luna, as her pussy made firm and not unpleasant contact with a curved item covered in black leather and shaped a little like a bicycle seat. It fit her just right, and the two composers now began pulling and stroking with a soft sort of insistent rhythm.

Luna rocked herself into it and she heard Chuck make a slight growling sound as he traced his fingertips over her neck.

"Chuck," she said, "seriously, what's going on here? This is getting down to the nitty-gritty."

Chuck laughed. "It's what happens at the House of Holes."

Luna thought, Why not? She let her head fall back again till she could feel some of Chuck's interesting groin bundle through his black pants. It pushed against the side of her head. Just then her attention was diverted by something stiff and warm tracing the curve of the arch of her foot.

"Mr. Borodin, is that you?" she said.

"Yes, that is my cock," said Alexander Borodin. "It is very hard and very famous."

"I see," she said. "It tickles a little. And you, Mr. Rimsky-Korsakov?"

"One moment!" said Rimsky. "And now, my cock, too!"

There was another resilient stiffness against her toes. Luna pushed back with both feet and felt both cocks standing hard against the composers' taut bellies. They both seemed surprisingly fit for musicians.

"How's the music going for you?" Chuck murmured into her hair.

"It feels good to have two stiff Russians pushing against the soles of my feet," said Luna, smiling up at him.

"Good," said Chuck. Then convulsively he whispered something in her hair that she didn't catch.

"What's that?"

"Nothing."

"No, Chuck, please tell me what you said."

"I said, 'I wish I could fuck you in the mouth with my cock and come all over your pretty lips.'"

"Woo, Chucky." Luna got a melty feeling in her shoulders. She turned and squashed her face against his lap, inhaling his warm cocoa-bean smell through his dress pants. The smell went right to her head. "Hurry, because this pussy cradle is feeling way too good."

Out flopped the enormity of Chuck's dick, poking stiffly between his white shirttails. It came to rest on her lips.

"Jesus, that's a nice dick, Chuck. My god. Rimsky, Alex, don't stop!" She bucked against the pussy cup. "Nnnnnng! This is way too good!"

She threw her head back and opened her mouth for Chuck's cockness. "Fuck my mouth!" she said.

Borodin and Rimsky-Korsakov were squeezing her calves and doing mad cocky things at her toes. "My penis is coming right now!" moaned Borodin. "My penis is coming, too!" said Rimsky-Korsakov. "Oh god, Chuck, I can't hold back much longer," said Luna. "Stuff my mouth with that fucking beast!" She ground her pussytwat against the crotchy holder, lifting her hips high to hold the moment in suspense. "Nnnnng-aaaaa!" She let her orgasm wave crash down just as she felt two hot blasts of white Russian semen drizzle against her toes.

"Phew," she said, breathing deeply, but she wanted more. She pulled her legs from the holes. "Now really fuck me, Chuck. No pussy cradle. I want to feel you inside."

Chuck turned the chair around. "You ready?" She nodded, feeling the Russian sperm cooling on her feet. Chuck's thundertube of dickmeat started sliding in. It pushed her frilly doilies of labial flesh aside, and it kept on going till it couldn't go any farther. She grabbed his hips and pulled him in, and then he pulled out, leaving her empty and waiting, and then he slammed into her train station again. His cock train was commuting in and out of her pussyhole, filling and emptying it by turns, and she loved it.

She heard him say, "Here it comes, oh, here it comes," almost in a whimper, and then he made a strange guttural cry that sounded like a tree cracking before it fell, and then a sound like a monster in a Japanese monster movie, and she felt a flowering of deep warmth inside her, and the sense of hot sperm that surrounded the prow of his still thrusting peckerdickcock.

"Thank you for the lovely concert of Russian piano music," Luna said.

Pendle Interviews for a Job

Pendle read about nuclear waste in *The Rooster* while he was waiting for the woman at the burrito store to make his burrito and wrap it in foil and put it in a paper bag so that he could go home and eat it while listening to the rest of a *Scientific American* podcast on the physiology of romance. In the *Rooster* personals an ad caught his eye. It said, "ARE YOU able to enter an alternative universe? ARE YOU friendly? CAN YOU interview people about their sexual experiences? Good money, pleasant living quarters, must like naked people and be willing to relocate." There was a small round black circle at the bottom of the ad—no address or phone given.

Pendle peered closely at the ad, and suddenly he felt a powerful air current pulling his hair and the whole of his head downward. He was vacuumed down into the black circle. He lost consciousness for a moment, and when he came to he was in Lila's office. Lila was the director of the House of Holes. She was large and pretty in bifocals, about fifty, with lots of loose light-brown hair. Pendle told her that he was there about the job in *The Rooster*.

"Ah, we filled that position yesterday," said Lila. "But just for the heck of it, why don't you give me a sample of your interview technique."

"I'd probably just say, 'So tell me what happened.' People seem to open up to me. It's been true my whole life. I don't know why, exactly."

"It's your eyebrows, I think," said Lila. "I see a forgivingness and a directness there. Now what if you were a client and I interviewed you? What if I said, 'Be honest, why are you here?'"

"I guess I'm here to see women naked."

"This is an unusual place, and it'll cost you a lot of money," said Lila. "I mean a lot, lot, lot of money."

"That's too bad," said Pendle, "because right now I don't have a lot of money."

"Maybe you better come back when you do," said Lila.

"How much money do I need?"

"How much nakedness do you want? Be honest. So few people are able to tell the truth."

"Let's see." Pendle took a deep breath and then poofed it all out. "I think I need twenty-four horny nude women at the same time."

"Twenty-four?" said Lila. "I don't often tell people this, but you know that a man can really only handle one horny nude woman at a time. Maybe two. Even with two, it's like that trick where you have to circle your head and pat your stomach. Do you want to reconsider? Think."

Pendle closed his eyes and visualized his dream of desire. He didn't need twenty-four horny women, he realized, only eight. He wanted some of them to have merry little breasts, and some huge soft heavy sad hangers, and he wanted some of them to be fairly old and some of them to be fairly young, and some to have throaty brunette voices and some wispy chirpy blond voices. He wanted them all to be on their knees on couches and chairs with their asses up and ready and their slippy sloppy fuckfountains on display. He'd walk in front of them holding his generous kindly forgiving dick, saying, "Do you want this ham steak of a Dr. Dick that's so stuffed with spunk that I'm ready to blow this swollen sackload all over you?" And they'd all say, "Yes, Mr. Fuckwizard, we want that fully spunkloaded meatloaf of a ham steak of a dick."

Pendle explained all this to Lila as well as he could. "They'd be supercharged and overdosed with horniness," he said, "because for eight days beforehand each one of them would have been imagining that eight guys were in front of her staring at her and pumping off their meatsticks, and each guy who's pumping his meatstick would have been imagining for eight days that he was in a room with eight lovely ultrahorny women, and those women would be imagining that they're in a room with eight ultrahorny meatsticks, and so on."

"Gee whiz." Lila reached for a calculator. "So far your dream involves slightly more than four thousand people," she said.

"If it does, it does," Pendle replied. "Actually my dream involves every woman in the world."

"Ah, does it?"

"Yes. I want every woman in the world to see my dick. I want you to see it, for instance."

"Not right now," said Lila.

23

"You could make a movie of me holding my dick and then project it on the moon. I'd like that."

"That's not really our style," said Lila, "but I like your ambition. Tell you what. Daggett! Daggett will give you a twenty-minute tour now, so you have a sense of what you're in for, and then why don't you go away and earn, say, thirty-five hundred dollars somehow, and come on back and we'll give you a work-study position here. That's a steep discount. How does that sound?"

"Good."

Daggett gave Pendle a brief tour of the House of Holes, and then Pendle went back to where he lived. He spent three weeks earning money at a landscaping company, spreading black mulch and digging holes and spreading sod. A woman came by in a van sometimes with flats full of purple flowers. She spent all morning planting the purple flowers, and then she washed the dirt off her hands and rested. Her name was Loxie.

"Why are you working here?" Loxie asked Pendle one day. "You look like your mind's somewhere else."

"I'm earning money to go to the House of Holes," said Pendle. "It's this incredible special place where sexual things happen and you get to see women naked. But it costs a lot, lot, lot of money. So I'm saving up."

Loxie was puzzled. "You have to go to a special house to see a woman naked?" she said. "Can't you just walk up to a woman and say, 'I'd like to see you naked?'"

Pendle was scandalized. "No, that would be rude. Plus it wouldn't work. And anyway I wouldn't do that unless I wanted to become boyfriend and girlfriend with her, and that sometimes leads down a long and winding road, if you know what I mean."

Loxie shook her head. "Whoa, tell me about it." Then she said, "Do women go to the House of Holes, not to work there as naked ladies but just to go? To meet a man?"

"Sure they do," said Pendle. "It's for everybody. Everybody when they're in that late-night New York state of mind. And any guy who brings a woman gets a fifty-percent discount."

Loxie sat for a moment, thinking. Then she sniffed. "Will you tell me something that happened at the House of Holes so I'll know kind of what to expect? I mean, if I ever go there?"

"Let me think for a second," said Pendle. "I just had a quick tour. One thing is you can get an ass-squeezer's license, which is a piece of paper that allows you to walk up to any woman you like and say, like, 'Hello, I've got an ass-squeezer's license, may I squeeze your ass now?' And she has to say yes. That on its own is worth the price of admission."

"What happens if the girl still says no when you show her the license?"

"Then the magical clothes-dissolving wind comes up, which is a special warm breeze that comes sweeping down the middle of O Street. It dissolves her clothes to a fine dust."

"So she's naked," said Loxie.

"Yes, she's naked. Which is not a bad thing, but maybe she liked those clothes. Women really pay attention to their clothes."

"I have to say the ass-squeezer's license does very little for me," said Loxie. "What else happens at the House of Holes?"

Pendle picked up a chunk of mulch and rolled it in his fingers. "There's the Porndecahedron, which is this special twelve-screen projection theater."

"Porn, ugh. So sick of it. What else?"

"Oh, let's see. There are the darkrooms, where it's all pitch-black and you talk. And there's the International Couch. Daggett showed me that one last."

"That sounds interesting."

"Yeah, it's a whole lot of women from all countries, all ages, all weights, Finnish women, French, Chilean, Canadian—Toronto women are so hot, I think—and they're all kneeling on this superlong stretch couch with their asses up, waiting, toying with their tender bits, and you get to hump your way right down the line."

"You mean you just say hello and start fucking?" said Loxie. "Isn't that a little cold?"

"No, it's more like, 'Hello, how are you today? What a lovely warm Tuesday afternoon.' And she says, 'Allo,' or 'Hi,' and you say, 'May I?' And she says yes, and then you ease yourself into her for fifteen seconds, and you get the incredible sensation of those first few humps—I call them the groaners. You get that fantastic new groaning feeling, oh, oh, fuuuhck, oh, and she holds very still or maybe not, maybe she tosses her hair around, and then you pull out and give your cock a quick breather so that it doesn't come, which it's threatening to do, and you say, 'Thanks, sweetheart,' and you move down one and do it again. Groan it in."

"Hm, I wonder how much the women enjoy the international stretch couch."

"I think it depends on a number of factors."

They were silent for a while. Then Loxie asked, "I take it there's something similar for women?"

"It's called the Squat Line. All these international dudes are lying on beach towels on the grass, aroused, with their dicks doing the Hokey Pokey, and the woman sinks down on one dude, humps him for a bit, then pulls off, goes to the next, humps that guy, etcetera."

Loxie sat up. "The Squat Line? Don't you think we should go together? I'd love to work my way down that line of guys and then maybe you'd be at the end, and I'd feel myself opening to take your hot wanky stick inside for a look around."

Pendle lay back on the grass and laughed. His erection was doing obvious things in his jeans, but he didn't care. "I wish that could happen, but I still have a thousand dollars to earn. I've got mulch to spread."

"I'm a portal, silly," said Loxie. "I thought you'd figure that out by now. Come into my van and I'll show you my pussy. That's the hole you're looking for."

Shandee Learns How to Wash a Penis

Shandee climbed the steps to the porch of the House of Holes and rang the doorbell. A dreamy leggy woman, barefoot, wearing only a man's blue shirt and yellow wooden beads, opened the screen door. Her name tag read "Zilka—Intake and Interview."

"I'm here to find the man who belongs to this arm," said Shandee, holding up Dave's arm.

Zilka, toying with her beads, looked Shandee over and led her to a waiting room, where she gave her a clipboard with a legal agreement to sign. "Lila will see you soon," she said. "She's the director." She walked away.

The waiting room was empty. There were two couches and some lamps with fringed lampshades and some pictures on the wall of sheep in fields. Shandee hummed along with Sade's "Smooth Operator," while Dave's arm, resting on her lap, gently stroked the back of her hand.

On the low coffee table in front of her was a pile of magazines. She began flipping through a copy of *Contemporary Crochet*. There were some very impressive crochet patterns—for dresses, scarves, leggings, and strange lumpy works of art—and then in the middle she came to a section called "Adult Crochet." There followed four pages of sultry men with perfect T-shaped chest hair staring off at the horizon wearing little crocheted ballsack pouches with their semi-erections hanging through. Then there were four pages of women smiling at the camera and wearing crocheted thongs and crocheted bikini tops that were tiny triangles over fleshpots of breast and crinkled nipple. The world of handicrafts had changed a bit, Shandee thought.

When she looked up, Zilka was leading in another arrival, who took a seat on the couch. Shandee stole a glance at him and gasped inwardly: *such* a beautiful boy—ascetic looking, with a shy large toothy smile and high cheekbones and large bony knuckles and heartbreaking shoulders. His hair was cut very short. He wore a frayed sweatshirt and torn jeans. Shandee nodded at him in a friendly way and casually tossed the crochet magazine back onto the pile.

"Hey, I'm Ruzty," he said, blushing, with a hint of a Bulgarian accent. "This is my first time here. It's kind of a crazy thing. I was in a parking lot putting some plywood in the truck, and this girl walks up and gives me a flyer for a festival."

"What kind of festival? I like festivals."

"Eh, it's a little embarrassing for me," he said, waving and looking away. "But she had big silver earrings on her ears, and she said that the first three winners got five thousand dollars—wow! And she said if I wanted to compete in the festival I would have to go with her to the House of Holes. She was very nice to me, all whisper-whisper. Very tall, too, like a supermodel. And then she pulled out her earring from her ear and told me to look real close at the little hole."

"The hole in her earlobe?" said Shandee.

"Yeah, so I looked real close, and then, voom, I was taken into the hole, and now here I am."

"That's like what happened to me," said Shandee. She told the story of finding Dave's arm in the quarry and how they communicated by writing notes and how Dave's arm had made an O with his fingers. "Dave's arm, meet Ruzty. Ruzty, meet Dave's arm." She held Dave's arm out.

"Hey, dude," said Ruzty, and gave the arm a thumb-to-thumb handshake. He smiled at Shandee—dazzling teeth. "Good for you to travel with somebody who is a friend."

"That's very true," said Shandee.

Just then Zilka reappeared with two more men in tow. "This is Dune," she said. "And this is Hax." She handed Shandee a folded men's blue shirt and some crocheted leg warmers. "Put these on now." She walked away.

Shandee's heart fluttered as she shook hands with the new arrivals: Dune, absurdly handsome in an old suede jacket, with an ironic, off-kilter smile, and Hax, West Indian, keen-eyed and devastatingly white T-shirted, with a broad forehead and long tawny dreadlocks and a light beard.

"Hello," said Hax.

"Hey, folks," Dune said, as he signed the form on the clipboard, after which he took several long seconds to look Shandee over. "You're pretty, shit. Tight little body on you, too. Look at you! Your mama must be proud." Then he cocked his head to the side. "Is that somebody's arm you've got tucked away in your lap?"

Shandee told the story.

"So you're a little bit in love, that's sweet," said Dune. "Makes sense to go for just an arm, though. Forget the head. Men are bullshitters. They'll always feed you a line."

"Hey, man," said Hax, turning, "don't go all loungey on the girl. Relax."

"Loungey? Who are you, shrimp locker?"

Hax looked at him. "I'm a masseur."

"Oh ho, a masseur."

"And I remove tattoos as well, manually."

"I've got a tattoo on my asscheek that says 'Remember Sputnik,'" Dune said. "I forget why. Can you get rid of it?"

"Hey, hey," said Ruzty, looking nervously from Dune to Hax.

"I cannot help you," said Hax to Dune. "Only women."

Dune snorted, then repented. "Sorry, I'll be nice," he said, and he looked back at Shandee. "So can your arm lover hear us chatting?" Whereupon Dave's arm flipped the bird at him. Dune chuckled and said, "I guess so." He picked up the copy of *Contemporary Crochet* and began flipping through it. "Oops, dicks in hammocks," he said. He handed the magazine to Hax, who grunted and put it down.

To be conversational, Shandee asked Hax how he got there.

"A fine woman came up to me on the street where I sell my belt buckles," answered Hax. "She asked me would I like to go to a handjob festival."

"You as well!" said Ruzty.

"Me, too," said Dune. "Smackdown. Longest cumshot wins the prize."

31

"It's a cumshot contest at a handjob festival?" said Shandee, puzzled. "Goodness, that's rather crude."

"Maybe it is crude, or maybe it's very beautiful for some people to see a healthy man showing all his healthy ways by letting a woman shake her boobies for him and pull out all his jizm," said Hax.

"Five thousand, I could pay off my motorcycle," said Dune.

Shandee stood. "Guys, please look away for a moment, I have to change." The three men looked politely away while Shandee took off her jeans and pulled on the leg warmers. Then she took off her shirt and put on the men's shirt, buttoning three of its buttons.

"Okay to look now," she said. "Ta-dah."

"Nice!" said Hax, sitting up. Dune sprawled and smiled, lifting an eyebrow of approval. Ruzty blushed. Dave's arm drummed his fingers.

Zilka reappeared. "Director Lila is ready to talk to you," she said to Shandee. Together they went into the inner office. There was an oscillating fan going. Director Lila was on the phone, toying with a banana in a fruit bowl. "Well then," she was saying, "we'll just suck it all out. If we have to we have to." She hung up.

"Shandee, sweetheart, I'm sorry it's so hectic today. And this must be Dave's arm. Yes, yes. Aren't you cute together. May I?" Shandee handed Lila the arm, and Lila pressed Dave's hand against her face. "Mmmm, gentle touch he has."

"I think I'm a bit in love," said Shandee, "and the weird thing is I don't know what Dave looks like, or what his voice is like, or what his personality is like, or anything."

"Ain't that the way it is sometimes," Lila said. "You don't know a damn thing about them and yet you love them to pieces."

Lila gave Dave's arm a pat, sighing, and handed it back. "There are times when I just don't know why I'm doing all this," she confided.

"It's not easy for you, I would imagine," said Shandee.

"No, it isn't. The sex happiness of so many people—it weighs on you. We have our fun, sure, but we have our problems, too. The Pearloiner has been on a spree lately, stealing clits. She is one sick bitch. Zilka got her clit stolen clean away."

"That's terrible," said Shandee.

Lila leaned forward. "That's why she's so vague sometimes. She's lost her focus. And yet life does go on. You see that light?" Lila pointed to a small red light that blinked above the words PLEASURE FIRST. "Every time somebody has an orgasm somewhere in the House of Holes that light lights up. Whenever that light lights up I feel happy. I was working in hospital administration—I was seeing my friends get old, my life go by. Now I'm living. Don't you wish you were having an orgasm right this second?"

"I guess so," said Shandee.

"Well I do. After I have an orgasm I get so darn much work done. However." She thought briefly, tapping her pen lightly on her nose. "Do you know how to fly an airplane?"

"I'm sorry, I don't." Shandee waited.

"That's too bad." She clicked a button. "Zilka. Could you bring those three arrivals in from the waiting room?"

Shandee thought she should bring the conversation around. "So how do you think I should best go about searching for my Dave?" she asked.

"Let me muse on that further," said Lila, taking off her bifocals. "I'll need to hold the dear one again." She sniffed Dave's arm's knuckles and pressed his hand lightly on her breast. "Hmmm. Let me just consider awhile. Mmm."

Zilka opened the door for Hax, Ruzty, and Dune.

Lila quickly lowered Dave's arm and looked over the crowd. "My goodness," she said, "this *is* a pleasant afternoon. Dune, hello again, you rogue. Can any of you three fly a plane?"

"I can sail a boat," said Hax.

"I drive a stunt motorcycle," said Dune.

"I can bend my thumbs backward, like this," said Ruzty, demonstrating.

"That settles it. Hax and Dune, you'll fly the pornsucker ship to Baltimore with one of the pussypilots. Daggett will give you pointers. Daggett!"

A dark-haired man appeared with a heavy bag on his back.

"Daggett, we've got an emergency overload," said Lila. "We're going to have to suck all the bad porn out of Baltimore, Maryland."

"Not Baltimore!" said Daggett.

"Yes. Buildings and Grounds says there's a sentient mass forming in our main settling tank. We need dilution. Take these two fine men to the pornsucker squadron right away. I will brook no delay!"

Daggett bowed and complied.

"Have fun with that dude's arm, girls!" called Dune as they left.

"That boy is fresh," said Lila cheerfully. "And now, Zilka, will you please help this lovely young man here, with the flexible thumbs"—she gestured at Ruzty—"to kick off his pants and lie on the massage table. It's a nice solid table, bamboo."

Shandee, watching out of the corner of her eye, saw Zilka

begin to busy herself with removing Ruzty's wardrobe. She was curious to see Ruzty naked, but she forced herself to look back at Director Lila. Meanwhile, Lila was frowning and squeezing the length of Dave's arm. Eventually she said, "Shandee, here's your best course of action. A lot of our armless men end up at the Hall of the Armless Men Who Still Want to Fuck Twat. That's way across the salt marshes."

"Oh, okay," said Shandee.

"With those legs on you, you'll have to get yourself a tall pair of waders. They're sold on O Street, at a little place called Wade for Me. Ask for Angelo, he's a sweetheart. He'll measure you all over. But first I'm going to ask you to give us some help right here in Intake. Because we are busy."

"Sure, I'm game," said Shandee.

"You've arrived here on what's called a work-study scholarship," Lila said. "We've got dozens of men arriving every day, with their wallets. The rush is on. We scan them for badness when they rematerialize—we'll find any of nineteen diseases, cough, runny nose, STDs, of course. Is it nineteen, Zilka, or twenty-three now?"

"I don't know," said Zilka.

"At least nineteen diseases, plus any tendency toward thieving, scamming, or violent behavior. Which doesn't mean some real a-holes don't get in."

"For instance, what's his name, Pootie," said Zilka, folding Ruzty's pants.

"Pootie was awful. So we screen them. And we know that some of these arrivals are nervous and uncertain, as well as extremely good looking, and they need a good friendly penis scrub. That's what we want help with at the moment. From you."

Ruzty was standing completely naked, his hands crossed over his crotch. "Excuse me?" he said. "Hello?"

Lila turned. "Hon, what's your name, sir?"

"Ruzty. I'm from Vermont."

"Well, Ruzty from Vermont, I don't see how you can have a problem with getting naked for a brief Penis Wash tutorial. We need to show Shandee the way we do it here at the House of Holes—the old-fashioned up-country way. Zilka?"

Zilka guided Ruzty onto the massage table, and the three women leaned over him. Zilka stroked his short hair. Lila stroked his chest muscles and right shoulder. "Aren't you a smooth sight, oh my," she said. "A regular Marky Mark."

Shandee caught Ruzty's eye and smiled at him. He rolled his eyes. "Sorry," he said, in his fetching accent.

Zilka held up two orange mittens. "Okay, so your job is to put on these sponge mittens and go out and wash the men who pass by you on the line. It's like a car wash. And the way you do it—"

"Excuse me, let me just interject," said Lila. "It's like a car wash with only luxury sport coupes, Ferraris, Miatas, etcetera. The men who go through the Penis Wash are personally selected either by me or by Aunt Maven or by somebody in charge. They are some of the tip-toppest-looking men who come in. So it's an honor to be washed on the Penis Wash, and it's an honor to be a penis washer. Both. Now carry on, Zilka, you're doing good."

Zilka held up her mitten. "Now we don't have any warm-water sprayer in here to show you, but on the wash station you have a sprayer that hangs from the ceiling, and you have foot pedals and you spray the man down, like this, *shpffffffsssssh,* all around his crotch and his scrotum, get it all wet and sloppy, and then you pull down the soap hose, and you spray that on him and then you take your gloves and work the suds all up like this, squoosh squoosh squoosh." She made pretend scrubbing motions an inch over Ruzty's crotch. Ruzty crossed his hands over his chest and beamed at Shandee.

"Can I talk to the man as I'm scrubbing him?" asked Shandee.

"Yes," said Zilka.

"Of course you can," said Lila. "They don't really know what's happening yet. They've just arrived, and this is the first time that they've been naked here. So yes, talk to them if you want. It's a matter of style. This experience is important, and your job is to make sure that they're clean and they're happy. Happy and clean."

"But you can't take too long," said Zilka, "because you're at a spray station and you only have a few minutes, and you have to be sure they're all rinsed off."

Lila made a conceding nod. "You don't want to be leaving them soapy," she said. "And you can scrub them all over, not just their crotches, obviously. But try not to spray directly in their faces, unless they want you to."

"I think I've got the basic principle," said Shandee. "Can I see how the gloves feel?"

Zilka handed them to her, and Shandee put them on. She winked at Ruzty and began an aerial simulation. "So I spray him all over, *ffffff,* and then I suds him up, like this, and I suds around all over his nice chest and his stomach and I suds all around his thighs, and higher up, and I get to his balls, and I suds his cock, like this—"

"Look at him," said Zilka. "And look at his cock, wow." Ruzty's cock was leaning dramatically to one side.

"Oh my goodness, our boy's got a banana cock!" said Lila.

"That's why I am shy," Ruzty said. "When it gets hard it curves sharply to the left. Almost a full ninety degrees when it's very hard, as it is now. It has been true my whole life. Once I had a girlfriend who said it was my progressive penis. But actually I'm a libertarian." He lifted it to show them. It was heavy and hard, like a shepherd's crook. "It can straighten some, you see? I am trying to overcome many years of embarrassment because some women say that they like a strong curve."

"Oh, some women love a curve," said Lila. "Am I right, Shandee?"

"Sure, I guess," Shandee said. But she was in shock. She hadn't seen that many penises in her life, and she had never seen one shaped like that. It was extreme, and it was extremely exciting. Also there was something distracting happening low down on her leg. She looked toward the floor. Dave's arm was gripping her ankle and squeezing it fussily. "Oh, I'm sorry, Davie," she said, "did you crawl all the way over here from my bag? Oh, my dear. Isn't that sweet. I'm sorry." She gave the sponge mittens back to Zilka and lifted Dave's arm. Then she felt flummoxed. "You two have met, I think," she said.

Lila wanted to wind things up. "And we will help you find Dave," she said. "But now it's time for you, Shandee, to go to your hotel and check in. Tomorrow you'll do the Penis Wash for real. I'll watch over Dave's arm back here, if you don't mind. He's such a heartbreaker, isn't he? I do love a veiny hand."

"I think I'll take Dave with me, if that's all right," said Shandee, a little crisply.

"Of course, hon," said Lila. "And Ruzty, thank you for being our teaching aid. I really think you're going to have to adopt a sideways stance at the cumshot competition."

Ruzty sat up—his penis, fortunately, had subsided. "Yes, I will stand almost sideways," he said. "But I will still make my come go quite far that way, I think."

"Good for you," said Lila. "And thank you, Zilka, for your tips, and let's see if we can get Ruzty in on tomorrow afternoon's penis scrub with the other men, if there's a slot, and we'll put Shandee on the main station, okay?"

"Is this how I should be dressed tomorrow?" asked Shandee. "Just a man's shirt and crocheted leggings?"

Everyone nodded enthusiastically. Ruzty couldn't take his shining eyes off her.

"Oh, I almost forgot the most important thing," said Lila. "Tomorrow, if you're inclined, go ahead and stroke the men's penises. Make them feel good. But gently. Do not ever, ever jerk them through to a climax. If you do, their enthusiasm will flag, and they won't spend their life savings on activities here at the House. Scrub, don't tug."

"Scrub, don't tug, got it," said Shandee. "I guess I'll get back to the hotel now." Like never before, Shandee felt the blood slamming in her bursting clit. She was beside herself. She had to get somewhere private. "See you soon, Ruzty," she said, putting every emotion she had into her good-bye smile.

"See you," said Ruzty.

Zilka took her to the hotel room. Shandee said good-bye to her and closed the door and took off her clothes. She pulled out Dave. "Oh, Dave, I missed you so much," she said. "I want to sit on your hand so bad. Can I sit on your hand?"

Dave's fingers wiggled yes. Shandee positioned his hand on the corner of the bed, and she sat down on it and crushed her pussy into his fingers and worked her hips in circles. "Give me a couple of stiff fingers up there, Davie," she said. She felt them slip up inside her, and whoo that was good! She bounced up and down on Dave's hand for a while, and then saw a bowl of fruit and said, "Wait, Dave, I want you to hold this orange." She put a navel orange in his palm and then she lowered herself onto its thick bumpy skin, cool against her opening pussyhole. She circled around the orange for a while—rocked and rolled on it—crushing Dave's knuckles into the bedspread.

Then she pulled a green banana off the fruit bowl. "Dave, please hold this big banana straight up for me."

He did, of course, being a gentleman of an arm, and she admired how curvy and upsticking it was—"a banana cock," Lila had said of Ruzty. She remembered the sight of Ruzty's cock getting hard in Lila's office. "Dave, I want to fuck this green banana so bad," she said. She pulled her pussy open so that she could see it push in, and Dave's arm held it steady for her. She felt the unripe fruit drive curvingly deep inside her till she was well and truly socketed.

"Dave, please help me come," she said. "Please fuck the banana in me." Dave moved it and jiggled it, and she circled her fingers one way and then the other over her crimson clit. She started to come with her legs and her hips, and she smashed herself down on Dave's banana fist and ground into it and said, "Grrrr," and watched herself in the mirror humping on the corner of the bed. As her orgasm found its way up her legs, her whole body went *clong, clong, clong.* "Oh, that's it, Dave," she said. But in her mind she was thinking, Ruzty, Ruzty, I love your eyes and face, and I wish you could see me coming.

Cardell Has a Sherry Cobbler

Cardell worked at the planning office of a small city, planning brick crosswalks and trying to figure out where people could park. It was interesting work, but he wanted to meet a nice, smart, sexy woman, so he went to a lecture on the history of the municipal water supply and sat down on a folding chair next to a woman with mustard-colored stockings. There was a good crowd, but unfortunately the lecturer had a boring singsong voice. Cardell's assbones hurt from sitting and his mind was aswirl with obscene imagery, cocks being stuffed everywhere, women's eyes suddenly going wide in surprise. He began to think more and more about the woman next to him. He liked her mustard-colored knees poking out from the hem of her skirt. She had a little notebook and she was drawing a picture of a cocktail glass. Below that, she'd written "He doesn't know anything" and underlined it twice.

When the audience questions began, Cardell leaned toward

her and asked her to the roof bar of a nearby hotel. "I noticed your doodle," he said, in his thrummiest voice.

"You naughty man," she said. She gave him a speedy once-over and made a single nod. They left as unobtrusively as possible. Turned out her name was Jackie. She sat on a dark-red bar stool and addressed the bartender. "Can you make a sherry cobbler?" she asked.

He nodded, sure.

"I'll take one, too," Cardell said impulsively. He turned back to Jackie. "What's a sherry cobbler?"

"It's my life's work," said Jackie, and moved an eyebrow provocatively. She told Cardell where she taught, and they talked about a big video store near there that had closed recently.

"Rented a lot of movies there, back in the day," said Cardell, closing his eyes in nostalgic reminiscence. "Before everything streamed."

The drinks came, with straws poking out. Cardell took three enormous sips and nodded, blinking and smacking his lips. The drink was incredibly sweet and strong. And good. "So that's a sherry cobbler," he said. "Not particularly subtle—but then, who needs subtle?"

Jackie sucked hers down greedily. "Damn delicious. I never tire of it. Would you like me to tell you the history of the sherry cobbler?"

"Tell it in the minutest detail," Cardell said.

But Jackie had an odd look. "Wait a sec," she said. She began breathing strangely and put her hand on Cardell's arm. "I need your help with something. Stand behind me."

Cardell stood behind where she sat on the bar stool. She

leaned forward, so that her head was almost on her arms, and pushed her bottom back toward him so that she was almost off the stool.

"What's happening?" Cardell asked.

"Put your hand under my dress."

"Here?"

"Yeah, just pretend you're whispering something to me. I'm trying to lay an egg."

The end of the bar where they were was dark and nobody else was sitting nearby, so it was possible to do as she asked.

"Now what?"

"I'm not sure." Jackie sat for a moment, leaning forward. Then she straightened and brushed the hair out of her eyes. "Nope, not quite yet."

Cardell sat back down and finished his drink. "Ah, Nelly!" he said.

"The great breakthrough," Jackie was saying, "came in 1842 when Charles Dickens came to the U.S. on his speaking tour. Somebody served him up a big, ice-cold sherry cobbler. It was the first drink made with crushed ice, you know."

"No, I didn't," Cardell said.

"Oh, yes. And the first drink people drank through a straw."

"Doubly revolutionary," said Cardell. "Did Charles Dickens like it?"

"Loved it, and he had his character Martin Chuzzlewit drink one."

"Ah, old Chuzzlewit," Cardell said, in a wuffly English accent. "And where do you come down on the question of the size of Dickens's dick? Big? Little? Doesn't matter?"

"We just don't know," said Jackie, with a look of mild exasperation. "It's one of the great mysteries. Now shush and let me tell you about the sherry cobbler."

"They're real good," said Cardell.

"Then let's have two more immediately," said Jackie. "They're best drunk as fast as possible." She ordered with a practiced move of her fingers—this woman knew her way around a bar. "Watch out for the spins, though. There's a book of Oxford bar recipes that says that sherry cobblers have 'more than once induced vertigo.' Published in 1827."

"1827, that early, really?"

She pointed at him. "You see, the straw allowed you to drink the mixture in a supercooled state."

"And that's why Martin Chuzzlewit's eyes rolled back in his head and he said, 'Good Lord Nelson O'Reilly, what is this marvel?'"

"Right, he gets totally smashed," said Jackie. "I mean squashed. And that, you see, ushered in the so-called golden age of the sherry cobbler."

"Can I say," murmured Cardell, wobbling his head seductively, "that I loved feeling the hot heat coming from under your dress?"

"That's what it's there for," said Jackie.

"That's what what's there for?"

"My li'l pussy."

"Oh, your li'l private space heater. Your hot wet—pooter. Your kitten. Mhm. You know—"

The second set of drinks arrived. Cardell took a long, cross-eyed slurp from the straw and then sighed hugely. "Cold," he said.

"Very. They drank it through straws from a straw-hat factory, and they cooled it with crushed ice from a lake in Massachusetts," said Jackie.

"In England, they used American ice? That's kind of loony."

"No, it's rational, because the Wenham Lake ice was the best ice, and the ice salesmen went over to London and Oxford and Cambridge, and they got the word out. They said, 'Make this sherry cobbler from our recipe, but you have to use real imported American ice, not the dirty ice from the dirty fish shops and the dirty British rivers, because that ice will make you ill.'"

"And then of course you'll upchuck, and the spins are no help with that."

"Right, 'Buy our clean innocent ice from the land of America, where there are clean green tree frogs, and clean shiny fish, and a few noble savages going skippity doodah in their immaculate moccasins.' It was a big business, the transatlantic ice trade. Charles Dickens bought five pounds' worth of Wenham Lake ice in 1850." Jackie pointed at Cardell. "We know that for a fact."

"Interesting," said Cardell, rubbing his face vigorously. "You know, the English talk a good game, but they're such hypocrites. All that business about how vulgar it is to have ice in drinks. Look at this freaking peach cobbler!" He held his palms toward his drink. "Just have a look at it!"

"Now, Cardell," said Jackie gently, patting Cardell's hand, "the peach cobbler is a bit different. It's baked in an oven."

"Of course, what am I thinking? Peaches and you bake it. Very different. Very hot. So hot you have to let it cool on your fork or you'll burn your delicate mouth tissues. This is with ice and a straw and you suck it up greedily."

"Shall we summon another?" said Jackie. Again she made

one of her expert signals to the bartender. Then she paused, listening. Across the room, the pianist had begun playing.

"What song is it?" asked Cardell. "It's very familiar."

"It's Hoagy Carmichael, of course," she said. "'I get along without you very well.'"

"God, these names. 'Martin Chuzzlewit,' 'Hoagy Carmichael.' You know, when I'm sitting in some lecture hall, listening to some talk by some really deadly historian—no offense to your profession—my head just gorges itself on obscene images. I can't help it."

"Like what obscene images?" Jackie said. "Be specific."

"Oh, you know—" Cardell did some quick self-censorship. "Specifically two people tied together at the knees. Loosely tied together."

"Not tied. Oh, please."

"What?"

"That's such a tired trope—people tying each other up and peeing in mayonnaise jars and whatnot," said Jackie. "You don't want that, do you?"

"Well, no, of course not, but." Cardell could feel a joywave gathering, a tingling in his lips at the exhilaration of saying what was now in his head. "Imagine two chairs, facing each other. I'm in one, you're in the other."

"Please, Cardell, let's not make it quite so personal."

"Okay, Charles Dickens is in one chair—"

"Not Dickens."

"Okay, that hunky bar pianist is in one and you're in the other, but you're not really you, because your mind is gonzo on apple cobblers. I mean sherry. Shorry. And you're both in your fashionable underwear, and your knees are tied together with long colorful scarves."

"Indian-print scarves?"

"Absolutely. Not tightly, but not loosely, either. You're toying with your slobbering kitty, and he's doing his bulldog—and your mouths are murmuring filthy nothings that neither of you can quite hear. Then he takes hold of your waist and tries to pull you toward him, and you hold his shoulders and try to pull him toward you. But no can do."

She frowned. "Why?"

"Because of the scarves. His knees and your knees are made to share the same fate. You see? Their bony places and their soft places. The knees are your point of mutual contact. You're kneecapping. The harder you try to pull toward him, and the harder he tries to pull toward you, the more it forces your legs apart. It's sad, really. Then he sees your hand going fast and you start to go, 'Ooh, mm, ah, mm, oh,' and your brow goes all furrowy, and your eyes go all glittery, the way they are now, you throw your head back, exposing your swanlike neck, and just when you're at that moment when you're starting to feel yourself come, suddenly you really desperately need him inside you, and just at that moment the scarves come loose and Charles Dickens is there—I mean the bar pianist—and you feel his dick find you, and it starts to push and to muscle its way in, slowly at first, and then *wom,* oh shit, he's slamming it up there, old twinkle fingers is in you, and his hips are humping, it's out of his control." Cardell did pelvisy things on the bar stool. "Ngong, bong, ung, fung!"

Jackie closed her eyes and smiled. "Well," she said, "you've made little missy pussy just a little bit horny, baby, because you talk dirty, and I sure do love a bar pianist."

"Good," said Cardell. Jackie held her head still, averted, listening to the songs; then she relaxed and got a sad look. "They play their hearts out in hotel bars where nobody can hear the twelve clever things they're doing with the harmony." She pointed. "See the big brandy snifter for tips there on the top of the piano? Not much in it."

"So maybe we should casually drop a ten-spot in the snifter as we walk on by."

"When?"

"When we leave together in about ten minutes to kiss and look into each other's eyes while we fondle each other and tie colorful scarves around our knees. Oops, did I say that?"

"Hold on." Jackie squinted and grabbed his arm again. "I think it's coming." Again she pushed back on the bar stool and turned red. A vein stood out in her neck. "Get behind me again, and slide your hand in my pantyhose and hold it right at my pussyhole."

Cardell obliged, cupping her bush, which was slick and swollen.

"Good," she said, "this time it's really happ—" Her throat squeezed to silence and she made a strained pushing sound, turning even redder. "Now! Uhhhhh!" Something heavy and smooth and warm fell into Cardell's cupped hand. "There you go," she said, straightening and sighing with relief.

Cardell pulled his hand from under her skirt. He was holding an egg. It was silver in color.

She handed him a bar napkin. "Wipe it down. Don't let people see. Put it out of sight."

"Is it a silver egg?" he asked, pocketing it in his jacket.

"Yes."

"Is it solid?"

"No, there's a tiny silver man and a tiny silver woman inside. You can watch them make love if you like that sort of thing."

"I do," Cardell said.

"Me, too," said Jackie, and she giggled and shook herself. "Phew, egg laying takes it out of me." She ate half of a pretzel. "Cardell, I'm sorry to be a tease, because you've been nice, but I'm buzzed now, and I'm going to have to say good-bye."

"Forever?"

"No, of course not forever. I'm just going to make an excursion to the House of Holes, where I can be a total tramp for a day or two. They let you do what you want there, you know."

"And what is it you want?"

She leaned forward confidingly. "I want two lovely Brazilian stonemasons in overalls, with huge smiles and warm hands— four warm strong hands that know how to fit stones together— and sad brown eyes."

"And they can offer you that kind of specificity at this so-called House of Holes?"

Jackie moved her lips to her straw, remembering something good.

Cardell asked, "Well, what are you going to do with these men? I like a woman who knows what she wants."

She thought, then frowned. "I'm going to idolize their cockpoles," she said. "I'm going to slide their foreskins back, so that the heads of their cocks pop out all pink and heart shaped. I'm going to gorge myself on as much of their deliciousness as I can stuff into my mouth without gagging. I don't enjoy gagging.

I'm going to look up into their eyes and feel them pump their come down my throat."

"Yee." Cardell tried not to look shocked, although he was a little. "Maybe I could tag along and sort of—watch? We could get some dinner first?" He touched a menu.

Jackie heard the brokenness and despair, but also the excitement, in his voice. She took pity on him. "Everybody's got to find their own porthole," she said. "It's harder for men to get in than women unless they pay and pay. Although you're pretty cute—you'll have a chance."

"Any hints on where to find a porthole?"

"Try the fourth dryer from the left at the laundromat at the corner of 18th Street and Grover Avenue," said Jackie. She waved. "Bye."

Her face began to blur and liquefy, and then she poured herself down into her straw and was gone.

Cardell picked up the straw and looked through it. There was no blockage. "Jackie?" he said. The bartender stood watching him, holding a glass.

"What just happened?" Cardell said.

"Your lady friend seems to have been sucked into her straw," the bartender said.

"That's what I think, too," Cardell said.

The bartender shrugged. "It happens, man."

"Well," Cardell said, "I guess I'll be heading out."

"Have a good night."

Cardell dropped a twenty in the brandy snifter and waved at the pianist, humming along to Hoagy Carmichael.

In the elevator down, Cardell smelled his fingers. Then he felt in his pocket. Yes, the silver egg was still there.

Marcela Admires Koizumi's Sculpture

Marcela, an art critic, was in the sculpture garden. Koizumi, the well-known Japanese artist, was mounting one of her newest wooden sculptures onto its base. The sculpture was of a woman resting on all fours—large thighed and stylized, with a wide bottom and a moon face. She was carved out of black wood with yellow streaks.

Marcela wore a boatneck shirt and white Bermuda shorts. She brushed her hair from her face, watching Koizumi bolt both of the wooden woman's knees to her pedestal. Then the sculptress pulled out a big manual drill with a kink in it where the handle was.

Marcela opened her notebook. "And what are you going to do with that?" she asked.

Koizumi, a slight woman with a small mouth, said, "Once I get the sculptures mounted, I do the last step, which is to drill this auger bit into their asses."

"Can I watch?"

Koizumi almost said no. She preferred to work in private. But then, struck by Marcela's fresh, curious face and generous hips, she changed her mind. She took a metal poker and tapped it lightly into the wooden seam of the sculpted woman's bottom. Then she removed it and fitted the tip of the auger into the tiny guide hole she had made.

"Now I will drill her asshole," Koizumi said simply.

She pressed against the handle and began slowly turning the crank of the hand drill. Curls of wood came twirling up off the spirals of the bit.

Marcela walked around to look at the wooden woman's face. "She looks like she's enjoying that pressure," she said.

"She likes to get her ass drilled," said Koizumi. "All my women do. It's the very last thing I do with each sculpture."

Marcela looked around the sculpture garden, and, sure enough, each of the four Koizumi women had a small hole drilled in her bottom. One had a drill bit left in place.

Marcela looked from the moon face of the sculpture to the thin, intent face of the sculptress.

Koizumi saw her and smiled. "Would you like to give it a few turns?"

"Can I?"

"Just apply steady pressure while you turn the crank—not too hard."

Koizumi put her hands on Marcela's hands and showed her how to hold the pommel and the handle of the drill.

Marcela leaned and turned the drill and it ground into the wooden woman. A long curl of wood peeled up and fell away.

"It's rather straightforwardly erotic, isn't it?" said Marcela. "Are you her, in this case, or are you the drill?"

"Both, neither, I don't know," said Koizumi. She raised her hand. "That's probably deep enough."

Marcela pulled the drill out, and Koizumi bent and blew away the sawdust. Then she took a rag with some linseed oil on it and pushed the rag into the hole with her pinkie and worked it around. "Do you want to try oiling the hole, too?" she asked.

"Sure." Marcela moved her pinkie finger in the wooden woman's new hole and felt a strange tingling clench deep in her bottom. "When I push the rag I feel my muscles tighten," she said. "Is that normal?"

"Which muscles?"

Marcela patted her behind. "These. The back ones."

"Yes," said Koizumi, solemnly, "that happens to me, too."

"Oof, I'm all confused," said Marcela in a small voice. "I feel like I want to fuck a football team."

"Put your finger in the hole for a moment and wait, and you will be taken to a place where you can be made love to any way you like, by anyone you choose," said Koizumi.

"Okay." Marcela pushed with her finger and waited. She felt herself turning sparkly and growing narrower. Her finger, and then her hand, and then her arm flowed into the carven woman's asswood, and then she found herself swimming deep into the wooden woman's body. She smelled the smells of linseed oil and cherry bark. Things went dark for a moment.

When she became solid again, she was facedown on a wooden rolling table with a soft, thin mattress, moving down a dimly lit hall. Two nice-looking naked men with towels around their necks were pushing the table by its railing. To the first naked man, Marcela said, "Where is this?"

"This is the House of Holes, where you can do whatever you want."

"Whatever I want? For instance, I can just reach out and hold your penis right now if I want?"

"Bono, wait up," the boy called. "She wants to hold my peeny wanger." He paused and stood with his hips canted forward, his peeny wanger close to her hand. "Go ahead."

She rose on one elbow and held the cock like the handle of a trowel and pulled slowly on it. She felt it thicken and was filled with longings in various directions.

"What's your name?" the nice-looking young man asked, gasping slightly.

Marcela decided to make a name up. "My name is Lucky Eyes," she said. She pointed his cock up and then kissed its tip and filled her mouth once with it.

"Oh, please don't do that cause I'll shoot for sure in two seconds. I'm real full of come cause your tits make me hot."

Marcela lay down and breathed. "Where are we going?"

"Into the massage room."

"Oh. Who will be massaging me?"

"Lanasha, the head masseuse, while Bono and I watch in the other room." He pointed to a one-way mirror. "Then we're supposed to take you to the groanrooms."

"Oh."

In the massage room there were Japanese screens and a pile of folded cloths, and bowls of water and liquids. "Is it okay to leave my bra on?" said Marcela.

"Lanasha will take care of everything," said the boy. Then he shyly squeezed her and said, "Thank you for holding me. It felt really good. I'm Ross." Some trance music came on, and Marcela lay on her stomach feeling very peaceful, still in her bra, with a towel covering her butt and throbbing cuntspot. Soon she heard the sound of a sliding paper door.

Lanasha, a large Filipina woman in a red dress, came in and sat in a chair next to her table.

"I am here to give you a teaching massage," Lanasha said. "What would you most like to learn?"

"Everything, I think," said Marcela. "I've not been to a sex resort before. Last week I let a man hold my breasts, but besides that I've been pretty darned nonsexual lately. It's been almost a year. I've started to worry about it, actually."

Lanasha unhooked Marcela's bra and tickled her back with the loose ends of it. Then she began making odd paddling motions over her shoulder blades and down the small of her back. Once, she lifted the towel. "You have a very lovely bottom—all men will like it," the masseuse said.

"Thank you."

Lanasha squirted oil on Marcela's bottom.

"Do you know what the Gumuz boys sing in the Sudan?" she said.

"No, what?"

"They sing, 'My girl's got big boobies and a big soft ass; she is the shapeliest woman in the world.'"

"Catchy song," said Marcela. "Can I ask you something?"

"Sure."

"Do you enjoy having a man behind you? Because I miss seeing his face make those nice twisty expressions that I see men make in dirty movies."

Lanasha smiled. "What you do is you send your whole self back to your bottom. Your bottom has a lot to say to him, by its shape. To him it doesn't feel cold. It feels as if you are talking to him in a new round soft language."

She pushed the cheeks of Marcela's bottom together as she said this, and then she released them. Then she pushed her thumbs deep into the muscles.

"Wow, that's a deep massage," said Marcela, pressing her delta bone into the thin mattress.

Lanasha made a growly sort of sound, and then her hands went back to Marcela's back, and she began kneading the younger woman slowly down each side of her spine.

"Tell me a sexy thing a man did to you," said Marcela.

Lanasha's hands paused for a moment. "One time I was giving a massage to this short man who was very fit," she said. "He was like a little Egyptian statue. He wanted a happy ending, and when I turned him over his penis had already half filled, and it was almost too big to seem like a penis, until I got used to it. It had a vein that forked off in two directions about halfway up. I took a little dipperful of oil, and I poured it on the underside of it and watched it trickle down, and then I put both my hands around his cock, and I began moving my fists around and together and apart, and he began making an odd, snorting sound and then he said, in a strong accent, 'I want to push it in you.'

"I said okay, but I showed him how to put his hand around his penis at the base so that he wouldn't go so far inside me that he would hurt me in my cervix."

Marcela said, "Boy, he must have been big."

"He was really huge, and glorious," said Lanasha, "but with

a delicate, shy face and long eyelashes. That was what was so interesting about him."

"So what did you do, you got up on your knees?" asked Marcela. "Would you mind if I did that?"

"Go ahead," said Lanasha. "I'll massage you that way."

So Marcela put her bottom up as high as it could go. She felt Lanasha's strong hands squeezing the oil into her ass muscles.

"So I was pretty much just like you are now," said Lanasha.

"Wide-open?"

"Yes. And I felt his hands on my hips. I said, 'Don't forget to hold the base of your penis because I can't take all of you.' Because I've been with men sometimes who are big and it's quite uncomfortable. One of his hands went away from my hips and he found me, and he began to push himself in. It was a combination of wide and deep, and I've never felt so full of anything in my life, it was like a complete Thanksgiving dinner of cock. Then I felt his fist coming up against me, and he said, 'Would you like to have a thumb ride?' I said sure, because I was ready to say yes to anything. And then every time he drove his dick in, he let his thumb push, at my bungee hole. Not in, just pressure here, pushing, moving, like this."

"Oofy. Feels like a meteor shower. Did you like it?"

"I had three little tiny orgasms and then suddenly I had this huge shuddering orgasm that was bigger than anything I'd had before. It was like the god of pleasure had punched me in the pussy."

Marcela whimpered and pulled the hair out of her face. "Mmm, I'm almost ready to be fucked now," she said.

"Do you want me to squeeze the Magic Kentucky Lime fruit

on your pussy? It will make you feel extreme cravings for stiff cock."

"Is it safe?"

Lanasha said it was. "Some people call it the Purple Cometwat, but its real name is Magic Kentucky Lime."

"Go right ahead," said Marcela.

Lanasha took a large yellow-and-green fruit and cut it in half on the side table. It didn't look anything like a lime to Marcela. Lanasha gently helped Marcela turn over so that she lay face up. She gently massaged Marcela's stomach and around her hip bones, and then she drew her knees up, and she said, "Hold your labia open." Marcela held herself open and Lanasha pressed the fruit between her hands.

Cold drops fell on Marcela's little thumper bean and trickled down. And then Lanasha took the whole half of the fruit, and she pushed it down over Marcela's mound so that the pulp of it was mashed into her folds. Marcela felt an incredible almost burning warmth flow back into her body and down her legs.

"Ooooh," Marcela groaned. "I don't just want to be full of a cock, I also want to have a cock. I want a cock of my own. Can you arrange that for me?"

"Ah, no," said Lanasha. "That's called a crotchal transfer. You'll have to ask Lila about that."

"Oh, okay. Well, can you put a trickle of the Kentucky Lime on my bottom, too?"

"Yes," said Lanasha, "but if I do, I warn you, you're going to want to have something in there."

"That's fine." So Lanasha held Marcela's knees together and pushed her legs back over her stomach. Then Marcela could feel the cut edges of the Kentucky Lime on the tender skin around her bottom hole. "I'm going to squeeze the fruit now, don't freak," said Lanasha.

She frowned and Marcela felt her bottom flooded with juice. Her asshole opened blindly for a moment and gulped some of it. She could feel the burning warmth going far inside her.

"How do you feel now?" asked Lanasha.

Marcela didn't speak for a moment. She cleared her throat. Then she said, "How do I feel? Lanasha, frankly I need two yellow school buses of dick to drive right through me. Each filled with a whole soccer team."

Lanasha made a satisfied chuckle. "I thought you said football," she said.

"Okay, one football team, one soccer team."

Lanasha rang a bell. "I think she's ready for you, Ross," she called.

Ross and Bono walked in. "Hot show," said Ross. "I loved when your titties were hanging."

Marcela began to turn slowly, smiling, and put her ass up. "You liked it when I was like this?"

"Yeah, just like that!"

Bono was standing to the side, staring at Marcela while Lanasha gently stroked his pecker. "Ross, sweetheart," said Marcela, "where's that nice young peeny wanger of yours? Is it still full of gobs of nice hot come?"

Ross said nothing, but Marcela watched Bono's eyes follow something happening around back of her. Then Marcela felt two hands on her hips and a heavy, knobby pressure moving around the folds of her pussy, seeking a way in. She arched her back and suddenly, because she was so wet, a stiff immensity went deep and filled her up. She made a surprised groan and answered instinctively by slapping her ass back hard against Ross's hips, then she pulled partway off his cock and let him slam into her again—once, twice, thrice, four times, and then she heard Ross say, in a fierce whisper, "Shit, baby, I'm coming!" She felt the thickness twitch hard inside her. "I'm sorry! Your pussy was just too hot for me."

"That's okay, honey, I like that you had to come right away—that's supersexy." Marcela turned and smiled at him reassuringly. He gave her an embarrassed shrug and grinned.

Lanasha spoke. "I think Bono's got something all ready for you," she said.

"Bono? You got something for me? My ass is still up. Lanasha, can you help this nice boy find his way? I'm still open for business."

Ross slapped hands with Bono. Marcela felt Lanasha's strong practiced hands pulling her asscheeks open, and then she felt a middle finger twiddle purposefully in her ass. And then, finally, Bono's length of badness stuffed her gasping twat full of warm, brown dick muscle. Bono had more control. He said little, but he developed an oval rhythm, angling and slamming his smooth musclemeat in and out. He slammed fourteen strokes, and then he said, "It's gonna pop soon!"

"Wait, stop, not quite yet," she said, freezing. "I want to frig myself off while you're still hard in me."

"Okay, but if you move the tiniest bit I'll come for sure."

Marcela held three fingers together and circled and swizzled over her clit hood, while Lanasha's finger darted and dithered in her ass. As she began to come, her cunt muscles tried to close around Bono's motionless blood-pulsing truncheon. "Now!" she said. Bono pulled out almost to the helmet and slide-slammed back into her slippery salope, then out, then back in, and once more, and then five hard short strokes. "UHLLLLLLLL!" he said, followed by lots of snuffling. She felt a cold spray of sweat droplets on her back, and, inside, she again felt the long warm twitch of liberated jizm. "Oh, that's it, fill me up with all that goodness."

She lay panting on the massage table. Lanasha rubbed the backs of her legs with a cool washcloth.

Shandee Wears the Sponge Gloves

Shandee left Dave's arm to sleep late in the hotel room. She met Zilka for melon and a croissant at the terrace restaurant overlooking the Garden of the Wholesome Delightful Fuckers. Zilka was wearing a striped shirt with the collar up. Her hair was amazing. Shandee wanted to know more about how she had lost her clit, but she didn't want to ask her about it right away, so instead she asked how Zilka spent her days. Zilka said she helped Lila, and after work she went out to the Trou or hung out at the Darkrooms. "The Darkrooms are good because you can just talk to a guy," Zilka said. "Before I lost my clit I would have been dancing or sleeping with somebody—not now."

"So—how did it happen?" Shandee asked.

"When I was a stripper, I headlined at the Wiggle Room in San Antonio for almost a year, and I flew all over the Midwest. I was going through security, and this awful woman with bad hair stole my clit from me."

"That's terrible," said Shandee.

"Yeah, it kind of is." Zilka was sad and silent for a moment, and then she pointed. "You see that cable over there? That's a ride called Fuck the Lake. Over there's the midway, where you can do Spank the Pretty Ass, or Hold the Young Hung Hard-on. The Masturboats are over on the river. They're moored right now."

"Zilka, can you tell me how it happened?" said Shandee.

"Oh, I was at the airport in St. Louis, and they told me my flight was out of a certain gate in Terminal O. I thought, Hm, I don't think I've been to Terminal O before, even though I'd flown through St. Louis a lot. But there was a security line, and the guy checked my ID, wearing the pale blue glove, and I got in line and took my shoes off, took my belt and my necklace off, and my bracelet off, and I put them all in the tray, and I walked to the metal detector, which was like a doorway, and I saw the man on the other side. He had a classy smile and short hair, and he lifted his hand and said, 'Come on through.' So I walked through in my stocking feet, and when I did I was fwooshed into a different mind zone, and all the men around me were the same but they were naked from the waist down."

"That's strange," said Shandee.

"Yeah, isn't it? They didn't seem to care that they were naked below, but they definitely were. They looked up and nodded at me, because I like to dress kind of sexy, and I was amazed because I'd never seen so many penises on public display. Cocks were swinging everywhere, every size and shape. Even though I'd been a stripper for a few years, I really hadn't seen all that much in the way of cock. Then I heard 'Bag check on three,' and the nice guy who'd gestured me through started going through my carry-on in extreme detail, and every move he made made his thingy bobble around a little.

"He said, 'We're professionals. I know it may seem a little strange to you that we don't have pants on.'"

"I said, 'Well, it's not a bad thing, really.' Then he said, 'Uh, we're going to have to perform a secondary. Would you like it in private or in public?'"

"I said, 'Well, what are you going to do?'"

"He said, 'Well, we have to check your tits and your nipples, make sure you're not concealing anything in your undertit area, and we're going to have to inspect your mouth with our dicks to be sure you're not concealing anything in your mouth area.'"

"Jeez!" said Shandee.

"I know, and I said, 'What the hell?' And he said, 'Of course we'll perform the search very politely, with full consideration of your privacy, blah blah. But we'll probably have to ask you to ease open your tight crotch hole so we can check what you've got down there, too.'"

"Oh, please," said Shandee.

"And as he said this I looked down, and his cock, which had been uninterested up till then, seemed to be doing a strange loop-the-loopy thing. It had come alive. I said, 'Give me a break, Mr. Airport Bag Check Man.'"

"And he said, 'You know how important national security is.' And then he called out to one of the other security guys, and the two of them took hold of my elbows and steered me into a room that said 'Official Business Only.' I knew I was in trouble then."

"Did they search you all over?"

"Let me tell you, 'gangbang' would be another word for it. I thought it was over, and then one guard, the less nice one, said to the other, 'We're going to have to call in the Pearloiner.' And the nice one said, 'No, let's not.' But then the Pearloiner came in. She was about forty-five, superpatriotic, big hair, big high heels, big patriotic tits, fake. And she goes, 'I'm sorry, but we've determined that your clitoris is not a carry-on item.' She's like, 'It's swollen and oversized, and it's over the weight limit, and it's a security threat, and I'm going to have to remove it now.' Then she clapped her hand to my crotch, and I felt this sharp painful tugging, and I saw my clit go into a tiny clear baggie, with a numbered label on it, and then a gloved man took the top off of a large jar."

"That's just so sad and so wrong," said Shandee.

"Yeah, and since then I've only had three good comes," said Zilka, "and they were all in my sleep. I used to come so big. I used to shout and kick, sometimes even fart if I was by myself and really bearing down. Now I can't come at all. Nothing to rub against. I still think about sex a lot, though, and I still get incredibly turned on. It's about as frustrating a situation as you can get."

"So what are you going to do?" said Shandee.

"Well, a few months ago I was dancing at Carbon Fiber in Chicago, and this girl Cheyenne who'd also had her clit stolen at the same airport said she'd heard the Pearloiner had gotten in big trouble with the FBI, finally, for abuses of her authority, and that she'd gone AWOL and somehow managed to sneak over into the House of Holes, where she'd been making a nuisance of herself—stealing more clits, of course. So Cheyenne and I decided to track her, and that's when I came here and met Lila, who said she'd help if she could. I worked the Penis Wash for a month—that was a kick. Now I'm a greeter."

Shandee was moved. "We must help you get your clit back," she said, socking her fist. "You can't just have that pleasure stolen from you. You have rights!"

"Thanks," said Zilka. "If you spot a woman with big hair and spike heels and a jar full of stolen clits, let me know. Precious baggage."

They were still for a moment, listening to the clink of plates from other tables. The warm wind sang in the gorse.

"Thanks for telling me," said Shandee.

"I guess it's time for me to take you to the Penis Wash, eh?"

The Penis Wash happened in a concrete-floored room. Five recessed floor tracks emerged from five openings in one wall, their low archways covered by flaps of cloudy plastic. Men lay face up on massage tables that rolled slowly forward on the tracks. Drifts of foam moved on the shiny wet floor. A sound of clinking filled the air; the massage tables were being drawn forward by loops of chain under the floor. The soap smelled wonderful.

Each woman had a washing station, with several pedals to control the spray of water.

"The right pedal is soapy water, the left pedal is rinse water," said Zilka. "Enjoy." She left.

Shandee tested the sprayers and the pedals. The water was warm. A man emerged through the dangling plastic flaps and was slowly pulled toward where she stood. A preliminary curtainlike blast of warm prewash water drenched him, and as he reached Shandee's station and came to a stop, he lay dripping, strapped to the table, his eyes closed. Shandee looked at the other women, who were all busily spraying their men. The speakers were playing something without words and with lots of twelve-string guitar. She cleared her throat.

The man opened his eyes and smiled at her. "Hi," he said.

"Hello," said Shandee. "Welcome to the House of Holes. I guess I'm supposed to spray you. Are you okay with that?"

"Yes," he said. He closed his eyes again, and she sprayed him all over with soapy water and then began scrubbing down his chest with her orange sponge mittens. She reached his genitals and scrubbed his short, thick penis, which lay against his stomach, lengthening, and his balls, which were warm and heavy and loose. Then she scrubbed down his legs and back up to his balls again, trying to maintain a professional frown. She noticed as she straightened that his penis was no longer lying back, but was now pointing diagonally at a corner of the room.

She sprayed, rinsing it. And then, with a clink of dragger chains, the massage tables lurched into motion.

"Bye," she said.

"Bye, thanks," he said.

Another man emerged through the flaps. She washed his penis. Then another. Most of the men lay quite still. One tried to grope her, and she said, "Oh, stop it," and sprayed water in his face.

More men to be washed. She was really starting to get into the rhythm of it. Just when she felt relaxed, Ruzty appeared. He was propped up on an elbow, looking around for her. When he came through the flaps he broke into a relieved beaming smile. He wasn't quite so muscly as some—built more like a snowboarder than a bodybuilder—and he lay with one knee up. "I'm so lucky to see you," he said.

"I'm lucky to see you. I thought about you yesterday. I did rude things to an orange."

She gently put his knee down and washed his stomach. She

washed his legs. She didn't touch his cock, although it was the most beautiful cock she'd ever seen. It lay there.

"This is pleasant," he said. "I'm lying here while a woman scrubs me."

She scrubbed his calves and thighs.

"Uh, would you mind also washing my private places?" he said.

"Oh, I'd like to, but I'm afraid I can't," said Shandee.

He looked at her with eyebrows raised.

"If I start washing your private places," Shandee explained, "I'll get carried away and want to jerk you and watch you come, and you heard what Lila said—we're not allowed to."

He made a whimpering sound. "Just look at my cock. Look at how bad it needs you. Is it really true that you don't mind that it curves?"

"Believe me, I don't mind," Shandee said. "Your cock is a revelation. Some have a hammer, and some have a sickle." With this she pressed the spray pedal and drenched Ruzty's body with warm soapy water. The cock still stood, hunched over, proud and pale and purple tipped. She sponged his forehead gently. "You poor thing," she said. She hit the spray pedal again and drenched his balls with warm unsoapy water, watching them metamorphose. His mouth was open so she kissed it, and then she looked down at his cock again. She simply couldn't stop staring at it.

"Just hold it for one second, will you, please?" he said. "I'm quite desperate."

"Oh, okay," she said. She held his cock in her orange sponge mittens. In a flash he grabbed a sprayer and sprayed her shirt.

"You!" she said. She looked down. The dark buttons of her nipples were visible through the white fabric.

"Watch what your nipples do to me," he said, and he tightened his cock muscles so that his scythe squirmed and nodded like some strange plant.

"Whooo!" said Shandee.

"Take off the mittens and hold it, please, please!"

"I'm going to get in trouble, but okay." She pulled off her sponge mittens and held her hands under the soapy water till they were slippery. Then she took hold of Ruzty's cock, which was as hard as a summer squash. She splayed her fingers and moved them over his balls and then over his stomach. She could see his thigh muscles tighten. His cock was straining, and she had to stroke it. She took it in her hand and felt its thickness and its sense of certainty. It was like the Arch of St. Louis. It had one thing to say to the world: "I am a stiff swervie." She slid her hand up to the tip—it was like sliding over a steering wheel—and slid it down again, enjoying the sheen of the soapy water on his cockknob.

"This is a big, beautiful dick you've got, Ruzty," she whispered.

"Thank you," he said. "You're nice to say it."

She began moving her hand slowly, then faster. "Ooh boy, I want this dick inside me," she said, "I want to be fucked by this dick, I can't help it, it's so perfect. It's literally THE perfect dick for me."

She gave it a number of good quick pulls and then she noticed that Ruzty was quivering and trembling. Suddenly he said "Ohhhhhhrrrrr" in his beautiful accent, and several white glops spouted from the end.

Immediately there was a buzzer and a ringing. "Uh-oh," said Shandee. She blew Ruzty a kiss.

"Bye-bye," said Ruzty.

An assistant named Krock appeared and led Shandee away.

"Why in heaven's name did you wank him off?" Krock asked.

"I didn't mean to. He begged me, and I obliged him."

"Did you take off your sponge gloves?"

Shandee nodded. "We had a rapport. I'm sorry."

Krock reassured her. "I think it'll be okay. Lila will give you your reassignment tomorrow."

"Is there any chance that I'll be able to see him again?"

"You never know," said Krock. He gave her a sly look. "I'll put in a good word for you."

"Thanks." Shandee shook her head wistfully. "I really wanted that cock of his so bad. God, I still do. I can't stop thinking about it. I had to hold it. I'd give that cock everything."

"I wish people said that about my cock," said Krock, as they reached the lobby of Shandee's hotel.

"I'm sure it's nice," said Shandee.

"Do you want to see it?"

"Um—" Shandee checked the wall clock. "No, thanks. Dave's arm is going to be needing his meal."

Rhumpa Unbuttons Her Shirt

Rhumpa was her name, and, yes, she paid a visit to the House of Holes. The people she was staying with in New Haven were wealthy and under-read. Although they were middle-aged, their minds were very young and she couldn't take them seriously. She saw a pepper grinder in the middle of the table, and while they talked about the price of tires she unscrewed the little knob on the top, and when it came off she lifted the wooden part off the central spindly thing and looked inside, where she could see in the shadows of peppercorns. She thought, The peppercorns are waiting to be ground up. They're still round, like little dry planets, but not for long.

Rhumpa held the machine to her nose and smelled the distant sharpness of the pepper, which made her smile. And then the pepper grinder got bigger and she jumped down into it and fell through tumbling peppercorns, and she smelled a hundred dinner parties of the past.

Then she was herself again, but standing on the porch outside the House of Holes. She rang the buzzer. A man with a bag on his back answered. He introduced himself; his name was Daggett. He took her into a small room with a round wooden table and, referring to a clipboard, began asking her questions. He asked her to describe her ideal man.

"I like men who are intelligent and witty," Rhumpa said. "Also kind to animals and interested in other people and able to hold a conversation of a reasonable length."

Daggett frowned and looked at his clipboard. "It says here that you favor a man with a heavy, dark dick. It quotes you as saying, 'Some nice things are just not possible with a small, pale dick.'"

"Where did you get that piece of information?" Rhumpa asked, outraged.

"During reassembly they do a spectrum analysis," Daggett said. "They screen for diseases, of course, and comb through for lurid thoughts. What's your ideal sexual encounter?"

"Oh, touching, kissing, caressing," Rhumpa said, at a loss.

"It says here that you would favor having three Italian airplane pilots in uniform shoot their comeloads onto your belly while you cup your clitoris with a wooden spoon."

"They don't necessarily have to be Italian," Rhumpa said. "And they can be race-car drivers if that's easier."

"Because of your interest in pilots, we thought you might be a good person to fly one of our pornsucker ships."

Rhumpa asked what a pornsucker ship was, and he explained. "It's an airplane that flies around sucking up bad porn from cities."

"Why?"

"Because bad porn is bad porn—it's depressing and drowns

out good porn. We store it, letting objectionable content settle out. The less porn there is overall, the more likely people are to come to the House of Holes."

"How sordid," Rhumpa said. "I don't want to spend time doing that."

"Oh? It says here that you'd definitely like to steer an airplane with your crotch."

"I do believe you've got the wrong clipboard," Rhumpa said.

"I don't think so," Daggett said, a trifle testily.

Rhumpa asked him if she was a prisoner or a guest.

"Do you want to be here?"

"I'm not sure," said Rhumpa.

"If you do, then you're a guest," said Daggett.

He looked at his notes again, and then at her. He seemed a little hesitant.

Rhumpa asked him, "Are you a guest, too?"

"Yes, but I'm on an intensive work-study program because I accumulated a great deal of debt and they assigned me to do intake."

"I see," Rhumpa said.

He changed his tone. "You're very pretty," he said, leaning forward. "You have a lovely spicy smell. Excuse me." He sneezed.

"What else does it say on your clipboard?"

"It says you'd like to dance in a solo porn video and hold your pussy folds open with your hands, and then you'd like to watch nine men watching your video and getting completely out of control."

"Hm, is that so?"

He tapped his finger on the page. "I'm just going by what it says."

"Well—I do like the idea of men being out of control at the sight of me."

"Ah."

"But I don't want anybody to watch me making the video."

"Of course. You can do it in your hotel room. I'll take you there now."

They rose, and Daggett led her to an elevator and down several hallways and then they came to a catwalk. "Don't be worried," Daggett said. "We're going through a visual privation area. You'll probably hear some shouting. The men are Deprivos. They haven't been able to see nude breasts in any form for three full weeks. This is the last day of their treatment, and they're in pretty sorry shape."

Below was a crowd of men looking up at her. "Take off the top, baby!" they called. "Show us the titties! Flash them, honey, just for a second! Shake them, jiggle them, squeeze them together!"

Finally, Daggett exploded. "For gosh sakes, men, Rhumpa's not going to show off her titties right here! They're way too hot for that. Have some sense. If you want to see her nude you'll have to go to one of the booths in the boothbay after you get out of Deprivo. Check channel six, where, if we're lucky, she'll be doing the homemade amateur nasty for us and showing us her hot fat warblers. Right, Rhumpa?"

Rhumpa shrugged, a little nervous. "Maybe."

"And congratulations, men, on making it through the program." That quieted them down, and Rhumpa and Daggett passed on without incident.

They turned down a hall and reached Rhumpa's room,

number 715. Daggett opened the door for her and ushered her in. He set the bag down on the bed, massaging his stiff fingers.

"What's in your bag?" Rhumpa asked.

"This is the bag of bras. Aside from intake, my job is to carry this bag on my back and help women choose a new bra for their time in the House of Holes."

"That must be fun for you," Rhumpa said.

He nodded. "Yes and no. The bag is a burden to me at times, because of the conditions of my assignment."

"You must like breasts."

He nodded. "Of course. All sizes. And I do believe I have a bra for everyone." He began grabbing handfuls of them from the bag and made a huge mound of every color and style. "If you're going to make a solo amateur sex video, which bra you wear is important. It may be the most important choice you ever make."

"And you'd like to help me choose?"

"Very much. But the unbreakable rule is that I can't ever look at your breasts."

"What—you're a Deprivo, too?"

Daggett hung his head. "Unfortunately, I am, yes."

"You mean that if you see my breasts you'll be turned to stone?"

"No, of course not."

"Then what?"

"If I see your breasts," he said, "they'll take me away and perform a reversible orchidectomy on me."

"What's that?"

"They remove my balls and put them in storage for a couple of weeks."

"That's harsh," said Rhumpa. "The empty sack?"

"Yes, it happened to me once, and it was bad."

"Who takes care of your balls while they're in storage?"

"Aunt Maven has a number of female helpers. They're called 'ballkeepers.'"

Rhumpa took this in. "So how will you help me choose?"

"Take a shower, and when you come out I'll have all the bras arranged on the bed, and then you can try them on, and if we need to we'll use the Silken Flesh Communicator." He held up a finger. "But first, of course, I'll need to see your current bra."

"On me?"

He nodded quickly.

"You mean, unbutton?"

He nodded again, waiting.

Rhumpa began unbuttoning her shirt, and to overcome the awkwardness that she felt—along with some excitement, for what woman can avoid feeling a thrill as she unbuttons her shirt in front of an attentive stranger?—she asked Daggett what the Silken Flesh Communicator was.

"It's hard to describe. It works pretty well if you know what you're doing. You'll see."

Rhumpa's shirt slid off her arm onto a chair, and she stood looking at the corner of the room, a little embarrassed, with her palms toward him. "Me in my bra," she said.

Daggett exhaled and slowly sat on the bed, staring. His eyes were large, and they were fixed on her breasts. He began muttering to himself. "Oh, those are so beautiful and generous and so lonesome and shy and so full and soft," he whispered, almost inaudibly.

"Sorry?" Rhumpa said.

He made an effort to collect himself. "A fine T-shirt bra," he murmured. "With a lovely woven starfish pattern. Is it a Luleh brand or is it an Olivia Wallenstein?" He made a brief show of looking into his bag of bras and then gave it up and returned to staring directly at Rhumpa's titboobs.

"I think it's an Olivia Wallenstein," she said, smiling.

"Make the porno in it. It's perfect for you. You don't need any of my bras."

"Ah, but I do. I need to feel like a different person. This old bra is too—autobiographical." She pulled down on it to seat it better, and then shrugged. Daggett's breath caught at her motions, and she laughed at her casual power over him. "They're just breasts," she said. "I wish they were a little bigger."

"Nonsense," he said. "You mustn't say that around here." He leaned forward and whispered, "Be careful what you wish for." His eyes moved hungrily from her right breast to her left, and then back.

"So you're saying if right now I took this bra off in front of you you'd really have your balls removed?"

"An alarm would go off in Lila's office," Daggett said. "Two headless men would come and take me away to be reversibly castrated. My testicles would live in a little mesh bag in a special lobster tank filled with a charged nutrient broth."

Rhumpa was appalled. "You mean with the lobsters in there?"

"No, no, no," he reassured. "Just a special tank."

"Oh."

"And meanwhile I'd wander around visiting museums and, you know, reading travel magazines and listening to choral music and feeling sorry for myself."

"Sounds not so bad," Rhumpa said.

"Oh, it's bad." He cleared his throat and stood. Rhumpa thought she saw a distinct hump in his corduroys. "So—why don't you have your shower and I'll get to work out here choosing and sorting. It's not easy to lay out a selection, and I'll need at least four minutes of complete concentration, I'm afraid."

Rhumpa went into the shower and was stepping out of her panties when he knocked. "Yes?" she fluted through the door.

"Sorry, I'll need your bra, as well, for comparison," he called. "You can just hand it out."

So Rhumpa opened the door and swung the bra out through the crack.

"Got it," he said cheerily.

While she was waiting for the shower water to adjust its temperature, she took a moment to look at herself in the mirror. Not too terrible, she thought. Admittedly her thighs were on the verge of jiggly, but her skin was smooth and almondy-brown, and her dense black bush was shiny and not unattractive. She pulled out her hair clip and looked at her face. Men liked her lips, she knew. No, she thought, it wasn't inconceivable that she could be in a solo sex video.

Rhumpa's hearing had always been keen. As she was about to step into the shower, she heard a tiny clink from the hotel room. Noticing that she'd left the bathroom door slightly ajar, she peered through the crack, at an angle, and was surprised to see Daggett with his back to her and his pants around his ankles. He looked around at the bathroom door to be sure it was closed—it wasn't—and as he turned she saw that he was clutching his erection in one hand and her bra in the other. He turned back and paused, evidently undergoing an inward struggle. Suddenly, with a moaning expression, he began wrapping her bra straps around his erection, which was startlingly large and curved upward slightly like some exotic purple tusk. Holding his hands motionless around her bunched and jumbled brassiere, he rocked his hips, poking and shoving the head of his cock into its waddedness. Then, doubling over, he folded one cup around the length of his cock and made several long gimbaling strokes.

Rhumpa watched, fascinated. Daggett seemed almost on the verge of coming, but, with what seemed to be an immense effort of will, he straightened and gained control of his compulsions. He flung the bra on the bed and pulled up his pants and buckled himself away. In a trice he had himself more or less arranged. His wary eye then darted once again to the bathroom door, but Rhumpa was too quick for him—she'd already pulled back from the gap. She got into the shower and began humming. Who could blame the poor man? Forbidden as he was to see any living breasts, he yet had to spend his life carrying around a bag of bras. It was no wonder that he developed what seemed to be a fetish. Rhumpa felt sorry for him. She liked him.

Cardell Goes to the Laundromat

Cardell put on a black corduroy jacket and went to the laundromat at 18th Street and Grover Avenue. A woman was peering into the dryers. "Do you know which dryer leads to the House of Holes?" she asked, giving him an appraising look. She was pretty in an ethereally wavy flaxen-haired way.

"Well, I was told it was the fourth dryer from the end," he said.

An old man spoke. "It is indeed the fourth dryer from the end," he said. "But stay away from the House, both of you. Lila will suck you dry. You ever heard of King Nynus?"

Cardell shook his head. The ethereal girl nodded.

"That was me. I wasn't a king, but I was rich. I had a harem with eighteen women, each lovely in a different way, and I spent my days eating watercress sandwiches. Now that's all gone."

"What happened?" asked the ethereal girl.

"Debts. I couldn't get enough of the summertime Tit Swarm.

That's when they put a lot of women in a dark room and tell them, 'Okay, tops off, girls, it's a tit swarm!' Then they let in one guy—me. The speaker says, 'Man entering, repeat, man entering,' and then the man gropes around, feeling everyone's breasts. It's so damn much fun."

"What do you do now?" asked the flaxen girl.

"Now I sit here and tell people never to go to the House of Holes."

"You're kind of a naysayer, you know," said the flaxen girl. Her curiosity piqued, she opened the door of the dryer and peered in.

"See anything?" said Cardell.

"Looks pretty ordinary to me," she said.

"It's not ordinary," warned King Nynus.

The girl climbed in and pushed with her fingertips against the back. Cardell stared at the pockets of her jeans. "I think I found the way," she called excitedly. Then suddenly she disappeared.

"Don't let it close up, hold it open for me!" said Cardell. He climbed in after her, but when he pushed on the back it didn't budge.

"It'll be shut for a while now," said King Nynus. "They never listen."

"Damn," Cardell whispered.

"Don't worry, you'll find a way in." King Nynus pulled a small vial from his pocket. "Let me give you this."

"Thanks, what is it?"

"It's a powerful aphrodisiac. Lila sometimes sprinkles it in the water at the House of Holes. That's one of her little secrets. It's made from Prince Bohuslav's beard. Give a gal a drop or two of that, and powee boom bang."

"Fireworks?"

"Oh, heavens, yes. Do you know the story of Prince Bohuslav's beard? Surely you must."

"No."

"Then I'll tell it to you."

The Story of Prince Bohuslav's Beard

Bohuslav was a powerful prince in the country of Bohrania. When he was nineteen, he married a tall comely princess, with pale eyelashes and freckled shoulders, who bore him a son. She had an unusual habit during their lovemaking: At the point of her climax, she would bite hard on his luxuriant braided beard. As a result of this repeated act of passion, Prince Bohu's beard began to develop a memory.

For the most part he ruled with fairness, and he loved his tall pale queen, but every few weeks her perfect beauty and her perfect goodness made him restless, and he became possessed with the need to plunge his purple cameroon into an ugly-but-lovely woman. He liked them plump and awkward and shy and full of jokes, with a gap between their two front teeth. He called them Uniques. When his queen visited the sick in the northern colonies every other Thursday, he would whisper to his court, "Find me a new and wonderful Unique for tonight," and then he would begin washing and singing and braiding his enormous beard. When the candles were lit, he sat on his throne, wearing a tiny toga, and the Unique was brought in, holding a penis sandal made of heavy black ribbon. She had been bathed and scented and told strange stories about mountain zebras mating, and she had been closely instructed in the art of lacing the penis sandal.

The king would ask her to kneel before him and he would open his legs, and she would lace the ancestral sandal around his swelling penis, telling him the new jokes that were circulating in his kingdom. He would laugh loudly, and his penis would become as hard as applewood and knotted with veins, whereupon he and the Unique would begin kissing eagerly on his throne. Then he would say, "Untie the sandal," and with one pull, as she had been trained to do, the girl untied it, so that it hung dangling for a moment from his royal turgidity.

"Stuff me full of your hot substance, oh mighty king, for I am Unique," the girl would say, as she knelt over him on the throne, planting her hands on his enormous chest. And at the moment of their perfect union, King Bohuslav would seize his black braided beard and hold it to her mouth, whereupon she would clamp down on it to stifle her cries. Thus the memory of innumerable couplings entered his beard.

This went on for almost ten years. Bohu's beard by now had a huge double braid and looked like a loaf of pumpernickel challah. It was said by some in the court that if you held your ear to his beard, you could hear the pleasure cries of a thousand women.

One night, though, a Unique of uncommon intelligence was lacing up the penis sandal. King Bohuslav groped for her breast and tried to kiss her, but suddenly she pulled out a large pair of shears and lopped off his beard with one powerful snip. King Bohuslav let out an agonized bellow and lost consciousness. The girl ran out the side door and hid carefully for a week in the hills with a friend.

Meanwhile the prince had sent guardsmen and black dogs out in search of his braided beard. "How can we hide it?" asked the girl of her friend. The friend knew the arts of pharmacy, and the two young women boiled the beard until it dissolved. Then they skimmed off the purple scum and buried it, and they purified and distilled the barbaric essence, mixing it with the liqueurs of fennel and saps of wild spinach, making of this mixture an uncommonly powerful aphrodisiac. The two women fled to Paris and grew wealthy selling Prince Bohu's beardwater, under the name Gouttelettes de Bonheur, or Droplets of Happiness. Even much diluted, the liquid had a startling effect on anyone, male or female, who tasted it.

The prince, meanwhile, took the loss of his beard as a warning. He ended his dalliance with Uniques and built a large hospital so that his wife wouldn't go away on Thursdays. Seventeen of his penis sandals are on view in the museum of the House of Holes.

Rhumpa Makes Her Come Video

Rhumpa emerged from her shower in a hotel bathrobe, with her hair in a towel turban. Daggett had arranged fourteen bras on the bed, sorted neatly by color. "These are all roughly your size, I believe," he said primly.

She looked at them with a secret smile. "They're all very nice," she said.

"Does one in particular call out?"

She shook her head no.

"Well then," he said, "there's only one way to make the right selection." Daggett drew from the bag a large piece of patterned silk. "This is the Silken Flesh Communicator," he said. "If you allow me to place this over your naked breasts, it will help me determine which of these bras is ideal for you." Gently holding Rhumpa's shoulders, he had her stand facing away from him. "Open your robe," he said. "Wait! Good. I just had to check that

I couldn't see you in any mirror. Now open your robe. Let it fall open."

Rhumpa did as he asked.

"Thank you. Now I am going to gently unfurl the Silken Flesh Communicator and draw it back against your breasts so that it surrounds them and cools them and makes them feel exactly the way your breasts most want to feel. Are your breasts ready for the silken touch of the communicator?"

Rhumpa looked down at them. She smoothed her hand over them and jostled them a few times. The nipples had tightened and were pointing off, as they did. "Yes, they seem to be quite ready," she said. "Unusually jiggly today, in fact."

Daggett made a small whimper and gently flung the piece of transparent silk over her head so that it fell in a U in front of her. Very slowly he pulled it back, so that the folds opened. She watched her breasts fill them. He held the ends of the fabric with a light touch, not drawing it too tight. He paused. "There," he said. "I can feel them resisting my pull."

"Mm," she said. The pattern on the silk was of peonies and birds of paradise. As he pulled, she felt the silk coming alive against her skin. It was clearly not just an ordinary fabric; it had an intelligence.

"I can sense the nervous vibration in your hands," she said.

"Yes, sorry," Daggett said. "Now we wait just a bit, and the silk will conform itself exactly to your shape, and it will understand your weight. But you must walk with me for a moment for it to work."

Rhumpa walked slowly around the room, and Daggett followed behind her. She could feel her breasts bouncing a little in their sheer halter, and she knew that the fabric was recording how they moved. Suddenly she felt a surge of warmth that began deep in her breasts and burned upward till it reached the tips of her nipples and was gone.

"That's it!" said Daggett. "Your breasts have communicated." He withdrew the silk and Rhumpa hiked her robe back on and tied the sash.

Daggett dangled the fabric over the bras that he'd arranged on the bed and waited. Nothing happened. Then all at once there was a twitching, a tugging, a movement similar to that of a dowsing rod. "It's working," he said. "Watch."

The very end of the fabric quivered and reached in the direction of a pale-yellow-and-white plaid bra with a white band of lace over its top. "This yellow one?" Rhumpa said. "I wouldn't have chosen it."

"It will fit you well and make you feel so beautiful and so new to yourself that you will make a movie that will cause many men watching it to bring out their cocks and yank on them till the jizz flies everywhere."

"Okay," Rhumpa said. "And, uhm, Daggett? I don't know quite how to put this. You can have my old bra if you want."

Daggett, reddening, reached under the pillow for it. "I just put it away for safekeeping."

"I saw you manhandling yourself with it."

Daggett moaned and dove facedown on the other bed. "I'm so sorry," Rhumpa heard him say, muffled in the pillow. "I'm so utterly mortified."

She put her hand on his shoulder. "That's okay. You wanted to see my breasts and you weren't allowed to. You were a big bundle of pent-up desire."

Daggett peeked at her. "Thank you for understanding," he said, visibly relieved.

Rhumpa took the yellow plaid bra to the bathroom with her and put it on. And it was true, this bra fit her perfectly, and her breasts looked full and luscious and slightly squeezed together, and she had a feeling it would drive a man crazy to look at what she was carrying in that bra.

"What should I wear below?" she asked.

He handed her the Silken Flesh Communicator. "Tie this around your waist, it can be your skirt. Leave your panties on."

Daggett helped her set up the tripod, aiming the camera so that she could dance next to the bed or on the bed. And he showed her how to turn on the music. Then he left.

Rhumpa danced at first on the balcony. Because it was so bright outside she was in a silhouette. Then she paused the camera and came inside and closed the dark-green drapes. "I'm going to do a pussy dance for you guys," she said. She slowly took off her robe and shook her jerries in the bra for the camera. She danced with one finger up her stash, danced while circling her clit, danced with one foot up on the edge of a chair seat.

She knew it was good. She phoned down. "Daggett? I'm done pussy dancing."

He came back to her room and retrieved the camera. "Have some dinner," he said. "I'll edit the tape and load it on channel six."

Rhumpa had an eggplant panini down at the café, and then Daggett led her down a hall inset with sixteen square, mirrored windows. There were green and red lights above each window. "In each of these little rooms is a man," said Daggett. "He has control of a video screen that has sixteen possible tracks. By clicking a button he can switch from one track to the next. You can look in any of the windows, but only when the light is green is someone looking at the movie of you dancing."

She nodded. She stood for a moment. All the lights were red, and then one was momentarily green, and then it went red again. Another light changed from red to green and stayed at green. Rhumpa walked to the window and peered in through the one-way mirror. In it was a man she hadn't seen before. Rhumpa was watching him from the side so that she could see a little bit of her own dancing performance. Mainly she saw him, sitting in a chair, squeezing his united parcel through his pants.

She looked at his face and saw how intently he was looking at her dance, and she saw that when she turned around and lifted the scarf he undid his belt. He stood and pushed his pants down and out flopped a heavy, ugly dick in the shadows of the little room. He stroked on himself several times and then he clicked the channel-selection button with the back of his hand. He began watching someone else strip. That was a rude shock.

Rhumpa stood back and looked at all of the doors: Three lights were on the green. She hurried to each window. In one room, a man had entirely removed his pants and underpants. He stood in his dress shoes, naked from the waist down, his feet tightly together, his fist shuttling over his small tuber. In the next one, a guy in jeans was leaning way back, his jeans unzipped and open, his dick-ball ensemble flaccidly out and about. In the third was Dune. He hadn't yet taken his pants down.

Breathing softly so as not to fog the glass, Rhumpa watched Dune remove his suede jacket and hang it on a hook on the back of the door. She watched him study the video of her dancing with her finger in her snatch patch. For a while he didn't move, and she couldn't tell what he was thinking; then all of a sudden he wrenched open his belt, unbuttoned his pants, and slid his boxers down. His dick bobbled once and stood still, its tip angling up slightly. He enclosed it with two hands and looked back at Rhumpa's movie.

"He's gorgeous—what a penis!" said Rhumpa to herself, enraptured. She was desperate to nibble on his pectoral manslabs; desperate to knead his suede-soft balls. She wanted him everywhere, in all holes at once—she wanted to show him the real her and not a movie of her.

Dune now leaned with his left hand splayed flat against the wall, holding the other hand fisted and motionless in the air about a foot in front of his crotch. He nosed his free-hanging cock into the tightness of his fist and began pumping his hips, driving the unyielding dicklength deep into his hand tunnel. His long hair hung in his face. When, in her video, Rhumpa put one foot on the chair and held her pussylips open, Dune started thrusting hard. Again and again the head of his cock poked out, dark and bull-necked, from his immobile fist, until finally, at the end of one long plunge, he held still for an instant and sent a hot and heavy lasso of manstarch slapping against the video screen. Even through the soundproofing, Rhumpa thought she could hear his primeval cry. He squeezed his Pollock one last time, shaking the orgasmal dregs onto the floor.

Breathless, elated at what she'd seen, Rhumpa wandered in a daze of dicklust back to her hotel room. She put on a dress, one dangly earring, sunglasses, and a soft sweater with big buttons, and then slowly she took everything off except the sunglasses. She lay on the bed and stuck two fingers up her simmering chickenshack and shook them. She found a can of Red Bull in the mini-fridge and humped its coldness. She thought about plaid patterns and polka dots. She could feel her ovaries and her hipbones dying for dick.

She called the front desk. "I don't want to come alone," she said. "I want a forest of cocks around me. I want to see them up close—I want to wear my sunglasses and have dick juice splurt all over them. I want ball loads of hot cockslurp landing on all my soft parts. This is an emergency top-level request for dick."

"You got it, ma'am," said the man at the front desk. She heard him make an announcement. "H.O.H. H.O.H. Emergency H.O.H. Hotel room 313. Eighteen stiff dicks needed."

Rhumpa heard the thumping of many feet, and then a crowd of dudes of all ages in green T-shirts arrived and began hopping out of their cargo pants. They formed an oval around the bed, where Rhumpa lay teasing herself, wearing red fingerless gloves.

"Now start ragging," she said. "Rag on yourself as fast as you can. Faster! Faster!" The men were puffing and blowing, their cheeks pink, a fine sheen of strain on their foreheads. "Who's first?" Rhumpa said. A little man of about forty-five wearing a baseball cap said, "I'm gonna juice big-time!" Rhumpa grabbed the back of his leg and pulled him close. "Come all over these britneys," she said. "They need it, shoot right here." She pinched her nipples and pointed them around the crowd. "Here it comes!" the man croaked, and a long whipflick of silly string curved through the sparkling air.

Then one very hairy man pulled off Rhumpa's panties and clapped them to his nose and went, "Aaaah!" He jerked out his putz and splashed on her pussyfloss.

"Next! I need more come—more come!" Rhumpa said.

Just then Daggett burst in, naked, wild-eyed, with Rhumpa's former bra twisted around his huge purple erection.

"Daggett!" she said. She clapped her hand over her breasts.

"I don't care, I need to see them, I don't care."

She let her hands fall, and he stared feastingly at her breasts while he slowly unwrapped the straps of her bra from his pulsing hellhound. He waved the other men back. "Take me and fuck me good!" Rhumpa said. She threw her legs open and he slowly socketed himself deep in her famished slutslot. Somewhere alarm bells and buzzers rang, but the lovers fucked for a moment with joyous sweaty abandon, laughing. Then two headless men appeared and pulled Daggett away.

"Is this it for your balls, then?" Rhumpa asked.

"They're going back in the tank," he said, "but it was worth it. It's only two weeks."

"I'll go to the opera with you," Rhumpa called as they dragged Daggett away.

When he was gone, she gestured the other men back. "More come, more come!" she said. "Jerk it out! Ice my cake, dickboys! I want to feel like a breakfast pastry!"

Wade Learns about the Cloth of Ka-Chiang

Wade's vesicles were jumping, and he felt sunny inside. He wanted to be near a woman he didn't know, but he felt a little shy, so he called up the House of Holes and said, "Hi, this is Wade, and I'd like to be able to be friendly with a woman."

Wade was transferred to Lila, who said, "Honey, why don't you come on by?"

Wade said, "Because I don't know how."

"Do you have a penis, Wade?"

Wade said he did.

"Then grab hold of it."

Wade grabbed hold of it.

Lila said, "Now make it hard and stare it down. Is it hard yet?"

Wade said, "No, it shrank way down while I was making this call."

Lila said, "Well, you're not going to get anywhere without a dependable boner."

Wade said, "I realize that. Okay, here it goes. It's hard now."

"Good, now stare right down at the hole in it. That'll open up time and spice for you. We're out here in spicetime."

Wade stared at his cockhole and zoomed down into it. It was kind of an odd, juicy, self-referential experience, but at the end he emerged as himself in the waiting room outside Lila's office. Lila's assistant for the day, an intern named Crackers, opened the door and asked him in. Wade said hi to her. Crackers, dressed in black pipe-stem jeans, was not bad at all—in fact, she was perfect—and he wanted to fondle her or touch her shoulder but it didn't seem the right moment. He sat down in the office chair. There at her desk was the famous Lila, a large and lovely gal of a certain age.

"I'd like to be able to help you, Wade," said Lila. "How long are you going to want to be busy here at the House of Holes?"

"I'd say three, four days," said Wade. He was tightening and loosening his thighs while Kegeling his love muscle, making his balls rearrange themselves. It all felt good in a crowded sort of way. "I figure maybe a girl will take a liking to me, and then I'll get over my shyness and go home with her and then I'll have a girlfriend."

"Now there's a plan, Wade. Four days, nine thousand dollars a day," said Lila, calculating. "That'll be thirty-six thousand dollars for room and board."

"That's too much. I can't pay it."

Lila said, "Can you drive a truck? Because if you look good enough naked I can offer you a half-time paid gig here in which you drive the sludge truck. That's the truck that drops off the pornsludge after we've let it settle in the settling tanks."

"Where do I drive it to?"

"We spread it over fields at the Triple O Raunch, and we grow all kinds of yellow and red and blue cornflowers there. Women walk through the fields after the flowers have bloomed and they get all hot and bothered, and they don't know that there's a layer of sanitary pornsludge underneath their feet. It's a pretty good system. But it depends on how you look naked."

"I see. Well, let me take my clothes off." Wade handed Crackers his Hawaiian boxers, and she tied his penis back with a rough strip of burlap.

"Good, now I'll weigh your testicles, if you don't mind," said Lila.

Just then Hax walked in and slapped his head. "Here she goes again, feeling the balls," he said.

"Hax, please be quiet and let me do my job." Lila cradled Wade's balls. "Hmm, good temperature," she said, frowning slightly. "You seem strong and resourceful." She lifted one ball, let it fall, then lifted the other and let it fall. "They're heavy, and they're independent. I believe you've got naturopathic potential. Your balls are holistic. You pass the testes."

Wade asked what that meant.

"Some men's come—young men's come—can develop special healing powers," Lila answered. "Did you masturbate yet today?"

"I haven't," said Wade. "I was too busy thinking about calling you up."

"Good," said Lila. She opened a wooden box on her desk and lifted out the top part, which held old coins and stamps. Underneath was a folded green cloth with ancient symbols on it. "This is the sacred healing cloth of Ka-Chiang," Lila said. "I'm going to tie it loosely around your balls. If you wear it for twenty-four hours you'll develop a crop of new sperm—very, very special sperm."

"Special how?" asked Wade.

"If the cloth works as it should," said Lila, "your new sperm will have the power to reattach human limbs or heads."

"That's interesting," said Wade.

Gently, with her head held slightly to the side, Lila tied the green cloth around Wade's balls. As she worked its corners into a small knot, the tugging made him smile slightly. His penis grew under the roughness of the burlap and pointed off to the side. "How does the Ka-Chiang cloth feel to you?" Lila asked.

"Not bad," he said.

"Not too tight?" she said.

He said no, just right. "Burlap tickles, though."

"Now," she said, "you're almost ready to go, but first you must, absolutely must, empty out the crop of mature sperm in your system, so that you will have a fresh, new generation formed under the powerful influence of Ka-Chiang. Crackers, could you please do a sexy lap dance to help Wade while he gives himself pleasure?"

Wade made a noise. "You mean I'm supposed to wank while Crackers does a lap dance?"

"If you'd like to give yourself pleasure privately in a different room you can do that instead."

"No, it's not that. It's just that you tied this handkerchief on my balls and now this. It's happening rather fast is all I'm saying."

"It must happen fast," said Lila, gesticulating. "We must clear out the old regime. The old tired ways of sperm must go. The young ones need their room to flourish." She handed Wade a small jade cup. "Ejaculate your sweet salty hotness in that, if you like. Or in my hand. I'd love to hold your seed." She held out her hand.

Wade put the jade cup down. "Maybe I'm too shy to have you watch me," he said. "Maybe I should go back home."

"Crackers, flash Wade your marvelous smile," said Lila. Crackers smiled a marvelous smile. "See, you're a prisoner now. You can't escape. You're going to have to come in this jade cup."

Lila's hands went down to Wade's knees, and then she slowly brought them up, touching only the hair on his thighs. Meanwhile, Crackers hooked her thumb under his cock and began moving it around.

"Tell me about a girl you think about at night," Lila coaxed.

"Well, at night," Wade said, swallowing, "sometimes I think about this girl in my Ancient Civilizations class. She listens to my ideas about the Phoenician traders, and we don't agree but it's okay. I've talked to her in the cafeteria a couple of times. She has a baggy blue T-shirt that says Froot Loops." Crackers lightly touched Wade's hipbones and his chest. Wade tightened his pectoral muscles when her fingers passed over them.

"What do you imagine doing with her?" Lila asked. "Grip your cock with both hands and tell me."

Wade gripped his cock like a flag bearer. "I think about putting my hand up under her Froot Loops T-shirt," he said.

"And what about her ass?"

"It's sacred ground. It's so loose and so jiggly it isn't even funny."

Lila smiled at his shyness. "You're a sweet boy, Wade, and I want to see those handsome white teeth when you come. We're going to coax all the old jizz out of those hot young stones of yours. Don't be shy now, let's see you work it. I want you to look me right in the eyes and stroke that big meat wagon for me. Isn't that a nice dingaling he has, Crackers?"

Crackers felt Wade's cock and smiled and nodded. "Nice," she said.

Wade smiled at her gratefully, then pumped himself.

"Oh, yeah, I like when your balls hop like that in the cloth!" said Lila. "You want to see some tit cleavage to keep that dick hard? Here's some tit cleavage for you. Make those balls jump for me. That's it."

Wade stared at Lila's boobs, one and then the other. He was as hard as a flügelhorn by now. He put his thumb on the side of his dick at the base and moved it and watched his dick wang lewdly this way and that.

Lila leaned forward. "Pardon me, I want a whiff of that." She tipped her nose and sniffed as Wade pointed the head of his dick at her face. "Mmmmm, that is a musky little fucker, isn't it? Makes me want to shake my boobs around for you. Want to see them really shake? Crackers, help me free up one of these bad babies for Wade."

She pulled off her sweater. Underneath was a huge pink-and-white bra. She reached into one of the bra cups and pulled out something shaped a little like a baby seal. Wade had never seen anything so big and so beautiful in his life.

"Oh, my, that's a massive tit!" Wade said.

Then Lila and Crackers scooped the other tit out, and Lila leaned forward, and when Wade touched the crinkly skin around her nipple she shivered and said, "My cookies are very sensitive." She hauled the tits together and pointed them at Wade and shook them. Then she held the shallow jade cup under one of her huge pancake nipples. "Now, my young friend, empty your stones all over this nipple and fill up this cup. I want to see the miracle of your come."

"I don't know if it's going to be all that miraculous," Wade said.

"All orgasms are marvels, so shoot that wad for me, darlin'," said Lila.

Wade, pumping slower and squeezing harder, approached the moment of abandonment. He could feel his squirter chamber filling as his sack crinkled and his balls tossed everything they had in the jizz hopper. "Mgonna come, mgonna come," he whuffled, and then he said, "Nnnnnngggggggggaaaaaaaw!" and there came the fluid catapult. His dickhole pushed open and a doublethick sackshot pitched out onto Lila's nipple and dripped down into the jade cup.

"Ooh, cream my tit, milk that cockmeat all over it, get it all out!" Lila said, frowning and shaking drops of come from her nipple into the cup. Then she handed Crackers the jade cup and smiled at Wade. She began putting her unforgettable wonderbreasts away.

"Now sleep and let the magic ball-hanky do its work," she said. "It will give you confidence." She slid on her sweater and fluffed her hair. "Take him to the hotel," she said to Crackers. "He'll be staying the night."

Wade followed Crackers to his room, hugged her, and got into bed. The sheets were cool and clean. He slept happily and soundly with the cloth of Ka-Chiang tied around his balls.

Cardell Buys a Gel Pen

Cardell still wanted to meet a nice, smart, sexy woman. His best bet, he decided, was to go to a coffee shop he knew called Tribe of Bean, where women sometimes wore dresses. Cardell had noticed that when a woman wore a dress at a coffee shop on a Saturday afternoon it often meant that she wanted to meet somebody. Of course, it didn't necessarily mean that she wanted to meet Cardell in particular—but she might.

First what he needed, though, was a pen and a notebook, so that he could be absorbed in writing in his notebook in the coffee shop when a woman in a dress came in. So he went to an office-supply store, and he walked to the wall where all the pens were. A petite, fine-boned women was standing there looking over the display. She had dark hair with lots of body and bounce, and she had big eyes and a small bottom and a little black purse. She was wearing a dress—black with thin vertical stripes.

Cardell wanted to be closer to her, so he began to move

sideways. He looked at the roller-ball pens, and then moved sideways some more, to the pastel gel pens. And then he was at the metallics. He was quiet for a while, and she was quiet, as if by mutual agreement.

Finally Cardell cleared his throat. "I'm going to the coffee shop," he said, "and I need a pen to write with. Do you have a recommendation?"

She pointed to the roller-balls. "If you just want to jot down notes, then I'd say go with one of those." She had a soft, thoughtful voice, with a hint of South Carolina in it. "What kinds of things are you going to be writing?"

"Oh," said Cardell, "everything I want in a woman, I guess."

The woman looked him up and down and then said, "Is that an egg in your pocket?"

Cardell nodded.

"I guessed as much," she said. "You'll want something a little more exotic, then." She shook the pen that she'd been holding. "These are the best."

Cardell glanced at the package. "Silver gel," he said. He looked at her questioningly.

She leaned toward him. "You know that if a man signs his name with one of these," she whispered, "something interesting happens. When he comes, his come squirts out molten silver."

Cardell was surprised. "Permanently?"

"No, for a day or two. I had a friend a while back who showed me."

"Do you have a friend now?"

"Well, I have a husband," she said. "He's very wonderful and very successful and very jealous. Sometimes we rent a condo at the House of Holes beach, and when we're there I get a little—ah—urgie-splurgey." She squeezed his biceps muscle.

Cardell thought it was time for a compliment. "Has anyone told you that you look a lot like Marlo Thomas in her prime?"

She thanked him. "Buy the gel pen," she said. "See you later, I hope. I'm Betsy."

Cardell watched her small bottom cheeks shake under the dress as she walked quickly away. He bought the pen and a notebook in a hurry. When he went out to the parking lot, her car was already gone.

At the café he got a huge cup of coffee that he didn't want, and he sat at a table and hauled out the notebook and tore open the packaging around the silver gel pen. He looked at the white page open in front of him, and he looked around the coffee shop. There weren't any women in dresses. There was an old guy sitting on a couch, staring. He had a Parcheesi board open in front of him. Cardell didn't want to play Parcheesi, so he bent over the notebook page and wrote "nice, smart, sexy ass." He tried to sign his name, but the pen went dry halfway through. He unscrewed the top and looked down into the hole at the top of the cartridge. Then he felt a very strange warm feeling in his testicles. His whole body began to lengthen, and suddenly he was flushed right down into the tiny penhole.

He swam blindly through silver gel particles for a minute, and when he came out at the end he was standing on a beach in front of some footprints. A sign said: "House of Holes Harbor. Swim at Your Own Risk."

Jessica Has Some Tattoos Removed

Jessica went for a walk one day wearing not enough clothes. Why? Nobody knows. She didn't know. It was summer, that was all, and she looked good and wanted the world to see. She was wearing a T-shirt and a pair of shorts with wide cuffs and some striped sandals. Only the sandals were the right size.

She walked into a store where they sold windup ears and windup noses and other windup body parts and lots of jokey decorative objects that she didn't want to own but would be willing to give to someone as a birthday present. A man of about thirty was in the store, standing looking out at the street, seemingly lost in thought. When the door jingled to announce Jessica's entrance, he turned toward her and started. She saw several emotions cross his face. He grasped a display of tiny stuffed monkeys to steady himself, panting.

"Is everything okay?" Jessica asked him.

"Yes, fine," he said, breathing in little shallow breaths. "It's just that when I see someone with a certain kind of beauty I can come just looking at her. Would you mind?"

"No, go ahead," said Jessica. "I'll just be browsing around the store." She turned away from him and picked up a pack of political-corruption playing cards. When she turned back she saw his eyes on her rear end. They quickly flicked up to her face, and his lips parted. A little stifled pained sigh escaped his mouth, and he leaned forward, shuddering. He wiped some spittle from his mouth.

She went up to him. "Did it just happen?" she asked.

He nodded. "I know it's strange. I'm freakishly open to a certain kind of beauty. Which you have, obviously."

"Well, I'm glad that it worked out for you," she said.

He took a long, deep breath and laughed and shook his head. "I'm Bosco. I want to paint you," he said, handing her a card. "I don't think I've ever wanted to paint anyone more than you. What's your name?"

She told him.

"Well, Jessica, I hope you'll come to my studio sometime and take off your clothes and pose for me."

She thanked him, and then she hesitated. There was something in his eyes of pleading and of hope that she hadn't seen in a man before. "Where can I see your paintings?" she asked.

He was in a group show in a gallery not far away, he said. "Do you want to go there now? That way you can see if you like my paintings."

"Well, sure, okay," said Jessica.

They walked up the street. Bosco asked Jessica what she was doing in school and whether she'd ever done any modeling before. She said she'd posed for photographers but never for a painter.

"It's very different," Bosco said. "Photographers take lots and lots of pictures. Painters look at you for a long, long time and make one picture. It's more like giving birth. Not that I know what that's like."

"Me neither," she said.

"All in due time," he said.

They turned into a small track-lit gallery. There was a table with some crackers on it. Most of the dip and the carrots and celery had been eaten. She took a cracker and cracked it in her hand. "Which are yours?" she asked.

He touched her back, directing her to a wall with five paintings. They were all of women sitting on chairs, wearing pants but not wearing anything over their breasts. Some sat relaxedly, some seemed tense. He'd caught something unusual in their expressions, which were sad and human. "I like their faces," Jessica said.

"Thanks, will you excuse me for a moment? My underpants are wet with my come, and I'm just going to take them off and throw them out."

Bosco went into the back and reemerged in a few minutes. Jessica had stood standing, looking at the women. She sensed someone looking at her, and when she turned she saw that he was staring once again.

"Do you offer a modeling fee?" she asked, in order to preserve her dignity.

"Name it," he said.

"When I modeled for the photographer, he paid me two hundred dollars."

He shook his head. "I'll sell the painting for eight thousand, of which the gallery will take fifty percent. So I will gross four thousand dollars. Nothing that I paint would exist without your beauty. How about two thousand for you, two thousand for me?"

She thought. "That's generous. But sure, yes."

He nodded. "Good. Now?"

She took a moment to reflect. "I'm kind of sweaty from walking," she said.

"Take a shower at my studio," he said. He said he wouldn't bother her or make any moves. He just wanted to paint her in her cuffed shorts, he said—but topless. "You know I've just had an orgasm so I'm obviously not going to wig out and attack you or something," he said.

Jessica said okay, and then she had a thought. There was a store across the street. "I'm just going to run in there and get some panties," she said. "I hate getting out of the shower and putting on the same pair. Wait here."

She bought a three-pack of panties, and they walked four blocks over to his studio. He said that he'd been painting for fifteen years. He was a little older than she'd thought at first— maybe thirty-eight, fit and kind of craggy with a confused boyish look that she liked. Every so often as they walked he'd lean toward her and say something like, "This is the best day of my life. I'm so eager to get painting. I understand everything about beauty now, now that I've seen you."

His studio was on the third floor. There were ten chairs on one side of the room and a bunch of canvases leaning against the wall. She recognized several of the chairs from the paintings at the gallery. "I haven't painted anyone in this chair," he said. He positioned it on a bare stretch of floor with windowlight coming in.

"I'll just have a shower," she said.

"One thing," he said. "When you come out, please don't put your bra on. It leaves red marks on your skin."

"Okay," she said. She went into his shower and washed using his soap and tore open the packet of panties and put one pair on. She didn't put her bra on but just her shirt, buttoned once.

He gestured her to a chair—white, covered in a nubby fabric. "Sit here and take off your shirt," he said.

Here she hesitated. "I warn you, I have tattoos," she said.

He froze. "You do?"

"Yes. Is that a problem?"

"No, of course not," he said. But he was clearly lying. She could hear the unhappiness in his voice, and she could see it in his face.

"You're disappointed," she said. "Admit it."

"It's just that—I haven't yet fully come to an understanding with tattoos. They tug at my eye, and I have to resist them. They distract me from the line."

"Well, I have a bunch, in various places," said Jessica. "Sometimes now I kind of wish I didn't, but I do."

"Do you really want them gone?" Bosco asked eagerly. "I know a way. You go to this tattoo-remover man, Hax. He has a suite at the House of Holes. He removes them completely, no ghostly traces."

"He must charge a lot of money."

"It won't cost you a thing."

He handed Jessica a card with a hole punched in it. "Tell Lila that you want to see Hax."

The address was way out along the shore. Jessica drove there, and then she saw an exit she'd never seen before, Exit 23-O, that went into a tunnel. When she came out the landscape had changed slightly. Everything had a brighter look. There was a house with several side buildings and wings and a gravel road in front of it in a horseshoe shape. She rang the doorbell.

Zilka led her to an office and introduced her to Lila.

"I wish my tattoos were gone," Jessica said.

"Why?" Lila asked.

"They're not right for me now. I'm done with them. I hate them."

"There is a way," said Lila. "But it involves sex."

"It always involves sex," said Zilka.

"I knew it would, somehow," said Jessica. "I suppose if that's what it involves, that's what it involves."

Lila picked up the phone. "Krock? Where's Hax? Can you ask him to come to my office?"

Hax looked a little like Bobby McFerrin, Jessica thought. He was tall and wore a white shirt. His shoulders weren't enormously muscular, but wiry and graceful. There was something infinitely appealing about his shoulders.

"Show me the tattoos you do not want," Hax said.

"Well, there are four."

"I can remove them."

He stood and held out his hand. "Come." He took her to a massage room. "Undress."

"All the way?"

"No, unless you have a tattoo under where your panties are."

"I do."

"Then take them off. Just common sense. I have to be able to see and touch your tattoos. Let me show you my body." He pulled up his T-shirt. His coffee-colored chest had a bizarre overlay of blue and green patterns. "All these designs were tattooed onto women at one time. I lifted them, and now they're on me. Such a sad thing that women tattoo themselves. It is a way of hiding."

"You think?" said Jessica. "In my case I did the one on my back, and then I liked it, and it was like building a collection of something."

"Yes. But it is collecting something that hides you. It is a way of not being naked while being naked. My job is to return you to your nakedness. Turn over and let me please see your pussy for a moment, if I may?"

She turned.

"Why do you have no hair on your pussy?"

"I don't know," she said. "I just don't. It's the fashion."

"That, too, is a way of hiding. No hair means you are dressed in hairlessness. You are finding a way to be clothed when you aren't clothed. Hair is your true nakedness. Do you want your true nakedness back?"

Jessica nodded. "Can you do that?"

He held out his hands. "These hands can do it. If we are lucky. You must make me feel your nakedness. If I feel it then your hair will grow and your tattoos will lift and come onto me. Try."

He put his hands gently on her hips and looked at her face. "Feel naked now." He circled his hands over her hipbones and then pressed his thumbs gently into her stomach. "Breath in and feel naked," he said. As he pressed she saw his chest muscles jump. "I will do this one first," he said.

He put both his hands over the flower on her breast. His touch was very light at first. "Feel," he said. She began to feel an urgency coming from his hands. Her breast was glued to them.

"You see how we are bonding." Suddenly he flinched. "Oh," he said, "here comes the pain of it."

"The pain of the tattoo?"

"Yes, all of it is going in my arm at once."

"I'm sorry."

"It's okay, it's what happens. It's lifting now. Wait, watch. Look in the air above your booby."

He removed his hands and lifted them. Following his fingers was a faint flower shape in blue and green ink, with a red blossom. He scooped it out of the air carefully. "Where shall I wear this flower?" he said.

She found a place on him that was still mostly free of other tattoos. It was on his rib cage just under his left pectoral.

"Touch it," he said.

She touched it. His skin was hot and very dry.

"Kiss it," he said.

She kissed the skin. He smelled smoky. He closed his eyes then and held the captured tattoo to his skin. "Ouch," he said. He drew his hand away. "Now it is on me, and your breast is naked. Look."

She looked, and her breast was entirely free. There was no ghost of the tattoo, no hint except the faintest tiny outline of what had been there. She sighed and laughed a laugh of relief. "I feel free," she said.

"Good," he said.

"Now my back? My back is the one I really don't want anymore. I hate it. Everybody has a butterfly."

"Stand and turn and I will see," he said.

She turned and he sighed with pleasure, lightly touching the base of her spine. His fingertips had a strange focused intensity.

"Ah, no. This is not merely a tramp stamp. This one was done by a hostile tattooer of great skill. He put a potent fingerblock on it. This will be most difficult. I think we must help you grow back your pussy hair first. You can't release such a tattoo with a bald cameltoe, it won't work."

"But that will take a week at least."

"No, I can help. It will mean my kissing your pussybone and then cupping my hands over it and blowing softly on it."

"Okay."

"You must close your eyes and ask to be naked and hairy again."

"Help me be naked and hairy, Hax."

"I can't hear you."

"Help me be naked and hairy, Hax!"

Gently he directed her to sit on the edge of the table. He knelt between her legs and brushed his fingers in peacock-feather motions over her stomach. He looked up at her. "I will kiss your pussybone now, very lightly."

"Okay."

She felt the kiss as a burning ring that made all of her discouraged and thwarted hair follicles scream and come alive. And then quickly he stood and cupped his large hands over her entire sex place, one hand over the other. He pushed hard against her several times. "Open your legs a bit more," he said. "Good. Now we wait. It will be very warm, almost hot."

All around her pussy the follicles were quivering and trembling and sending up shoots of hair. She looked down and watched her brown bush fill his hand. He pressed her and shook his hand, saying, "That's it. There it goes. Do you feel the tingling?"

"Sorry, I'm getting a little drippy," she said.

"Good, you're feeling naked again." He began swaying and moving his hands over her bush. "Now hold your arms up, and I will give you lots and lots of luscious hair under your arms, too."

"God, no!"

"Are you quite sure?"

"Very sure. No, thank you."

"Okay. But let's see." He removed his hands. "Spread your pussy for me?"

She reached down and felt the thicket of her hair, the feeling that she remembered from when she first became a sexual person. She spread her lips and then scissored her fingers closed around her clit. "Ooooh," she said.

"Better now?"

"Much, yes."

"Now maybe perhaps I will have success with your tattoo."

In one quick motion he turned her so that she was lying facedown. "I will lay my hands directly on your butterfly." She felt his warm dry long hands pressing at the base of her spine. "And now I lift," he said. "Rrrrrrr!" She was conscious of a force lifting her lower back up. "Come on, come on now," he said. He lifted her trembling until she all but hung from his hands. "Your skin is not releasing the ink," he said. "You must relax. I will put you on your knees. We are joined now, and we won't be able to unjoin unless you give up on the release of the tattoo, or the tattoo gives up. It is a battle now. You must choose nakedness. To do that you must play with your clitoris. I may perhaps be able to draw the tattoo out with my penis. Do what your clitoris craves that you do, and show me how open you are."

She slid her knees apart until she felt the tendons tighten in her thighs. "There," she said. "You can look at my cunt if you want."

"It's beautiful. The hair is slick—it looks newborn."

"It's naked, and it's open, and—Hax?"

"Yes?"

"I need you to please fuck me. I want your cock in me."

"Then you will have to pull it out of my shorts," he said. "I'm afraid I can't move my hands from your back."

He moved awkwardly around the table so that she could reach him, and with some struggle she pulled off his white shorts. His dick was shockingly enormous and covered with murky tattoos except for the head, which was bright pink. She gasped at the sight of it, and her shoulders involuntarily arched back to pop her boobs. "You need a home for that thing," she said in a sudden low fuck-ready voice. "Get back behind me."

She rose a little higher, centering his bow-curved dick just where it needed to be, and then she circled on it for a moment so that it was wet all the way around. Then she drove slowly back on it. A long low guttural cry was hauled out of her. "Fuck me, oh, my god, it's been too long. Oh, yes." She bit her lips and felt his hands burning on her back, and then she began to feel a lifting that began at her asshole and swirled and whorled up through her skin and into his hands.

"I must use my penis to pry the ink away under my hands," he said. He drew himself slowly out of her pussy, and then she felt his slickened seedstick slide up over the cleavage of her ass and, directed by her slippery crack, begin bumping against his hands. "I have an opening," he said. "I'm going to fuck your tattoo free now. Uh. Uh. Fuck it away, uh." He slid in and out from under his hands. At first she felt nothing, and then suddenly she could detect all the tiny microampules of ink withdrawing themselves from thousands of tiny holes in her skin. "Ahhhhh!" he said, "it stings, it hurts, it's okay, ouch."

And then he lifted his hands. "Your back is finally nude now." He held a mirror and she saw.

"Oh, baby," she said and she turned. The butterfly was gone. "I'm so free. I'm so clean." She held his dick in both her hands and spoke things to it. "You've made me new, you lovely dick. I'm going to suck you off, and I'm going to feel you come." And so she did. She opened her mouth and let all of his big tattooed dick inside, teasing the hole, and then she pulled back and pumped him several times and felt the come splash over her, and then she collapsed in a happy heap of complete artless pubic-hairy bliss. "My tattoo-removing wizard, how can I thank you?"

"Just tell people: Stop hiding, stop disguising, be naked for once. Be hairy down in the punany." He took her to Lila's office.

"All gone?" asked Lila.

"Gone," said Jessica. "But so are my feelings for the artist, I'm afraid. He didn't want to paint me the way I really looked, and that bothers me. I really want to see more of Hax."

"Well, that's unfortunate, because Bosco paid for your tattoo removal by having a voluntary head detachment."

"That's not good."

"He reveres you, but his head is, for the moment, physically separated from his body."

"Oh, dear," said Jessica. "How awful for him."

Wade Presses the Sex Now Button
and Koizumi Visits

Wade woke up in his hotel room and pressed W, for woman, on the Sex Now button of his remote control. Then he dozed off. About ten minutes later, he heard the door open—the woman had a keycard, he supposed. He heard her slip off her slippers and her bathrobe in the dark and get into bed next to him. He could tell from the way she moved in the bed that she was naked.

"Hi. Wow, that was fast," he said.

"Hello, my name is Koizumi. I'm a sculptor. I am also a collector of wet-dream memories. Do you have a wet-dream memory for me to collect?"

"I'm sorry, I can't remember. I had only a few, and it was a long time ago."

"Try to remember," said Koizumi. "You will remember if you try."

Wade shifted so that he was lying on his back, his arms on

the blanket. He breathed, thinking. "Okay, I remember one. A woman looked at me. I didn't know her. She was sitting under a red beach umbrella and wearing a black bathing suit. Nobody else was around. She held out her arms and I asked, 'Me?' She nodded. She liked me. She understood me. She wanted me. I walked toward her and knelt in the warm sand, and I put my arms around her, and then I felt this gulping overflowing fizzing of sexual goodness, and I woke up, and I discovered that I had a dab of something in my underpants. I went around for a week thinking, Wow, I've had a wet dream. It was great because it was a dream in which something real really happens. I didn't tell anyone. That's it. Not very detailed, I'm sorry."

"Thank you," said Koizumi. "I will let you feel my breasts now."

"Okay, great. Thanks."

Wade felt her breasts.

"I'm sorry they are quite small," Koizumi said.

"Nonsense, they're exquisite, and you know what the Be Good Tanyas say. 'The littlest birds sing the prettiest songs.' You know the Be Good Tanyas, right?"

"Yes, they're Canadian. I'm Canadian Japanese. I believe in supporting Canadian singers."

"Makes sense," said Wade.

"I believe in Canadian art. Also I believe in men who have quite big penises."

"Do they have to be Canadian men?"

"No, they can be non-Canadian. They can be from any country. When I said to the computer that I was ready for sex now I specified only men with quite large penises. So I hope you have one."

"Well, you'll have to see, won't you? Your nipples are hard, like dried peas."

"My husband was not honest with me," said Koizumi. "He had a large penis, and he was very nice, but he was a gay man and he pretended to love me but he couldn't. He wanted me to have my hair cut very short like a boy. He liked to do me in the anus."

"Did you enjoy that?" asked Wade.

"Yes, because of a time I ate a pinecone seed."

"Really? It was eating a pinecone seed that made you like anal sex?"

"Yes, it was," said Koizumi. "When I was thirteen, I wanted a boyfriend. We lived in a small town in northern Saskatchewan. The only friends I had were two sisters, Natasha and Brigid. I told Natasha that I wanted to see a boy without any clothes on, and she said she did, too. So we went to her sister, Brigid, who was older, and we said, 'Brigid, we would like to see a boy without any clothes on.' She said, 'You mean a picture of a boy?' And we said, 'No, not a picture, a real boy.' And she said, 'Then follow me.' So we followed her out to the hill behind their house, where there was a tree that had lots of large pinecones on it. Brigid said, 'Choose a nice pinecone and pull a seed off it and put it in your mouth and chew on it a little and swallow it.' We asked her what would happen and she said, 'A special pinecone will grow inside of you. You'll feel like you're constipated. In a few hours, you will need to take the biggest poop of your life, and it will hurt a lot when it comes out, but not unbearably.' And we said, 'Okay, but how will this help us see a boy naked?'"

"That would have been my question, too," said Wade.

"Brigid said, 'The pinecone is called a boycone, and the best place to allow it out is in the creek.' She said, 'When it comes out, wash the cone in the creek and it'll crack open and a miniature boy will hop out, and if you rub him he will grow rapidly until he is a full-sized boy, and you can talk to him and look at him naked.' We said, 'Can we eat the pinecone seed right now to get started?' And Brigid said, 'Go ahead.' And then she went inside to bake a pie. My friend Natasha got scared and said she didn't want to do it. But I said I would. I chose a nice big pinecone from the tree, and I pulled a seed from it and chewed it up, and nothing happened. We sat on the hill and looked at the telephone pole against the sky and talked about how much we liked boys."

"Nothing happened?" said Wade.

"Natasha kept asking me if I felt anything, and I said no. Finally she went back to the tree and got the biggest pinecone she could find, and she put a seed from it in her mouth, and she swallowed it. Meanwhile, I could definitely feel something going on inside my body. I felt this tremendous pressure in my bottom, against my anus."

"Did it hurt?" asked Wade, full of sympathy.

"No, not then. I pulled down my pants and lay facedown in the grass, and Natasha opened my bottom cheeks and looked. She said she couldn't see anything except that my pussy seemed to be very purple. I said, 'I need to go down to the creek.' So we went down to the creek, and I took off my shoes and my pants and held on to a branch and dipped my bottom in the creek, and I screamed because the water was so cold. Then Natasha whimpered a little and said her boycone was really hurting and needing to come out. I said, 'Mine's hurting, too.' But it wasn't hurting as much, because I hadn't chosen quite so big a pinecone. Then we both squatted in the creek for a while, and we pushed and pushed, and we could feel the boycones wanting to come out but not being able to. Finally we took a breath together and looked into each other's eyes and gave a huge push as hard as we could. She got very red, and then at last the boycones splashed into the creek. We were relieved, and we laughed and washed them off and laid the pinecones in the sun to dry, and we lay next to them. We were quite exhausted."

"I can imagine," said Wade.

"And a few minutes after that, we heard the two pinecones go pop, pop, and crack open. Just as Brigid said, there was a miniature boy in each one, wrapped in green plant folds."

"How old?" said Wade.

"They were about seventeen, but very tiny. We rubbed them and massaged them, and after half an hour they grew to one quarter size, then half size, and then they were full-size long-legged boys, but their eyes were still closed. They were sleeping. So we looked them all over while they gathered strength, and they had the most beautiful penises and thatchy patches. Then their eyes opened, and mine said, 'It's a beautiful day,' and he stretched. I stroked his chest, and I knelt over him and held the sides of his face and looked at his eyes. He was in the tent of my hair, and I could feel his hips trying to find a way in. He was very ready, so I let him in. He became my boyfriend that summer, and then unfortunately he went away. Now I make sculptures of women. I use very smooth hardwood. The women I carve have wide faces, and I always drill deep into their asses. I think the reason why it is so important to drill deep into their asses in my sculpture is because I pooped out the boycone when I was young."

"Maybe, maybe," said Wade.

"I would like to touch you."

"Okay."

Wade felt her fingers move lightly over his arms and chest. They converged and found his cock. Koizumi made a little startled happy sound.

"Oh, that is lusty," she said. "I feel like a lusty lady when I hold your cock. I get a very special feeling in my anus."

"I'm glad you like it," said Wade.

"Would you like to know what my wooden women look like when I carve them?"

Wade said he would.

"They are posed in the kundalini pose, like this." Koizumi threw off the covers and put her round bottom high, with her knees together and her wrists crossed at her ankles. A wisp of black hair fell across her face and stuck to her lips. "I believe that the anus is the center of life energy and of consciousness," she said. "I need to be drilled by a cock now. I hope your cock can be hard enough to fill my ass and anus."

"I hope so, too, for both our sakes," Wade said.

She had something in her hand. "I brought you a pinecone," she said. "Pull off a seed and chew it. It will make your penis very stiff, and then if you come inside my bowel I will make you a special souvenir."

"Oh, wow," said Wade. He pulled off a pinecone seed and chewed it. Almost immediately he developed a huge, almost painful hard-on. "Jeez, my cock's straining at the leash."

"Good," said Koizumi. She handed him a small vial of liquid. "Now put some of this on your finger and circle it around on my anus."

Wade did what she asked. She clenched her bottom cheeks and did a whimpery dance on her knees. "It almost tickles," she said. "Now drill me with your cock," she said. "Unh, unh, unh, put it right down into me. Sink it into me, please," she said.

Wade found her anus and pointed the almost sharp head of his dick into it. He let some of his weight begin to drive it in. He heard a buzzing. She'd brought a little vibrator that she'd clipped to her finger.

She began a mewing kind of chant. "Moon . . . moon . . . moon," she said slowly. "It's big, it's very huge, ouch, ah, slowly, drive it in. Moon. My kundalini body likes to be fucked in the ass," she said.

Wade began to do hip jerks that weren't entirely voluntary—they happened as his cock went deeper and deeper with each pull and push. Finally, he felt the cool pillows of her bottom on his hips.

"Now please continue to fuck in and out of my asshole," Koizumi said, "and when I come you will feel the ring tighten very hard and that is when you must come and put your seed in my bowel, so that I can push out your souvenir."

Wade pulled almost all the way out so that he could feel the blunt, strong rim of her sphincter clenched on his underdick.

Koizumi was in a dream world, and Wade could hear her vibration going rum, rum, rum and her little panting sounds. She said Japanese or perhaps Sanskrit words he didn't understand. Then he felt a sudden distinct spasm of tightness from her anus, followed by a catlike mew of orgasm. It was so primitive and pure and in a strange way mystical that his comesack clenched once, twice, three times, and he could feel the come shudders zithering down into her body.

She collapsed and he lay on top of her, smiling. Her asshole tightened one last time and pushed Wade's softening cock out of it.

"Ah, a good experience," she said. "Now we must wait. I am going to have a bath."

"I'll run it for you," said Wade.

He rinsed off his cock, which was surprisingly clean, and then ran her a warm bath. She came in holding her stomach. "I can feel it growing in me," she said.

She got in the water and held Wade's hand. After a moment's time, she reached down and poked into herself. Then her face contorted, and her upper lip pushed out, and she drooled a little. She practically broke his fingerbones in her grip. In the water was a large brown object.

She slumped back for a moment, resting. "That hurt very, very much, even more than your cock hurt," she said. "But I will recover."

"I think you may have just crapped the bathtub," said Wade.

She looked up. "No, I did not 'crap.' That is incorrect. You will see. This is one of my sculptures. It is made of asswood."

She washed it off and dried it with a towel and handed it to him. The sculpture was indeed in the shape of a woman, with a wide face, made of dark polished wood.

"It's beautiful, I stand corrected," said Wade.

"I will give it to you. I have others for sale in the HOHMA gift shop. Now I will go. I enjoyed our dream. Good-bye." She nodded to him.

"Good-bye," said Wade. "Thank you very much for the sculpture."

Henriette Surfs the Lake

Henriette was sitting in Lila's office. The book of men's faces lay open and unregarded on the glass table next to her chair. Poplars were waving their little leaf shadows on the floor. "I imagine a sensual man," Henriette said, "strong-jawed, financially secure, who understands my needs and is not threatened by them."

Lila snorted in disgust and flung a paper clip into a little dish. "Oh, for heaven's sake, honey," she said. "Can you please cut the boilerplate?"

Henriette, slightly shocked, thought for a moment. "I guess the truth is I'm sort of bored and scared. I don't want to go through life alone, obviously. I want a loving partner. I want a little more out of sex. I've made some bad choices. When I was with my ex I almost never came, because I can't come without my vibrator and the sound of it embarrassed me. I always felt I was doing the wrong thing around him."

"That's fixable," said Lila.

"That's not the real problem. I can find a new guy."

"Of course you can."

"The real problem is I've used the darn vibrator so much lately that it's made me numb! Not just numb, but I sometimes get really sharp tingling pains—not good tingles. Angry hurting tingles."

Lila picked up the phone. "Krock, could you ask Zilka to bring in the Cable of Induhash? The big spool of it, mm-hm." She smiled at Henriette. "Go on."

"So, yeah, I think I've damaged the nerves. It's just so hard to reach that delicious point now. I press and press, it's like my clit is not getting good reception anymore. And honestly, is it worth the effort? And if it isn't worth it, what is? Making a really nice soufflé, that's satisfying. Volunteering at the park cleanup, that's satisfying. But then there is the middle of the night, and my clitoris is just sitting there like a little numb pebble, and I'm full of filthy ideas, and I think, grrrrr!"

Lila stood and paced. She stared out at the horizon, pondering. "Now Henriette," she said finally, "you're an attractive young woman, with lovely smooth skin, wearing a lovely short skirt."

"Thank you," said Henriette, pleased.

"It seems that you have given yourself a tiny case of sleepy clit or even—clitordynia."

"You mean my clit has died?"

"No, that's just a fancy way of saying that it hurts you sometimes. So let's take a look under the hood."

"You mean right now?"

"Yes, I do."

Henriette opened her legs and pulled her underpants to the side and showed Lila her clit.

"How utterly precious," said Lila. There was a knock, and she opened the door for Krock and Zilka. "Take a look at this utterly precious pussy, you two," she said.

"It's nice," said Zilka.

Krock knelt and looked closely. "J'adore these lips," he said. "So dark, so fleshy."

"That's enough, Krock," said Lila, kneeling too and gently pushing Krock out of the way. "Henriette has been telling me that she's got numbness and sometimes pain in her tender clitty when she uses a vibrator. She's much too lovely to be suffering that discomfort." She leaned toward Henriette's vulva. "Can I kiss it a little, hon? To get a better diagnosis."

"Uh—yeah," said Henriette.

"She did this to me, too, when I told her my clit was stolen," said Zilka to Henriette. "What kind of vibrator do you use?"

"A Pocket Rocket," said Henriette. "Tangerine-colored Pocket Rocket. I just bear down, a little to the side, about here, against the sleeve."

Lila's mouth made juicy kissing sounds between Henriette's legs.

"Oof, careful—it does hurt a bit," said Henriette.

"Pocket Rockets are powerful," said Zilka. "Also they're kind of loud. What about getting something with adjustable speeds?"

Lila emerged from between Henriette's legs. "That's a yummy lemondrop you have. Tiny but nice. Curiously refreshing. My advice would be to listen to your clit. If it's hurting, it's telling you something. Stop with the vibrator altogether for a while. Give those battered nerve endings time to regenerate, collect their wits."

Henriette nodded.

"And we're going to help you with a dose of the House of Holes's healing powers. You need a leg wrap with the Cable of Induhash, and you need the Belt of Jingly Bells, and you may need a squirt of my own titmilk. And you definitely also need a higher vantage. Much higher. You need perspective on your life." She gestured for Zilka to bring over the Cable of Induhash, which was a spool of soft yellow cord. "Can I ask what you think about when you masturbate? Krock and Zilka are going to wind this special cord around your legs. You can leave your skirt pulled up."

Henriette pulled her underpants back into position and considered the question. Zilka and Krock both began gently wrapping her upper thighs with soft rope. Their hands sometimes brushed against her pubic hair. "My mind's in the gutter a lot," Henriette said. "I'll remember some nice old man selling magazines near the bus stop, with bushy eyebrows, and I'll think of seducing him. Or I'll think of being a coke addict and having to give blowjobs in bus stations for money. I'm into animals, especially horses, beautiful strong brown stallions with very glossy coats and six-pack abs, I think about washing the ends of their long penises with a soft cloth and watching them sniff at a mare and nip her neck, and I think about getting them ready to mount the breeding mount." Henriette had a dreamy look, slouched back in the chair with her rope-wrapped thighs open. There was definitely something unusual about the Cable of Induhash, she thought—it was very pliant and soft and gripping, and she could feel a sexual current running through it. "I think about putting my hand on the underside of the stallion's penis just at the moment when he's coming, so that I can feel the pulses of the ejaculation forcing his hot come through the length of his penis and into the collection jar. Or into me. I'd give birth to a centaur."

Krock paused in his wrapping and sat back on his heels. "You've been watching cable."

"Now you're being honest," said Lila, unbuttoning her blouse. "Are you afraid of heights?"

"Heights? No. I love flying. I went parasailing once in the Cayman Islands."

Zilka finished wrapping the cable around Henriette's leg and then threaded it between her toes. From there she tied the end of the soft rope around one of Lila's huge white breasts. Lila was teasing her nipple, which was very dark. "Now I'm going to squirt you with my titmilk, if I can—sometimes it's difficult to get it to flow, and then I need a nipplerider. But let's see. We need just a drop or two for your clit, to start the healing process. Krock, honey, will you help me lift my breast? It's huge today."

Krock, grunting, lifted her breast, and Lila, leaning forward, squeezed out a tiny spray of titmilk directly onto Henriette's clitoris. Henriette shuddered, feeling an odd sensation that wasn't pain or pleasure, and wasn't warm or cold. It flowed through her pelvis and made her Fallopian tubes go squirmy. "Feels like it's working," she said.

"Fantastic." Lila untied the rope end from her breast. "Now can you stand up for me? And Zilka, I'll ask you to wrap the tinkly bells around Henriette's pretty waist. We're going to attack this on all fronts." Zilka arranged the bells. Lila sat in her chair, flicking the end of the cord that led to Henriette's legs against her crotch.

"Thanks for doing all this," said Henriette.

"We're going to get you back in the saddle, missy," said Lila. "Now, Krock, do we have a reasonably handsome and friendly arrival who could accompany our lovely friend Henriette up to the observation tower? The really high one that looks out on the White Lake? I think she needs a rejuvenating ride on the Pussyboard."

"I think we can find someone," said Krock. Henriette thanked Zilka and Lila for their help, and Krock took her through narrow passageways on a shortcut to the hotel. She heard someone practicing the drums, and she saw a man sitting on a bench eating a hot dog. As she walked, her waist belt jingled, and the jingling made people smile. Occasionally, as they passed an entryway or courtyard, she heard a sudden whoop of laughter or a stifled orgasmic cry. A large round building lit with many small lightbulbs loomed on the left. "The Merry-Go-Round," said Krock. "That's where the beautiful ladyboys hang out, swinging their cocks around and hoping for a brass ring."

They went down more streets, into another hotel lobby, and up an elevator, and they knocked at a double door. A man answered in his socks and boxers—it was Ned, the golfer. "Ned, this is Henriette. Would you be willing to take her up to one of the ultrahigh multicolored rock crags?"

"Sure, absolutely," said Ned. "I've just been sitting in here—uh, well—give me one second to get my pants on. Sorry about this." He pulled on his jeans and buttoned up a shirt and stuffed his wallet in his back pocket and shoved his feet into his shoes. "Will I need bug spray or sunblock?"

Krock shook his head. "Neither."

Ned grabbed a pair of sunglasses from the side table, and he put on his hat. "Ready, steady, go!" he said.

They rode the elevator to the top floor of the hotel, where there was a sign that said "Observation Crags" and "Pussyboard," with pointing-finger arrows. "Here's as far up as I'm allowed to rise," said Krock. "You two will go up on one of the lifts to reach an observation plateau on one of the chemical crags." He pointed to a little yellow door. "I'll be down here reading if you need me. You have an hour. Any questions?"

"May I ask—what's the Pussyboard?" asked Henriette, pointing.

Krock gestured off in the mist. "That's when your pussy becomes a surfboard. You glide down in that direction along a cable, in a spread-pussy harness, and you land in a lake of white rejuvenating oil. You skim along gently on your pussylips over the lake, making soft spreading ripples."

"Oh," said Henriette.

"It feels very wonderful, so I'm told, and it heals numbness. An aquatic animal lives in the lake, but he's kind of a late riser."

"The Cock Ness Monster," said Ned. "I read about him in the guidebook."

"Yes. And there's a restaurant where people stand on the balcony to watch the pussyboarders come zooming downward to the lake one by one. Men, mostly Deprivos, line up afterward, if that's what you want. It's totally up to you. Some women feel so fresh from the lake that they want sex immediately."

"Got it," said Henriette.

She looked at Ned and Ned looked at her, and they shrugged—what the hell? Then a small cable-car gondola arrived, swaying and circling around on a metal track. The cables made gentle zinging sounds of tautness, and the door whished open. They got in, waving good-bye to Krock. The gondola rocked a little as the doors closed, and it began silently ascending toward a very high craggy tower.

Ned and Henriette smiled embarrassedly at each other. "This is fun, I think," said Ned.

"It's quiet," said Henriette.

"Very quiet," said Ned.

"Oh, look at the little herd of mountain zebra! So elegant."

Ned looked, but he couldn't see them. They rose up up up, till the trees thinned out and stopped, and the mountains changed color and became turquoise and orange and red, and then they turned past a tall tower where there was a sudden dinging and an urgent pull of acceleration, and then they went higher still, through an impossibility of mist, and then finally out again into very bright deep-blue daylight. As they slowed, Henriette yawned to adjust her ears. The gondola's door opened, and they disembarked on the flat smooth top of a crag.

There were two chairs and a table with a linen tablecloth, and each chair had a shiny chrome double-scoped observation telescope in front of it. It was sunny and, fortunately, not too windy. The strange swooshing silence was even deeper here.

"We're really up high," said Ned.

The table was laid with some fruit, some grapes, some crackers, and a bottle of House red and two glasses. Henriette looked out, chewing a grape, letting her eyes adjust. They seemed to be about a mile up on an irregular, brittle, wind-eroded obelisk with a flat top and a low railing. There were about fifty other pillars, or spears, needling up from the clouds around them—each looking like the chemical mountains that grow in toy aquariums. The closest mountain was about five hundred yards away. Henriette spied a couple sitting on it. They, too,

seemed to have a table with some delicacies set out. She waved.
They waved back.

"Have you got a quarter?" Henriette asked.

"I think so," said Ned, looking through his pockets.

They fed some coins into the slots of their sightseeing scopes.
Henriette frowned, looking through the chrome-hooded viewer.
At first she had a little trouble getting the hang of it because the
image hopped around, but then she learned to move slowly, and
she found she could see into the haze very far away. There was a
red Mustang convertible on one tower, with a sunbathing woman
on top of it wearing a red bikini bottom and no top. On top of
one green crag a naked man had painted a billboard with large
letters that said, "Show Me."

"There's a couple in this direction," said Ned. "Looks like
they're doing stuff."

Henriette swiveled her binoculars around. "Yeah?"

"Yeah, the man's got his johnny-stick out, I think. Yeah, the
woman's jerking it. Wow, fast. Now she's blowing him. He's
having fun."

"Where? Dang, can't find it," said Henriette.

"Way over there. I'd say he's going to pop the oyster pretty
soon."

Finally she found the right angle. The man was holding
himself up off the chair with his hands, and the woman knelt
between his splayed legs. It was difficult to see at this distance,
with the colors gone all blue and pale, but she thought she saw
the woman's lips relax and a gush of sperm flow back down over
her fingers.

Ned made a little noise. "What did you think?" he asked.

"Very nice," she said.

"Did you like to see her sucking on his bone?" Ned rubbed her shoulder in a friendly way.

"Uh, sure. Have you got another quarter? Let's find out what else is up here at the roof of the world."

They scanned the horizon.

"Another couple!" said Ned excitedly. "Oh, boy. He's doing her real nice. Mmmm-yeah, her boobs are jumping around. Jesus mama." He shifted the direction of his scope. "And there's a AR-24 Pornsucker ship!" He pointed excitedly. "See it? Out on a mission, sucking that pornstarch. You can tell it's an AR-24 Recon/Pornsucker because of the red tips on its wings. That's the giveaway. You can always tell."

"Mm," said Henriette. She wasn't listening. She'd swiveled her scope and was looking intently off to the south. "Mountain zebras," she said, in a small intense voice. "A herd. Two of them are getting ready to mate. How on earth did they get so high? Oh, they are such nimble climbers."

"Where?" Ned was panning unsuccessfully.

"Way way off, about halfway down a crag, on a little ledge. See them?" Henriette pointed, then hunched to see more.

"No, I'm not seeing them," said Ned. "Damnation!"

"Keep hunting, you'll find them. The female is holding her head down. Ooh, she's backing up. The male's penis has dropped. It's big but it's hanging. It's practically dragging on the ground. I don't see how—ooh, her pussy is literally steaming. And his balls are huge and luscious."

"I'm still not seeing it," said Ned.

"She wants it. She's switching her tail around. She's a hot stripy-assed zebra bitch in heat, and she wants him now. Mmm, so natural. She's not ashamed. She just aims her big swollen privates toward him and lifts her tail and winks her anus. She says, Hey zebra boy, have a look at this."

"Where? God! Where? Shit. You want some wine?"

"Thanks." Henriette took a sip and touched the cord wrapped around her legs. She felt zigzags of black-and-white zebra energy pouring into the flesh of her thighs. She looked over at Ned, who'd gone back to scanning the horizon anxiously for sex. She flipped up her skirt and pulled down her panties to let the air cool her pussylips. Ned missed it. Henriette squinted through the scope again, watching the zebras.

"They're so beautiful together," she said. "Oh, boy, his penis has flipped up now, my god, is it hard, and big. Big black zebra cock. Now he's up on her! He's holding on to her. Oh my god he's stabbing that big thing in—oooh, that's big. Oh, Ned, if you've got a dick somewhere on you, stuff me with it, this is your chance."

Ned leapt up, fumbling with his pants, breathing the clean thin crazy air. "Here it is, baby." He slid into her with bone-hard assurance and began bucking and slapping against her backside.

"Oh, that's good, Ned," said Henriette. "Mm."

But it was too much too soon for Ned. "Woops, can't hold it!" he said. "Sorry! Aaaaaah!"

Henriette was still watching. "He's down again, he's done, he's done, looks like a little clear dribble from his cock, poor old mountain zebra, he's shot his balls, and it's all over—but she's still keyed up!"

The quarter dropped in Henriette's binoculars, and she looked up. Her gaze rested on Ned's down-pointing cock, shiny with juice and come.

"I got carried away," said Ned, panting.

Henriette waved at the couple on the nearest crag. "I think they watched us."

"What about you? Can I, er, lick you?"

"That's sweet, Ned, but no thanks. My clitoris is resting right now. I think I might want to give the Pussyboard a try. Will you ride down with me?"

"Sure."

They descended in silence. Henriette flung her panties out the gondola's window and watched them disappear into the clouds.

Krock was waiting at the Pussyboard launching area, which was built like the decking at the top of a ski jump. He unwound the Cable of Induhash from her legs and helped her take off her jingly belt. Ned and Krock lifted her so that she could strap herself into the harness, which pulled her thighs apart. "Breezy," she said.

"This will go fast or slow on the cable according to your control," Krock said, showing her the control stick. "You'll want to go fairly slowly when you first skid down into the lake because the fluid is warm and it's heavy, not heavy like molasses but almost creamy."

"Is it toxic?" asked Henriette.

"It's inert," said Krock. "But still, I wouldn't drink it if I were you. It's just there to make the bottom half of your body feel good."

Henriette nodded. "I'm ready. Thanks for the lovely date, Ned. It gave me a new perspective."

"My pleasure," said Ned. "I'm glad you got to see the zebras."

Krock tightened a final strap on Henriette's harness. "So—are you ready to feel some deep lake love on your pussy?" he asked.

Henriette swallowed and nodded.

There was a whir and a clunk and she was airborne, sitting on a small U-shaped fiberglass support, sliding down the long curving cable. She went fairly fast at first, her skirt fluttering. The air was warm, and the sky was a startling blue, and she said, "Wheee!" She swerved around a pylon tower and then turned down into the mountain valley, in the midst of which stretched an enormous white lake. She could see several other cables that swept down toward the lake, and she watched the other pussysurfers slow just before touchdown.

She dipped down the last length of the incline and swooshed and splashed and slowed on a level liquid plain of dazzling white. The lake was warmer than she expected. It had the consistency of hand lotion but with tiny gold flecks. The lucky liquids burbled and creamed over her hydroplaning vulva and, as she slowed, churned purposefully over her clitoris.

Then the harness lifted her back in the air for a moment and swung her dripping in a long laughing kicky hemicurve past the pontooned restaurant with blue tablecloths and waiters wearing white tuxedo vests. All at once, out of the lake rose a hugely gigantic phallocentric dick-shaped monster cock. It stood for a moment, thirty feet in the air, and then toppled with an enormous splash and disappeared into the white water.

A group of about twenty Deprivos were following Henriette's progress with binoculars. They gestured entreatingly—down here, down here! She landed in their midst and climbed out of the harness, dripping. She knelt, breathing the rich air, feeling better than she had in months, listening to the rustle of stroking men around her. "Come all over me, guys," she said. One man jizzed on her cheek, another on her shirt, two on her lips, one on her nose, one on her shoulder, and another—a cute guy with blond spiky hair—came politely into her cupped hand.

Krock appeared with a towel.

"How are you?" he asked.

"How am I? I'm a jizm-covered princess, and I've just pussysurfed the lake!" she said, laughing and crying at the same time. She went to her room and had a shower and slept for hours, feeling her revived clit glowing like a summer firefly.

Dennis Explores Mindy's Purse

Dennis, a traveling teacher, went to a city to give his two-day fund-raising seminar for nonprofits, "How to Get Other People to Give You All the Money They Have." After he was done he waited in line at the hotel to check out. A woman got in line behind him. He turned and recognized her from his seminar.

"I enjoyed the class," said the woman, who had a kindly face and dark hair that didn't quite touch her shoulders. "I liked how few euphemisms you used. You never once said 'issue.'"

"Thanks," Dennis said.

"It was a lot of money for just two days, though."

He asked her what kind of nonprofit work she did, and she told him that she was working on a documentary about women in a remote region of Estonia who sing while they masturbate. "We've got some great material," she said. "It's just a question of editing it down. We're looking for investors."

"Ah," said Dennis. "What's your name?"

"Mindy."

Just then two different people at the counter said, "I can help you over here." Dennis the traveling instructor and Mindy the filmmaker went up and paid their bills and signed, and then they were done. They walked toward the door and stopped for a minute feeling a warm breeze.

"Your seminar has given me the confidence to ask for what I want," said Mindy.

She's smart in a certain way that I really like, thought Dennis. And he thought: I really don't want to walk out of this lobby without talking to her more. "I hate this feeling," he said finally.

"What feeling?" she asked.

"The feeling of having just talked to you for a moment and now you're leaving."

"Would you enjoy a stick of gum?" Mindy asked. "Sometimes gum can alleviate the pain."

"Yes, I would," said Dennis.

She reached in her purse and pulled out a packet of gum. He unwrapped a stick and began chewing it vigorously. Immediately, yellow and pink stars came twirling in from the edge of his vision.

"This is good gum!" he said.

"It's special gum," she said. "Every time you chew, a woman in Estonia is having a singing orgasm."

"Mmm!" He chewed, his jaw working noisily. "Utterly delicious. I could chew this all day long." He looked down. "What else have you got in that dark, strange purse of yours?"

"In here?" she asked, holding the flap open wider so he could peer into its depths. "Why don't you take a look?"

Dennis leaned, bringing his head close to the compartmented

opening. He could smell the leathery smell, and he thought he could also smell more sticks of gum, and her checkbook, and her lipstick. But he didn't smell any money.

"Do you have a tiny address book in there?" he asked.

"Yes, I do."

"May I reach in and give a squeeze to your tiny little address book?"

"You may." She held the purse out to him and Dennis gingerly reached in. He felt around for a moment, found her keys, and then under it came across the tiny book.

"Ooh, I'm squeezing it," he said. "I wish my name were in here."

"It can be," she said.

"How?" he asked.

"Become an investor in my film."

"I'll think seriously about that."

Mindy held open her purse wider. "Come inside where it's dark and warm," she said. He bent and gazed deep and then, shrinking, he fell forward and was enveloped in purseness. "Come with me, Mindy," he called as he shrank. He smelled the fumes of leather and bottles of nail polish, and he saw Mindy's driver's license picture staring at him behind plastic. Her eyes were generous and pretty. He lay for a minute in the jumble of her things, and then it occurred to him that if he didn't climb out, he would probably suffocate.

He grabbed the edge of the purse and hauled himself out onto the floor of a fancy hotel room. He sat, collecting his wits, until he had grown back to his normal size. The purse was on the floor next to him. "Mindy, are you in there?" he called. She wasn't. He felt an odd tickling or burning sensation in the tip of his penis, and he heard a tiny voice shouting something muffled. He got up and took off his chinos and peered into his striped boxer shorts. Something was definitely going on inside his penis. He stripped off his boxers and sat on the edge of the bed, lifting his penis so that he could get a better look. Mindy's head was protruding from its tip. Just her head and neck were visible.

"Good lord, are you all right?" he said.

"I think so!" Mindy shouted in her tiny voice. "Welcome to the House of Holes. I'm here stuck in your penis for some reason."

"Can you get out? You're so teeny-tiny!"

Mindy said something.

"What did you say?" said Dennis. "You have to really shout, I'm afraid."

"I said that I feel like a kidney stone!"

"Oh. We really need to get you safely out of there." Dennis thought for a moment. "I don't think I should try to pull on your head."

"No, you might injure me." Mindy struggled, trying without success to free her arms, which were pinned next to her body. "I just need a good push. Do you think you could try urinating? That would work, I think. I'll hold my breath."

"Well, I could try, but I'm warning you I've got a shy bladder." Dennis went into the bathroom and got a glass and held it under his penis and pushed. Mindy waited, moving her head around nervously.

"I'm sorry," said Dennis. "You're kind of jammed in there, and I always pee just before I check out of a hotel. I'm dry. This is really embarrassing."

"You don't need to be sorry," said Mindy. "I'm sorry about this horrendous inconvenience."

"No, it's fine, we'll beat this thing."

"What about if you—you know—do yourself proud?" said Mindy. "It might make it easier for me to wriggle."

Dennis held up his finger. "You know, that thought crossed my mind," he said. "Let's see what we can do on that front." He went back to the bed, lay down, and began gingerly stroking himself. "This is tricky because I don't want to squeeze you."

"You can squeeze some," said Mindy. "Just please don't waggle. That's better. It's much better for me when you're pointing up—otherwise I'm upside down and the blood rushes to my head and I get confused."

"What did you say?"

Mindy resumed talking loudly. "Nothing! You just really have to get hard. Is it at all erotic for you that I'm here, stuck in your dickknob?"

"Well, it gives me a chance to know you better, that's for sure. It's a nice first date. Are you naked in there? Or do you have your clothes on? Because if you're naked that's definitely erotic for me."

"I'm pretty sure I'm naked. Let me see. Yep, I'm totally starkers. 'Naked as a worm,' as the French say."

"That's good news, Mindy. I'm going to think about you being naked. Can you toy with yourself?"

"I'll try. I'm putting my finger down between my puffy pussylips. That's my little friend there, oh, yeah. It's warm in here. I feel like you're hugging me all over my body. I'm playing with my pussylips now. I don't feel panic anymore. You can squeeze me a little more. Squeeze me through your cock. That's it."

"This is better," said Dennis. He was gently stroking the

middle section of his cock, which had lengthened and stiffened. "Can you do a little hip dance in there, shake your hips for me?"

"How about this?" Mindy's head moved back and forth. "Can you feel it? I'm shimmying my hips for you." She bit her tiny lip with her tiny teeth. "I've got a finger going in my fuckalope now. I can feel your cock getting longer. That's good, when you do that I can feel you squeezing my hips."

"Mmf, getting some wood now," said Dennis. "You feel slightly painful in there, but good."

A froth of bubbly fluid surged up around Mindy's neck. "Woops, what's this?" she said. "Precum! Hah-hah! This is sick! My hair's all wet with it! Oh, you juicy, juicy man! Squeeze me a little more!"

Dennis squeezed some more, and this pushed her a little ways up, freeing one of her arms. She tried using the arm to lever the rest of her out, but it didn't work. "We're definitely getting closer," she said. "I think, though, you're actually going to have to come to push me out."

"Will do, I'm trying," said Dennis.

"Try picturing something dirty, really dirty," Mindy advised. "I mean dogfuck dirty. This is an emergency. What's the dirtiest thing you ever did?"

"Uh, I'm not that dirty. Once I came into this girl's guitar."

"Into the hole? Did she know?"

"No. I felt bad about it, but it sounded fine afterward, thank goodness. I like to think that my dried come was vibrating to her songs."

Mindy waited. "Is that memory helping you want to come?"

"No."

143

"Well, then, think some more about my sexy hips stuck inside your cock."

"Mm, mm, better."

"Think about me kissing the head of your dick like this—mwah!—and slapping at your cockhead hard, like this!" Mindy slapped. "And splashing your precum foam all over the place!"

This excited Dennis. "Oh, kiss my cockhead!" he said. "Oh, you're so fucking tiny. I wish you could free up your breasts."

"You're getting slippery enough now I think I can." She shook out her hair and then with some effort she scooped a tit out of the well of his cockhole. "There's one. And here's the other. Do you like?"

Dennis had a new, lower note in his voice. "Ooh, shit, tease the nipples for me, tease them, I'm real hard now. You're like a pretty mermaid coming out of my volcano." He started working long, steady dickstrokes, sliding the skin so it bunched up and then went smooth. He extended his tongue, and Mindy reached up for it but couldn't catch hold of it.

"Jack me out right into your hand," Mindy said. "Pump your lovely Lincoln Stiffins. Jack me!"

Dennis made a mooing sound, standing up, with his feet planted apart like an action figure. "You want to feel this come push you right out? You want a come ride? You want a flume ride of my burning jizz? Huh? I've never jerked a beautiful woman out of my hot dick before. I want to see your big sexy hips blow out of my cock."

"Oh, this is getting good," said Mindy. "Hold on just a second, I want to catch up. I want to come with you." She bit her lip again and frowned, her breasts shaking as she urgently frigged her tooter. She hummed a few notes of a wordless Estonian song,

144

then she said, "I'm almost there, Dennis, I'm going to come, I'm going to come. Ohh, make me shoot out of you, shoot me out, SQUIRT ME! AAAAH!"

Dennis grabbed his balls and made five smooth cock-pumpings, and then he felt the pulse of his come bulbing below Mindy's legs. It pushed her out of his screaming penis on a blast of jizz force. She fell slickly into his hand and lay panting in the puddle of his cumshot.

"Whew!" said Dennis.

"That was a man-jack adventure," said Mindy, shaking come off her arms. "I think if you rub me gently on my stomach I'll grow back to the right size."

Dennis moved his fingertip gently over her, and she began to get heavier. He had to set her down, and she got bigger and bigger, and then she was a naked smiling documentary filmmaker sitting on the floor in front of him.

"You are so fucking sexual," Dennis said. "Raugh!"

They went to the restaurant and the gift shop and got a House of Holes T-shirt. Dennis wrote his number in Mindy's address book.

Polly Visits the Hall of the Penises

Polly's boyfriend Jeff said, "We can have a conversation about that if you want." So they did. It was one of those "conversations" where both people are just steaming, just fuming, fighting each other for dear life—but even so they are doing everything they can to sound reasonable and fair-minded.

The cause of the disagreement was that Jeff had liked a play they'd seen together and Polly hadn't. Polly thought it was an hour and a half of insults, ill humor, and spurious profundities, while Jeff thought it was a work of cryptic, discombobulating genius. And what was worse, during the intermission Jeff had flirted openly with Polly's friend Helena.

The next morning when Polly woke up, she looked at Jeff in bed. His hair was curly—she'd always liked how thick and curly his hair was. But now his hair did nothing for her. Well, very little. What she was thinking was: If he liked that awful, awful play, then they were unsuited for each other.

That was a Sunday, and they had a lot of laundry to do, so they went to the laundromat. Polly was trembly inside because she was pretty sure that she wanted to break up with Jeff, and he kind of knew a major thunderstorm was coming. But still they had laundry to do.

So they were there sitting in the orange chairs, and Jeff was reading *The Rooster,* and Polly was looking around at people, as she did. Suddenly she saw a girl with long flaxen hair get in the dryer and close the door after herself. She thought, That's odd. The girl didn't reappear. Polly got up and looked in the dryer window. No girl. She went back to Jeff and she said, "Huh."

Jeff didn't look up. He was reading a review of a rock concert. He never wanted to go to concerts, but he read all the reviews. "Jeff," Polly said, "a girl just got in that dryer."

He looked up and frowned.

"Will you please take a look?"

They walked over and Jeff pulled open the dryer door. There was a pile of hot clothes inside—hot summery women's clothes— and an oven mitt, and that was it. She noticed a little card taped next to the dryer's controls. "HOH," it said.

"What's 'HOH' stand for?" she asked Jeff.

Jeff shrugged. "Hard of hearing? Water?"

She said: "I'm not kidding, two seconds ago a girl with long straight hair climbed into this dryer."

"I really don't see how she could have," he said. He sat back down and began reading his free paper again.

Polly shook her head in exasperation and climbed into the dryer. It was quite hot, but she could breathe okay. She pushed against the back, and she thought she felt it move. She grabbed a T-shirt from the heap of clothes, so that she wouldn't burn her hand, and she pushed as hard as she could against the back. It made a sound like a tight rusty spring and swung open. She climbed through and fell out on some grass near a lilac bush. She was lying topless on a hill, surrounded by wildflowers. There were women walking around with backpacks and hiking boots on and no shirts on. She thought she could hear murmured sounds of sex in the air: Suck it, pound me, squeeze it, that's it. Fortunately, she still was holding the long T-shirt she'd used to push out the back of the dryer. She put it on.

A minute later, Jeff tumbled out of the hole in the wall behind her. He was wearing just his shirt and underpants. He sat up in the grass and looked around. It was a beautiful day, with one tiny cloud and some bunched trees off in the distance near a creek.

"I told you," said Polly.

Jeff looked around. "Lots of interesting seminudity here," he said, pleased.

A woman appeared from behind a bush. She was wearing a very pretty long skirt—an I-want-to-go-out-on-a-wildflower-walk-with-you-and-fuck-you-later skirt—that was in kind of a forties style, with blue polka dots. She had a cute little mouth and friendly but calculating eyes and breasts shaped like breakfast muffins. She said, mostly to Jeff, "Do you need assistance?" Very sweet voice.

"Sort of," Polly said. "We've just popped on over from the laundromat."

The woman nodded and smiled, and then she looked down at Jeff, who was still sitting on the grass in his underpants.

"You bad boy, you lost your pants, and I can see your dickybird," she said. Jeff smiled goofily, looking up at her.

Polly felt a toxic wave of jealousy and hatred and disgust, and she turned away. And that's when she saw the most gorgeous cream-colored Cape house she'd ever seen. It had a huge wraparound porch, and it had dormer windows that reflected the sun, and it had big, softly sighing trees in front of it. Polly pointed. "I think we should go up there, Jeff," she said.

"I think I should stay here," Jeff said dreamily, "so we know how to get back to the other side." He lay back on the grass and looked up at the sky, smiling. Then he looked over at the girl in the polka-dot skirt. She was cutting bunches of white lilacs.

"You sit out here on the grass in your underpants," said Polly. "I'm going up to that house and investigate. We'll meet in about an hour and a half."

"Sounds good," Jeff said.

Polly walked up the hill toward the house, fuming. A man answered the door. He said his name was Mischa, and he was quite handsome, although his ears were odd—the inner parts poked out farther than the rims, which gave him an air of studiousness. He took her to a waiting room, and then she met Lila, a cheerful busty woman who wore bifocals.

"What do you want?" Lila asked.

"I don't know—a Cape house on a knoll and a husband?" said Polly.

"Can't help you."

"Then I don't want anything," said Polly.

"You're unhappy with your boyfriend because he's acting like a shit."

"Yes, and he and I have different taste in plays."

"Do you still like men?"

"Yes, I love men. I've always loved men."

Lila picked up the phone. "Mischa, our friend Polly needs to spend some time in the Hall of the Penises."

Mischa was there in a moment. He took Polly's hand and led her to a very large room—a kind of dance studio with a refinished floor, hung all the way around with green curtains made of shot silk. One wall had enormous windows that overlooked the hills. There were two other women in the room. Polly nodded at them and they introduced themselves. One was Saucie, and one had a name like Donna.

Polly said to Saucie, "What are those odd little bumps there in the curtains?"

"They're what you think they are," said Saucie.

Polly found a drape cord and pulled it to make some of the green fabric slide to one side. She saw many little toadlike things hanging out from holes in the wall at about crotch height. She said, "All those little brown toadlike things are penises?"

"Yep," said Saucie. "And balls."

"They go all around the room," said Donna.

"What are we supposed to do with them?" asked Polly.

Saucie handed her a tasseled knee pillow. "I think we're supposed to talk to them, or maybe even suck them off."

Donna whispered, "I think that one there is my husband."

Polly was surprised. "Is that good or bad?"

"Not entirely sure," said Donna.

"And I'm guessing that one there is my ex-husband," said Saucie.

Then it occurred to Polly to wonder whether one of the penises was Jeff's. She toured the rows carefully to see if she could spot Jeff's organ hanging out among the crowd. But she couldn't

150

be sure. Which was all in all a relief. He was probably still down in the glade, she thought, chatting up the topless girl in the polka-dot skirt.

"Do you think we should dance for them?" said Donna. Polly, feeling a little giddy, started in with a Diane Birch song, "Rise Up," and the three women danced and sang around the room. "Rise up, little sisters!" they sang—and soon they began to notice some changes in some of the wall toads. There was a new alertness about their attitude, no question about it. Several of them had started to do a little elongational leaning-forward sort of movement.

"I think they like us!" said Polly. The penises were in fact becoming visibly semi-erect at the sound of voices. Golly, Polly thought, I had no idea that my simple presence in a room could do that. It was kind of interesting and exciting, but also a little sad, because those penises had no clue what Polly, Donna, and Saucie were all about as women—what they believed in, what their plans were.

Near one corner, Polly came to an empty hole. She tried to peek in, but she couldn't see anything. "What's up?" she said into the hole. "Are you a little reserved today?" There was silence. Then she said, "I can wait." She looked back over her shoulder and saw Saucie kneeling on the opposite wall. Polly suspected that Saucie was in front of her ex's penis, but it wasn't easy to keep track. Donna was really getting into it—she was kneeling on her cushion with both hands on a wall and she was passing her face and hair all over a large, attractive petard.

Polly turned back to her empty hole and she said, "Can you tell me something about yourself?" Suddenly a tennis ball appeared in the opening. At least she thought it was a tennis ball.

When it popped through and she caught it, she felt how heavy it was, and then she knew it was the kind of ball they use in real tennis, or royal tennis, the game Henry the Eighth played.

"So you enjoy the sport of kings?" she said. "The old *jeu de paume*?" And then the end of a tennis racket came through the hole. She looked at the handle. It was very worn. He had really used that racket. She held it for a second and said, "Nice racket." Then the handle disappeared, and a bunch of purple turnips came through the hole and dangled there, held by their green tops. Polly squeezed them and she said, "I bet you could get some good blood out of these roots, you crazy fucked-up vegetarian."

Then the turnips disappeared. Polly looked back at Saucie and Donna. Both their heads were bobbing. They were sucking toad-in-the-hole with guiltless gusto. Polly said, "I wish I knew your name." There was silence. She said, "I'm going to call you Chief. Okay, Chief? Do you want me to do a private dance for you, Chief?" The racket handle reappeared and it nodded slowly up and down. "I can't unless you give me a present," said Polly. After a moment, a little leather pouch of gold sovereigns came flying out of the hole.

"Those look like nice pieces of money," Polly said, "but that wasn't exactly the present I had in mind." She waited. "You're supposed to put your babymaker through this hole." There was a pause, and Polly said, "Right now, please. I want you hard or soft, doesn't matter. Put it through, Chief, so I can see what you've got."

Finally a large dark semisoft penis flopped out through the hole. After some further fumbling, a matching ballsack was stuffed underneath. The three-pack hung there. "Hello, hello," said Polly, somewhat surprised that the man had done what she had asked for. "Pleased to meet you, Chief Cock and Bottle Washer."

She had to admit to herself that it was, in fact, quite a nice-looking penis. Not intelligent looking—few penises were—but the testicles did somehow have the air of being attached to a man of substance. And Polly had always liked confident tennis players.

"Would you enjoy it if I shook my bottom for you?" she asked. She turned and wiggled her bottom. "Now a bit of tit action!" She turned back around and flashed open her shirt for a second, so that the penis, if it had an eye, could see her bra cleavage.

She felt out of breath, and she started talking nasty, the way she always did when she got aroused. "Do you want me to be your little suckslut?" she asked. "Hm?" She never knew where the words came from—they just came out of her. And as she talked, the penis began lifting. She said, "Ooh, you're getting bigger for me, Chief. Yeah, yeah, I want you totally stiff for me. Is that all you have, you perverted gloryhole fucker? I want you as hard as that racket handle. Come on, baby. Do you like my mouth? Do you like my twenty-seven-year-old nasty cocksucking mouth, you twisted shitter?"

The more she insulted the penis, the stiffer it got. It was remarkable. She said, "Do you want to see me brush my hair?" The dick nodded yes. So she got her hairbrush out of her purse. "I have lots of dark hair," she said, "and this is how I brush it, like this. And I like to toss it around, like this. Do you like it when I pass my hair over you, Chief Cock? Hm?" She said, "I like when men look at my hair and then they go home and they beat off their gnarly dicks thinking about me brushing my hair." She said, "But you can't beat off, can you?" And she circled her hand around behind his balls and cock, so that she had him. "You're stuck out here with me, and you can't beat off, no matter how bad you want to, you hopeless sadsack dickjerker."

By now, after all this abuse, the penis was truly huge. "That's quite a heavy piece of machinery you've got," said Polly. "You are a fucking grotesque cuntsplitter." She put her lips close to it. "Do you like it when a suck strumpet like me talks nasty to you with my soft red lips? Do you see how full they are and how ready they are to glue themselves onto your knob? Hm? See how ready I am to take that big stiff fleshbone and jerk it off onto these soft full lips?" The penis went boing, boing. She said, "I bet you're crazy to see my tits, too. You can't stand it, can you? See that? That's my right tit. Sometimes I squeeze it a little bit. Sometimes I pinch my nipple through the fabric, mmm, like that. Sometimes I spank my tits a little bit, like this. Ouch, bad titties. They like to be spanked. Are you married?"

The penis nodded.

"How many kids?" Polly asked.

The penis waggled three times.

"You monstrosity! Three kids you've got? And you're here hanging out of this hole in the wall? Can you see me?"

The penis nodded again.

"High-tech, are you, you sick demented voyeuristic plaster-fucker!"

She was amazed. It was like his penis had a telescoping action—the more she taunted and reviled it, the more it kept adding intermediate sections. It was like a subway improvement project. And it had these knobby veins all over it. She couldn't resist holding it, so she pinched the skin right underneath its head, and the whole penis immediately leapt away like a shying racehorse. "Don't fight me now, shitbird," she said. She pinched the skin again, harder, and rolled it between her fingers so that its monocular eye gazed crazily around the room. And then she said, "You want me to jerk you off now?"

She really did want to wank that dick off—really wanted to jack the whole dick, from the head to the base, right off. She began fast-jacking it, using her egg-beating skills. And when her right hand got tired she switched to her left, and then she switched back to her right, and then she said, "I want you to come right here." She touched her lips, pouted them, and resumed cock pumping, and when she looked down she could see something major happening with his ballsack. It was lifting, the prune elevator was going up, and there was serious wrinkling, and she knew that meant he was almost there. She rested for a second and then moved her hand very fast and said, "Right here on my tongue, Chief." She pulled hard on his dick, and she could hear the Chief thump into the wall on the other side. "Let all that blookie out, slutfucker," she said. She opened her mouth as wide as she could, and she felt his whole body course down into his penis. A spume, a trilateral spray of jizm came out like light through a prism. It was a jizm prism, split into three parts, all of them white, and some of it slapped against Polly's cheek and some against the roof of her mouth. She could feel it running down the back of her throat, and as she was swallowing it she thought with a triumphant inner chuckle, *I have just busted this man's nut.* She gave the cock a few last love jerks and then released it with a final full-length squeeze, watching it subside and draw back on itself like an aged parliamentarian. "Bye-bye, Chief," she said, and then the penis was gone. She turned. Donna was putting on her makeup. Saucie was talking through the hole to her ex. Polly sensed someone else in the room. Jeff, her boyfriend, was standing at the door. He walked up to her and saw the shine of come on her face. He had a fascinated, horrified expression. Unconsciously, he checked his fly.

"It's all over, Jeff," she said.

Pendle Buys a Bathing Suit

Pendle called up Lila and asked her how he could improve his cumshot. "Mine just kind of curves over the tip and drips off. Can you recommend some kind of herbal supplement?"

"People talk a lot about lecithin," said Lila, "but lecithin only takes you so far. Here's what I'd recommend. Go buy yourself a Thompson Heftyshot bathing suit. It's got the patented Active Grid inner pouch. Wear that around for a couple of days. It goes to work on all your glands, and you'll be amazed. I've seen some sad dribblers transformed."

Pendle took a moment to think about that. "Where would I get this bathing suit?"

"At Big Top Sports on O Street. The blue ones with the big yellow flowers work best."

Pendle went to Big Top Sports on O Street and walked down the center aisle past the vibrating kayaks. "Can I help you find something?" asked a woman in a yellow polo shirt. Her name tag said Trix, and she was a nice handful of prettiness and eyelashes.

"Could you point me in the direction of the, ah—" Pendle consulted his notes. "Thompson Heftyshot bathing suits?"

"Men's?" Trix asked.

Pendle was surprised. "There's a women's Heftyshot?"

"Sure," the girl said. "Some girls want to be gushers. They don't understand that it's rare. All guys shoot, but only a few girls gush."

"I see what you're saying. Actually, though, I don't shoot. That's why I'm here. I sort of pour."

"Ew. Sorry, I don't mean that. Follow me."

They walked next to each other, and because they weren't talking Pendle could hear Trix's body move. He could hear her footsteps traveling up through her legs, bunka bunka bunka bunka, and he could hear her hips going slant slant slant, and he could hear her cheery little breasts jostling in their little tit-cozies, jostle, jostle, jostle.

He looked over at her. "This is a big store," he said.

"It's got everything," she agreed.

They kept walking. Finally they reached the men's bathing suits.

They turned the corner. "Do you like the display?" she asked. "I designed it."

Pendle made enthusiastic noises. "I like the way you offset one bathing suit over the other—that's fresh. That's fresh new work."

She thanked him and touched him lightly on the arm. "The Heftyshots are around this side," she said.

"I believe you just touched me," he said.

"Just a twitch of the hand." She beckoned him on. "These blue ones with the yellow flowers are nice, I think. What size are you?"

"Large," he said. Then he said: "Do you ever have crazy nights?"

"Sweetie pie, don't we all?"

Pendle thought, I love talking to this graceful eyelash girl at Big Top Sports on O Street.

Then there was a bling and a woman's voice came on the PA system. "Trix to the front for a price check."

"Oh, that's me, I better go," she said.

"Wait," Pendle said, "I want to try these on."

"With Heftyshots you have to buy what you try," said Trix. "Do you know how to put it on?"

"It looks complicated," said Pendle.

Trix held the suit open. "It isn't. You put your jacksons in the pouch, and then just hang pete out front, like that." She indicated how with curled fingers and index extended.

"Got it," Pendle said. "Can I wear them out of the store?"

"Come to my register, I'll scan you."

He could hear her shoes going tap tap tap tap, until he couldn't hear them anymore. He thought about how amazingly petite she was and how amazingly attractive, and he thought, I wonder what would happen if I gave her a drop of Bohu's beardwater?

He went to the changing room and stuffed his ballsack into the pouch and tied the waistband of the suit. It looked pretty good, but it felt strange—as if his testicles were trying to sing the song about a horse with no name. He pulled his pants on over the suit, leaving the tag flapping visibly.

At the register, Trix pointed her scanning gun at his pants, and it made the bleep.

"Two hundred and four dollars," she said.

Pendle pulled out his wallet, and he gave Trix some bills. She handed him back his change. He hesitated. He'd come to the test. Here was the moment. There were so many things that he could do wrong. For instance, if he leaned toward her and said, "Trix, I'd so like to munch on that apple ass of yours"—that would not be good. Even at the House of Holes, especially at the House of Holes, crassness didn't pay. If he said, "I have half a pound of prime Angus cockbrisket ready for you"—that would not be good, either.

And then he thought, You know, so what? He said, "There's something I want to say, but I don't think I should say it. I mean, it's not that outrageous, it's just that it's not something that you normally say at the checkout counter."

"You'd be surprised at what people say here."

Pendle said, "I was going to say that I wish I was a man who had a store where he made custom sequin pasties for exotic dancers and you were an exotic dancer and came into the store and ordered a set of spiral pasties and so I had to measure your aureoles for fit."

"How would you measure them, with a ruler?"

"Probably with my mouth," said Pendle, "and then I'd measure my mouth with the ruler."

"I see. How does the bathing suit feel?"

"Intense. Things are definitely hopping down there. But here's the thing. When I look at you my fingertips actually go cold on me. Your face is that powerful. Do you want to have a bowl of soup and half a sandwich?"

"Sure, I'd like that."

So at nine o'clock, when Trix got off work, she and Pendle went to a restaurant and had smooth soup and talked about working at the House of Holes. Pendle showed her the little purple vial of Bohu's beardwater.

Trix said, "What does it do, make you horny? I don't need much help with that."

"Me neither, frankly," said Pendle. "But I think it also makes the sexual experience more intense."

"Well then, I'll try a drop in my spritzer."

"I'll put a drop in my spritzer, too, so we're even," said Pendle. Then they went for a walk down Quim Street and turned right on Loulou Avenue. They talked about shipping lanes, the European Union, Trix's French grandmother, and what Trix did after she got home from work when she wasn't at the House of Holes. Bohu's beardwater was beginning to kick in by then.

"I walk around in my bare feet listening to NPR and eating soy crisps and cherry tomatoes," Trix said. "Gradually I take off my clothes. I open the fridge and look in the celery drawer, and I sometimes flash the fridge my pussyhair, and the fridge seems to like it. At least, its motor comes on and it gives me a breath of cold air. I like to have my breasts out when I eat soy crisps."

"And then a little later you . . ."

"Mhm. Close the curtains. Now here, it's different. Here I go to a groanroom with a friend. Sometimes I don't have sex, I just listen. I love sex sounds."

"I've never been to a groanroom."

"Oh, you should go. The groanrooms are like the darkrooms except bigger. There are four couples in each one, and you can't talk at all, not one word, and everyone wears a glowing wristband and a glowing ankleband. That's all you can see. Mostly it's just juicy sex sounds. I love when people make a surprised sound, 'ooh!' Basically I love to listen to people making out. That's why I don't understand about cumshots, frankly. Not that it's bad for you to wear a Heftyshot. But seeing a man squirt out into the air is much less exciting to me than the idea of a man shooting inside me and filling me up with wonderful hot streams of doodle-goo."

Pendle gave her an eager smile. "Just the sounds of people just—just doing the happy humperdinkle, eh? Just doing it and loving it. Hooooooo."

"Exactly." Trix sat forward politely. "So what about you, have you been having any fun here?"

"No fun at all," said Pendle. He plucked an aspen leaf. "Well, a little. I haven't been here that long. Lila asked me to be a nipplerider, and I shrank down and rode her nipple for a bit, but I wasn't good at it. The best time I had was when I went out with this woman for lunch on the terrace, overlooking the Garden of the Wholesome Delightful Fuckers. We were eating melon and blueberries and looking down, and there were all these wholesome fuckers having sex in among the palm trees and the bushes. It was exciting. They really take extra care with the grounds here—the grass is so green and the paths are so carefully tended. I like the landscaping."

"How many couples could you see?"

"Oh, gosh, eight, nine couples. I think our final count was eleven. I said to her, 'I have never seen this many couples doing it before.' She said, 'Me neither, I kind of like it.' I said, 'Do you want to go down and be a part of the action?' And she said, 'Well—let's just sit in the glorious sunshine and watch them being wholesome.' I said, 'Okay,' and we watched for about half an hour. We both got very turned on. I was saying things like, 'Woo, look at them go, look at them just boinking away like the crazy wholesome fuckers they are!' And eventually we went up to her hotel room and messed around, and it was okay."

"No anal?"

"No, should there have been?"

"There's just so much talk about it. Everybody's supposed to love assfucking, and live for assfucking, and frankly I just don't."

"No, no anal," said Pendle. "It was good but I don't think we're really soul mates."

"And what after all is a soul mate?"

"A soul mate is when you really think someone is great. You really like her a lot. You like when she explains things to you. You love her. That's a soul mate."

"Oh," said Trix.

"Will you take me to the groanrooms?"

They went to a groanroom, and in the darkness of the entry foyer they put on the glowing wrist and ankle bracelets, which were in plastic packets in baskets just outside the door.

"Just remember, we can't talk in here at all, only groan," said Trix, her hand on the door. "It's like meditation except it's more fun."

They went in together and closed the door very quietly.

Henriette Chooses the Cheekpump

Since she'd surfed the lake, Henriette had received two invitations to the Masturboats and visited the Hall of the Penises, but she still hadn't met a man who really attracted her. Lila suggested that she take a walk down the Man Line. Henriette thought that was a good idea.

The Man Line was a line of about a hundred single men who stood fully clothed in wedding suits, with numbers pinned to their lapels. She walked down the line, nodding at the men. Then she saw the one. He was smiling, trying to stare straight ahead. He was tall, with wide, even teeth and an easy, careless way of standing. His bow tie dangled. His number was 53.

She didn't say anything to him, but back at the office she told Lila that Number 53 was the one.

Lila promptly called up a video of Number 53's entrance interview. "Do you want to see it?"

"Of course," said Henriette.

On the screen, Number 53, slouching in a chair, was asked what type of woman he was interested in. "Honestly?" he said.

"Honestly," said the entrance interviewer, Mischa.

"Well, right now," Number 53 said, "I'm wanting a woman with a humongous oversized ass—not a fat ass but a big round wobbly huge ass that's busting out of her pants."

Lila turned off the video and Henriette sighed. "That's just not me," she said. "My ass is not humongous and oversized."

"It could be you if you wanted it to be," said Lila.

"How so?"

Lila called Mischa in. "The cheekpump," she said. She held Henriette for a moment. "If you let Mischa work on you with the cheekpump, you'll get a day with the biggest ass you could possibly want."

"Just one day, and then it goes back to normal?"

"Sometimes the ass lasts two days, if the fixative is properly applied. Here is a pair of jeans that will fit you after the procedure." She handed Henriette a pair of strangely roomy pants.

Mischa took her to a small, dimly lit round chamber with a low couch against one wall. He pulled down from the ceiling two enormous clear-plastic suction cups that looked rather like cymbals or dinner plates.

"You have to strip down so I can put these on," he said.

She shucked off her pants and scants and knelt on the couch. "Like this?" she said.

Mischa was frozen, staring. "My dear, dear friend," he said. "I don't know why you want to do anything to that rear end of yours. That is a lovely piece of craftsmanship."

"Thank you," said Henriette. "But I want it bigger."

"I'm going to have to ask Krock to come in to help position the suction pads. This is too much ass experience for one man. Krock!"

There was a slight pause, and then a man emerged, chewing a hastily finished sandwich. He washed his hands at a little sink, winking at Henriette.

"What do we got?" Krock said.

"One day cheekpump," said Mischa.

"For her?" Krock said. "I don't think so."

"Eh, she has a thing for a guy who likes a superbig ass."

"In that case," said Krock sadly, "let's do it. But first, a moment to look—okay, baby?"

Henriette nodded. She sensed them both looking at her exposed wonderloaves and felt a softening and an unfurling in her innernesses.

Meanwhile Mischa reached up and pulled down a black hose with a squirt attachment at the end. "This is the flesh-bulging oil," he said. He misted it lightly over her ass, and she felt strange things begin to happen.

"You hold the left and I'll hold the right," said Krock. Henriette felt the two suction cups embrace and conform themselves to her cheeks, and then there was a sound of a vacuum motor starting and jiggly vibrating sensations, and she felt pressure as both men leaned against the suction cups, holding the seal in place. "Oooooooffff," she said. It felt strange but strange in a delectable way and then, when Mischa and Krock together started rotating their suction cups—"to distribute the energy uniformly," Krock explained—she put her head down and gave herself up to their ministrations, feeling her privacies stretched and held open and then squeezed shut. "God dang!" she said. "Holy effing shitter wiggle."

And then she started to feel the growing—she felt a heaviness to her ass as it grew and grew and grew and grew and grew. "Don't let the cups slip off as she gets bigger," Mischa warned, "keep pressing."

Finally they were finished. The groan of the vacuum pump stopped. The vibrating suction pads released themselves with a juicy kissing sound.

"Okay, baby," said Krock. "You have now got some seriously heavy assjunk. Mmm, mmm, mmm!" He rolled a full-length mirror over. Henriette stood.

"Holy cow!" she said. She reached back and squeezed it—it was like squeezing two soft smooshy pillows. She tightened one crumpet muscle and then the other and felt how that felt. "I hope Number 53 likes this," she said, "because this is one major derriere."

She turned toward the two of them, wearing only her bra. "What's your verdict?"

They were both open-mouthed. Her eyes flitted to Krock's nethers, and she saw what looked like a stack of Duplo blocks. "The verdict is yes."

Mischa said, "And now, the fixative."

"What's that?" asked Henriette.

"I will excuse myself and Krock here will come on your new humongous ass."

"What? I didn't know about that. What happens if he doesn't come on my ass?"

"It shrinks back to normal size in ten minutes."

"No!"

"Yes. You have to have the fixative. For each man who comes on your ass, it'll remain humongous for a full hour, up to a total of twenty-four hours. How much fixative do you want?"

"The full twenty-four."

"Then you'll need us to summon the beginning of the Man Line. Kneel on the couch and Krock will come on your ass, and when he's done I'll wipe you down and send in the next man. Okay?"

Henriette knelt on the couch and waited, jiggling her amazingly huge ass a few times to get used to how it moved. "Okay," she said. "Bring on the Man Line."

Dave Trespasses

Dave was out for a walk in the middle of a quiet road near the House of Holes. He'd set out at about three o'clock in the afternoon, needing a little break after spending eight hours in the Porndecahedron watching amateur movies of women making themselves come. It was a lovely budding afternoon, and the sky was a perfect Pantone 2925 blue. Dave had a big plaid blanket in his canvas bag and a thermos of barley soup, and he unfurled the blanket over some matted grass and lay down and looked up at the clouds till he found one with soft breasts and a leg held alluringly half open, and he stuffed his hand down his pants and started working himself to the bone.

A young woman walked up and said, "Excuse me, what are you doing?" She had a large blunt-faced dog on a leash. The dog barked once politely and then sat down.

Dave whipped his hand out of his pants. "Just having my way with the clouds," he said. "My apologies."

"You shouldn't be doing that here in this field. This is a working farm. It doesn't belong to the House of Holes. Beyond that road over there is the property line. This is the real world."

Dave was horrified. "Very sorry, I had no idea I'd wandered off the range," he said. "You'd think they'd have a little border-crossing caution sign." He looked at the woman. She had generously messy hair and rough lips with no lipstick and a tiny scar on the bridge of her nose. "I'll tell you, it's one heck of a nice field you've got here. And you have some nice clouds, too. Nice soft luscious clouds just hanging in the sky."

"Thanks," she said, with some friendliness, looking at his missing arm. "It was the clouds coming over this hill that convinced my parents to buy this place. It has different weather on this side. And the oats grow well down on this slope."

"Do you drive the tractor?" Dave asked. "I'm Dave, by the way. I'd offer to shake your hand, but I've been, ah, having a meeting with the fondling fathers." He folded up his plaid blanket and stuffed it into his canvas bag.

"I'm Chilli," she said. "Yes, sometimes I drive the tractor."

"Good skill to have," he said. "Portable." He stood and brushed off his pants, holding the canvas bag over his lap. "Well, I'm off. I'm practicing for a festival."

"Was that what you were doing when I walked up, 'practicing'?"

"I like to stay in shape." They walked together down the rutted path toward the road. "Do you think there are certain fields on this planet that are sex fields? I feel that this is a sex field. It's not just the clouds. It's the shape of the land. You can't tell if it's a rectangle or a triangle or an oval. It undulates."

"It does," said Chilli.

"Can I ask you something impertinent? Do you ever come out here and just want to take your pants off? With the sky so huge and those clouds just hanging there?"

"Do I come out here sometimes and play with myself?"

Dave nodded. "Yeah. Do you do rude things to your little pulsing happy bloated clit, who's sitting there in the prow of the boat, looking backward at the rowers with her horn saying, 'Row, team, row, row the boat faster, and when you reach the shore, slide way up on the warm sand'? Do you do that?"

The woman looked down at her dog for a moment, and then she said, "Once I did sort of take my pants off."

"What made you do it?"

"It was a hot day, and I wanted to feel the breeze on my bottom—I think that's why."

"Don't you want to feel the breeze now?"

"Mm, but this is an awkward situation."

"I know it's awkward but, hey, that's what makes it fun. I've spent all day in the darned Porndecahedron looking at self-filmed amateur masturbation movies, and I've seen almost too much of it, if that's possible."

"You're at the House of Holes, and you're watching masturbation movies? I thought it was a sexual paradise."

"It is," said Dave. "People masturbate a lot in paradise, let me tell you. Have you been?"

"Nope, never have. We sometimes get people wandering over, so I've heard some stories, but I've never gone. My husband and I—" She trailed off. "And my kids."

"The whole family thing. I see."

"They're at school—and my husband's doing one of his trips to France to the cheesemakers' convention, so I'm here, and I'm—what can I say—walking the dog."

Dave had an idea. "Look, you're a neighbor to the House of Holes. You should pay a quick visit. I'll take you. You can just look around. I'm sure Lila—she's the director—would want to cultivate good relations with abutters." He peered at her rear. "And you're definitely an abutter."

"I've heard about Lila. But no, thanks. Maybe another time."

"Okay." They stood on the shoulder of the road. "Well, I'll be off, then. But will you walk me to the property line? I want to come back here, and I don't want to trespass."

"Sure. It's through here," she said, parting some shrubbery. Her dog made a brief yip of pain. "Oh, sorry, Gumball. Careful, Dave, there are some serious thorns here."

"Thanks, having the one arm makes some things more difficult."

"What happened? An accident?"

"No, it was intentional. I wanted a really big penis, and Lila said that I had a choice. I could either lose twenty percent of my intelligence or lose my left arm. And it's all totally reversible. I really wanted a bigger penis, a monster cock, I was tired of looking at my own. I'm not quite sure why. I guess all the Internet spam finally took its toll. And I said, Hell, Lila, take the left arm. So I had what's known as a crotchal transfer."

"Who with?"

"With this guy, he's an Australian wilderness photographer. He uses a giant eight-by-ten wooden camera. Glenn is his name. He has my penis and balls, and I have his penis and

172

balls. Meanwhile my amputated arm is out wandering around somewhere, having its own adventures."

"That's nuts," said Chilli. "How does the photographer feel about the swap?"

"Glenn's okay with it, surprisingly. I mean, my penis was fine, it was adequate, just not huge. Lila gave him two months free at the Hotel du Trou, and he takes boudoir pictures of women and indulges every whim. He's a good nature photographer, actually, and a nice guy. Are you sure you don't want to pay a visit?"

She looked indecisive for a moment, and then not. "I've got the dog, and I'll have to pick the kids up in an hour anyway. Thanks, though."

"What about tomorrow?" asked Dave. "I could meet you right here at, say, eleven. We could get some lunch, and maybe I could show you the Porndecahedron. I know you're married and all—you can set limits. We could just walk around. There's lots to see, believe me. Besides, you drive me crazy."

She looked at the clouds, which were doing something particularly puffy. "This is so wrong," she said. "But okay, I'll see you tomorrow at eleven."

"Good—and one more thing: If you go home now and get horny with yourself?"

"Yes?"

"Here's something to consider. It might be that at a certain point you think, Wow, I'm making these great expressions, and I'm making all these interesting noises, and I'm moving all around in this sexy way that's sexier than I've ever been—and nobody's seeing me play with myself. Well, in that case, just set up your webcam or your video camera, whatever you've got handy, and film it for me."

Chilli looked not at all sure. "I don't know if I can."

"You know you want to. And I'd love to see your eyes go all glassy, and I'd love to see that ferny thrusty feeling growing right down past your knees. I'd love to see your whole gaping snatch hole just munching on that orgasm, just chewing on that big sweet piece of half-melted pleasure that's hidden inside you until it's swallowed up by its own dissolution. Okay? If you play tonight, will you film it for me?"

"I've got to go pick up my kids now," she said. She was breathing, not moving.

"I know. Get yourself all filled with oxygen and nitrogen and helium and all the other special components of the air that will allow you to breathe out the best come you ever had right in your own bedroom, this afternoon. See you, bye." He squeezed her arm and ducked through the hedgerow.

Dune Visits the Midway

Shandee was standing up on a balcony on the midway, shaking her hips self-promotingly. She had white boots on and a small green cloth of Ka-Chiang hanging like a flag from her pussyhole. Out in front Krock was calling, "Forty to slap the pretty ass, sixty to spank it. Forty to slap, sixty to spank." Dune, strolling by, saw Shandee and immediately got in line for her. He paid and was given a pair of blue quilted oven mitts. "I'm going to slap that girl's happy ass," announced the man in line in front of him.

It was a long wait, in through a red door and around a series of small turns that led through a maze of plywood baffles painted black. Finally, Dune reached a small private room with a velvet curtain in it. Shandee was there—or part of her was. He couldn't see her face or upper body because she was leaning forward through a hole in the curtain that went around her waist; only her legs and bottom and pussy hanky were visible.

175

Dune sat down and said to himself, Will anything ever look as good to me as this girl's wineglass shape looks to me right now? Probably not.

"Shandee, baby," he called quietly. "It's me, Dune. How goes the search for your one-armed mystery man?"

Shandee's voice came muffled from the other side of the curtain. "No luck yet," she said. "Lila wants me out working on the midway while Dave sows his oats. She says I have to wait because Dave has a superlarge penis and he needs a little more time with it before he has to give it up."

"Too bad for him, he's missing out on you," said Dune. "Have you been going with anyone else?"

There was a thoughtful silence, then Shandee said, "Ruzty's paid a few calls."

"That sweet smiley kid with the accent?"

Shandee sighed. "It's embarrassing because whenever we finally get down to a little kissing, Dave's arm starts thrashing in his bag like a bad puppy. I put him in a drawer, but he starts thumping to get out."

"I can sympathize," said Dune, lightly stroking the back of Shandee's knee with his oven mitt. "You're so damn pretty I can barely swallow my own spit. And I can only see the lower half of you."

"That's sweet. Have you been well?"

"Oh, I'm rattled and cranky and horny," said Dune. "But I do have something that will be of interest to you." He tucked a scrap of paper into one of Shandee's boots. "It's the number of Dave's hotel room. Four thirty-four."

"Wow, thanks, Dune."

"And now, before my time runs out, I hope you'll let me slap or spank your ass."

"Sure, that's what it's for," said Shandee. "But wear the mitts, and don't spank too hard. Some guys spank me too hard."

Dune blew on her ass and rested both his mitts on it for a moment. "Shandee, honey, I'll spank you so soft you won't even know it's spanking, I'll spank you real tender, and you'll know it's me, because I'm really just touching your ass with a man's gentle touch and showing you how much respect I have for it."

"That's nice," said Shandee.

"And can I kiss your ass, too? And worship it?"

"Yes, you can kiss and worship my ass."

He bent close and kissed, closing his eyes, and then he whispered, "And can I pull out your hanky and stick one pinky finger in your pretty pussy? I know I'll find true peace if I do."

"If you do that with your pinky, Dune, they'll cut it off," said Shandee, putting her knees together. "Look up on the wall above you."

Dune glanced at the long, bony row of dried fingers that were nailed there. Then he noticed a small blood-stained chopping block in the corner. It was not a pleasant sight.

"Damn savages," said Dune. "It's almost worth it, except I play guitar and keyboards. Can't they make an exception for an old friend?"

Shandee shifted her weight fetchingly, considering. "Krock is a stickler," she said finally, "but you've been so helpful, I'll tell you what I'll do. Pull out the cloth of Ka-Chiang, and I'll push some fresh juice from my cunny for you."

Dune breathed. "Oh, that would be a welcome treat." He

pushed an oven mitt into Shandee's upper leg, softly, and palmed her left asscheek. Then he thumped the asscheek a little on one side, so that she jumped and her elegant flesh shimmied. He pinched her thighs gently three times and tugged on her hanky till it fell out. "Now let me see your pussy cry," he said.

Shandee was wet already; she arched her back up and pushed. Dune saw a tender shining weep of wetness that brimmed over her slit and leaked down one leg.

"Oh, my glory!" Dune said, losing control. Before he realized what he was doing, he'd flung off an oven mitt and slid one pinky finger knuckle-deep into her velvet draperies.

There was a bonging sound and a commotion. A disembodied male arm leapt up, twirled once in the air, and seized Dune by the wrist. Krock hurried in and grabbed the knife. Mischa set out the chopping block on a towel. "Dune, why did you do it?" said Shandee, full of disappointment and concern.

"I forgot myself, I'm sorry," said Dune, disengaging the viselike fingers of Dave's arm. He turned to Krock and Mischa. "Now hear me out, guys. I play keyboards and guitar, and to be honest I'd rather lose my pecker for a little while than my ability to make music."

That statement got Krock's attention. "Daggett," he said into his communicator, "tell Lila that Dune has verbally agreed before witnesses to lose his pecker."

Lila was pacing up and down in front of her desk when Dune was led in. "All right, Mr. Pussyfinger," she said firmly. "Just for that bit of defiance, we're going to do a switcheroo on you." She opened a door.

In walked Marcela, the art critic, in a black slip. "Hello," she said, with a nervous smile.

Chilli Goes to the Porndecahedron with Dave

Chilli met Dave at eleven o'clock at the border crossing. She'd put on a little makeup and was wearing sandals and a sleeveless white shirt with black buttons. "Hi there," she said. "I just wanted to tell you that I'm really sorry, I can't go with you."

"Oh, pshaw, sure you can," said Dave. "See the sights!"

"Well, just a quick visit then."

They walked through a thicket and emerged at a clearing and climbed a low stone fence and walked a little farther. Dave pointed out the White Lake and the midway. They bought some falafels and ate them, while Dave told her about the darkrooms, where you talked in utter darkness. Chilli seemed to like that idea, so they checked into a darkroom and sat.

"So how did everything go yesterday?" asked Dave in the dark.

"Just fine," Chilli said, enigmatically. "Now, tell me how this Porndecahedron works."

Dave said, "It's a twelve-sided projection theater, like a dodecahedron. You've heard of buckyballs, right? It's a big buckyball that you go inside of. There's a cluster of seats in the middle, either single or tandem seats, and you go in and sit in a seat, buckled in for safety, because you're suspended. You sit there and movies play on all the screens around you."

"Dirty movies."

"Well, you pick the playlist. Could be music videos, or a mashup from Brad Pitt movies, or handjobs, or beautiful Balinese dancers, or men having sex with each other—some women like to watch men having sex, it seems. Some people are into fetishes, so then there'll be twelve screens of, say, men coming on women's feet."

"Oh, wow," said Chilli.

"I personally think all fetishes are just a waste of time. All you need for good porn is a pretty smiley woman who's having fun, and a dude with a hard dick who isn't fat."

"And you watch this on your own?"

"You can, or sitting next to somebody you've not met, or hardly met, or somebody you know well. It's like a planetarium, except instead of planets and stars there are nipples, or cocks, or gorgeous faces, or flowers opening, or sped-up clouds, or whatever, you get to pick, and you're surrounded."

Chilli took these varied images in. "And you decided to spend eight hours watching movies of women making themselves come?"

"I love homemade come movies. But not pussy close-ups. You have to see the woman's face when she comes, pussy and face together, or it doesn't work. I thought about watching some more movies when I got back from your beautiful field yesterday, but my mood was totally different because of talking to you. Also Lila's got me on a deprivation schedule, which means I can't masturbate myself as often as I'd like."

"How sad for you."

"Yeah, so for instance right now my cock is dealing with a massive porn overdose. It's so full of home jizm brew it hurts."

"By 'your cock,' of course you mean the cock you got from the Australian photographer guy."

"I think of it as mine, but, yes, it's his cock I've been edging with. Do you edge?"

"I don't know, frankly, do I?" Chilli said.

"Edging's when you do yourself till you almost come and then stop. You keep right on the edge of the tipping point. Go, stop, go, stop. Do you do that?"

Chilli gave this some thought. Dave heard her crossing her legs in the dark. "If my husband's away," she said, "I'll drop the kids off with my mom, and I'll do a shop, and then back home, yeah, I have so many crazy thoughts in my head that it sometimes takes a while to get through them."

"Nice way to spend a Saturday afternoon, edging," said Dave. "Close, then away, then close, then away, till it really burns, and then finally, whammo bing-bangy ba-doom! Then, blip. Snerp."

"Um, I don't know how to ask you this, but—"

"Yeah?"

"Do you think I could feel this unusually large cock of yours that you had grafted on? Just for a second. I don't want to do anything with it, I just want to touch it for a second."

"Yeah, sure," said Dave. "It's not a graft, though. Let me clarify that. It's an interplasmic dual crotchal transfer. Very different process. I can explain if you want."

"No, that's okay. Let me just grope a little closer to you. Woops, where are you?"

"I'm here. My pants are down now."

"Oh my god, your balls are like sheep balls. Wow." She breathed in with a sipping sound, fondling Dave's cock. He moved his hips a little so that it poked and shuttled through her loose fingers. "It's been so so long," she said.

"Your fingers feel good. So long since what?"

"Since I've held a really nice big cock. I went out with a boy in college for about a month. He was big. Not this big, though. Uh. It's so heavy. I'm going to stop now though. Self-control. I have something for you."

"Your mouth?"

"No, here." She handed Dave a flash drive. "This is the movie I made of myself last night."

"Great, we'll pop into the Porndecahedron and watch it. I'm signed up for a block of time." Dave readjusted his clothes, and they walked out into the sunlight squinting and shading their eyes and smiling at each other.

"I'm so horny I can barely walk," Chilli said, giggling. "Where is this filthy Frigahedron?"

"Right through here," said Dave. At the upload station he keyed in his password and loaded Chilli's movie into his playlist. "I warn you, this is pretty immersive. It may just be too much for you. All I've got on this playlist is women making themselves come. Plus a few titty cumshots to spice the mix. I love those."

"That's okay. I'll be a part of it. I want to see what you do when you watch me."

Dave got them a pack of Red Vines and opened a door, and they walked into the staging area and sat together in a tandem chair. Once Chilli had gotten herself buckled in, they were lifted up into the center of the Porndecahedron. Dave tapped a button on his handrest and they started watching. There were movies above them and below them and on all sides, and all the soundtracks merged and mingled and were confusingly present, although some people muted all but one of them or overlaid a music track. "So this is it, huh?" she said. "She looks like she's enjoying it. Oh my goodness, that's a lot of sperm. Don't you find this a bit overwhelming?"

"Hell, I could probably handle twenty-four screens," said Dave. He was biting his lips, watching, his eyes ping-ponging around from clip to clip. "I love the way she moves her knees," he said.

"Now that woman looks sexy to me," Chilli said, pointing off to the left. "Whoa, was that her orgasm? She really came hard."

Then Dave spotted Chilli's face. It was on one of the screens just above his head and to the right. "There you are!" he said.

"Where? Uh-oh. This is incredibly embarassing."

"No, it's not, it's beautiful. Is that your living room?" On the screen, Chilli was taking off her shirt and undoing her bra and looking at herself in the mirror of her laptop screen. "You are so sexy! Jesus. Mmm. I'm going to have to do some serious edging. I hope you don't mind."

"You're going to bring your charley horse out right now?"

"Yeah, and I wish you would liberate your clit, too. Just set it free."

"But then I'd be masturbating to a film of myself mas- turbating."

"Exactly, and you'll enjoy it, too. Don't miss this opportunity to get serious with your entire cunt. It wants your attention."

"That's true," she said.

Dave angled out his Malcolm Gladwell.

"Ooh, you've got it out again," she said. "Can I hold it for a second, just the head of it? Oof."

He leaned back. "I don't want to come right yet, though. But, oh gosh, you're so so pretty up on the twelvemo screen. Look at that, you're so lusciously nasty with yourself. This is fantastic." In her movie, Chilli was holding her legs open with her elbows, and she was gripping one hand with the other and stuffing three fingers inside herself.

"I am getting down and dirty, aren't I?"

"And your eyes, look at your eyes, look at that fucky sex blur in your eyes."

"This is where I came, I think," she said. "Yep, that's how I come."

"You are ridiculously hot, wait, don't move your hand on my cock, don't move even a quarter of an inch or I'll spunk ham juice out everywhere, oh, oh, so close, let it work its way down—Zen, Zen, whooooooooo."

"But I want you to come."

"Not here," said Dave. "I've seen too much porn. I need to escape. I need nature. I want to come in your field with your pussy shoved in my face."

"I can't do that," said Chilli.

"No? Under the clouds in the sex field?"

"Well, okay," she said. "Briefly."

"Goody, just press stop on your handrest there."

The tandem chair lowered to the staging area, and they walked out.

"I'll get the blanket," said Dave.

"Hurry, because I'm here leaking right down my leg," said Chilli.

She and Dave had a breathless run—it felt like an escape—out of House of Holes territory and on through the briars and the bushes to the sex field.

"We can go back close to where you were yesterday," Chilli said, "but a little ways back. It's private."

Dave spread out the blanket over what Chilli noticed was an old dry hole in the ground. Probably a mole hole, she thought. Then she thought, Hmmm. She sat splaylegged on the blanket, and Dave brought out his massive, porn-maddened spunk-spewer. "Let me just stare at it," she said.

Very lightly and respectfully she touched it, as if less pressure made for less of a marital infraction.

"Can I fuck you right here on this blanket?" asked Dave.

"No, you absolutely cannot fuck me, no," she said. "But you can fuck my field. Stuff a bit of the blanket down that mole hole and then put your big cock in it. I want to watch your assbuns clench. Drive your cock into my field. Root yourself. I need to show you my whole pussy now. You want to see it?"

She scooted so that Dave's face, when he arched his neck up, was inches from her cuntgash. He listened to the luscious squelching at close range as she pulled the folds away from her clit. He closed and opened his eyes, and each time he opened them her succulent stovetop filled his vision, being stretched one way and another by her questing and well-practiced fingers. Supporting himself on his one arm, he guided his dick into the prickly wool of the blanket. He sank in deep. "I'm fucking the hole," Dave said, and he saw her gaze travel to his assclenching maximus cheeks.

She said, "Here's all of me, Dave, nurse on my big clit so I can come." He smelled her radiating vadge, and then, opening his soft lips, he slopped and slobbered his whole face into her pussy. He rolled his eyes up to look at her. Her head was thrown back. She was feeling good. He smiled into her pussy and then took a breath. "Look up at these great clouds," he said, "while I suck your pussy and fuck the planet earth."

Chilli breathed. "I love this," she said. She looked down at Dave's mouth at her lettuce patch and watched his tongue do its wonderful work. "Edge us as close as you can, loverman."

Dave said, "Gluddle-luddle-luddle-luddle-luddle-luddle-luddle, mmmm."

"Take it out of the earth and milk your huge cock off for me. I want to see it. Please milk it off."

Dave pulled out of the crumbling earth hole and knelt close to her. "Here you go, sweet woman," he said. "Haaahh!" Five days' worth of sperm flowered out all over her stomach and breasts.

"Now me," Chilli said. "Jab that wicked tongue back inside me—that's the way." She held his head and moved her cuntal hand in slow connoisseurial ovals, and then, making her fingers rigid, she DJ'd herself, as if her clit was a scratch record. "Nnnnn, nnnn," she said, frowning down at her frigging self. Her hips lifted off the blanket. "Oh, that's good! Oh, shit, Dave, I'm a pornstar! Oh, juice it, juice it, I'M COMING!"

Ned Undergoes a Voluntary Head Detachment

Ned the golfer had incurred terrible debts at the House of Holes, and he was called into the main office. "Let's see your body, please," said Lila.

Ned removed his shirt and pants.

"Very nice," she said. "And the underpants, please."

He stepped out of them with a smile, his jig swaying.

She looked at him for a long time, tapping a pen on the arm of her chair.

"Your body is adorable," she said.

"My face is not so good, though," he said. "Is that what you mean?"

"It's a perfectly nice face. You mean well, you're a nice man, but you don't have that smoldering puffy-lipped look that a lot of women like."

"I know. So what on earth do I do?"

"I would say that for you, with that body, the fastest way for you to pay off your debts is with the voluntary head detachment."

"What's that? I'd like to try it."

"Think about it carefully. Your head will be removed and put on a wheeled pedestal. Kathy will roll you around and change your plasma bags and be sure that your electricals are all shipshape."

"And my body?"

"Your body will go into one of the six headless rooms."

"Okay, and what happens in there?"

"Your body and a woman will get to know each other."

"How? My body won't have a head."

"No, it won't. These are women who don't want you to have a head."

"Oh, I see, okay."

"And your body will have a simple form of consciousness."

"How?"

"We put a cap at the top of your spinal cord, and we redirect your nervous system. Your body will be able to think, in a very limited way, with your spine, penis, and balls. Your ass will serve as a neuronal proxy as well."

"I see. Makes sense. Well, let's do it."

Ned took a pill and was able to remain conscious through the detachment procedure. He felt a faint tugging once or twice and then a powerful wave of vertigo. He closed his eyes, and when he opened them he was detached and positioned on the wheeled pedestal, his head strapped in a comfortable head-rig.

His body sat about ten feet away from him, in a chair. Where his head had been there was a low dome covered in artificial skin. Kathy, his pedestal pusher, was dressing his body, helping it to learn how to move with its limited neural resources. She rubbed the body's arms, and it stood. She patted them. "Good bodyboy," she said.

She tied a conservative tie around his body's neck and then planted his body's hands on her shoulders. She touched his leg, pulling, indicating that he should raise his leg, which he did. She held some khaki pants out for him, and the leg slid them on. Ned noticed that his body's penis was unusually tumescent. This seemed not to trouble Kathy. She grasped his zipper, stuffed his equipment into place, and zipped him neatly up. Then she slipped a tweed jacket on him. "There we go," she said. She turned to Ned's head. "What do you think of your body?" she said. "Cleans up pretty nice, eh?"

"Kind of strange," he said. "But I guess you get used to it."

"Oh, sure," said Kathy. "I used to work on a dairy farm. You just have to be patient and gentle, and sometimes they get excited. It's just a whole other way of being. It's very—bodily."

"What happens to me?" Ned the head asked.

"My sister Cora, the headmistress, will take care of you for a while."

Cora came in and put his head in a bowling bag. She carried him away.

Reese Visits a Headless Bedroom

"I want something where the man's not always judging me and criticizing me and disapproving of how I dress and all that," said the ethereal flaxen-haired girl, Reese, to Lila, in Lila's office. "I guess I want a good-looking man for a fun brainless time in the sack."

"Well," said Lila, "we do offer the headless bedrooms."

"What are they?"

"You choose a good-looking body whose head has been temporarily removed."

"That's horrible!" said Reese.

"Surprisingly it's not, really. What you get is a nice friendly extremely handsome male body that is very responsive to any stimulation because it can't hear or see or speak or think except with what it has, which is its spine and crotch."

"I see, I see."

"You and the handsome headless body are together in a

furnished room for fifteen minutes, half an hour, or even a full hour."

"Where's the head during all this?"

"You never see the head. The head is safe in the headroom. Cora is the headmistress, she takes care of eight heads. We'll put them all back on later."

"And the heads have agreed to this?"

"Yep."

"And the body can move and all that?"

"Yes, although some fine motor skills are not there. On the wall you'll see some how-to posters that Kathy has made. They'll help you handle these bodyboys, as we call them."

"Let's do it."

Daggett led Reese into a room where there were eight headless men sitting on couches. They were wearing long Japanese-style bathrobes. Kathy smiled at Reese and offered her a seat in a comfortable chair. Then she touched each bodyboy, helping it stand and walk in front of Reese and then open its robe, showing off its chest and underpants. "I can have him pull down his underpants, if you'd like," said Kathy. "He doesn't mind."

"Well, I'd kind of like to see his butt, if you'd have him turn around."

Kathy guided him around and held his robe to one side. Reese nodded. "Very nice."

She was disappointed, though. He was an extreme body-builder type with a tanning-bed tan and pectoral muscles that looked sort of like breasts except hard. She said, in a low voice, "Um, do you have any men who are more, you know, guy-next-doorish? Fit but not like a male stripper?"

Kathy smiled. "Ah, yes, there are a few. The first is Lonny, who when he had his head hung gutters for a living. Here he is."

Kathy helped Lonny-body stand. Reese feasted her eyes on a headless man with a set of callused hands and a wiry strong build that had come about by work and not by working out.

"Then there's Bosco," said Kathy. "Bosco is a painter."

"Hm, nice, trim, but too old," said Reese.

"And then there's Ned," Kathy said. "He's my favorite. Come on, Ned." She cooed at him, gently nudging his arm so that he would stand. "Look at this," she said. She pinched his nipple, and his arm flapped her hand away. "Ned doesn't like that, see? He's got a lot of personality left in his body. He knows how to move. Watch." She stood behind him and put her hands on his hips, and Ned's body swayed, his robe flapping.

Reese felt a sudden throb, which she masked perfectly. "They're all very nice," she said, "but I agree with you that this one is the most normal. If anyone can be normal when he's missing his head."

"I know what you mean. Just remember that even though he has been freed of his head, he still is going to have some feelings. Treat him well, and he'll treat you well."

"What do I call him?" Reese asked.

"Well, he can't hear, but it helps to have a name. His head's name is Ned, so call him Nedbody."

Reese walked up to Nedbody and took his hand. He seemed to sense that she was a different person from Kathy. When she lifted his hand, he didn't resist, but followed her movements.

Kathy showed her that two fingers gently squeezing his arm muscle meant "good."

The room was large and sparely furnished. Kathy explained

that furniture had to be kept to a minimum because Nedbody was blind, of course. Then she left.

There were some grapes in the corner, and Reese looked at them wistfully, thinking that she could eat them but Nedbody couldn't. She ate a grape, and then, feeling a little shy, sat down next to him on a couch and put her head on his shoulder. She inspected the low mound of his neck. It was surprisingly easy to get used to his headlessness. If you hadn't known what human beings looked like you would simply assume that this was the way they were.

She tweaked his nipple, as Kathy had done, and his hand brushed her away. That was good—it was a sign of his having preferences. She wanted to know what Nedbody wanted and what he didn't want. "I think I want you to have no clothes on," she said to him. She pulled, and he got up, and she slipped the robe off and slipped his underpants off, and he almost lost his balance getting out of them, but she held his arm to steady him. Then she walked him over to the bed and stood behind him. His butt was his best feature, it was quite amazing—two strong bouncy male musclecakes covered in a furze of hair. She helped him bend forward, and, showing him how to place his hands, she urged him to lie on his stomach on the bed. He did so, his legs hanging out over the floor. She wanted to look at everything about him. She punched lightly at his ass cheeks, and then she looked at the back part of his balls for a while. Then she lifted the phone. Kathy answered. "Kathy," she said, "I don't think I can do this. I really need him to have a head."

Kathy came back in. "I'm so sorry, Reese, his head is unavailable." She said. "You have to make do. But have a look at this body." She pointed to him facedown on the bed. He was sleeping. He seemed to drop off easily. A slight sound of breathing escaped from his neckhole.

"Can you at least give me some pointers?"

"Sure," Kathy said. "He likes to be massaged. The seat of his intelligence is his lower back, so I massage there first to get his attention. It's like getting eye contact." She parted his legs and stood between them, squeezing her thumbs into his back. He stirred slightly in his sleep.

"Another thing is he likes you to tickle just behind his knees. Watch." She tickled, and Nedbody's legs jumped. She tickled again.

Reese noticed that now Nedbody's hips were grinding into the bed. She turned to Kathy. "He seems to be getting into the bed action there."

"That's what he does, poor guy," said Kathy. "Anytime you put any pressure on his genitals, he dry humps you."

"Oh," said Reese. "Well, I can live with that."

"I'm going to leave you now," said Kathy. "It's a little traumatic for me because I take care of him. I can't help it. Sometimes I feel jealousy. But I want him to have as good a time as he can have, and I have to do an oil change on three of the other guys."

"What's an oil change?"

"All the bodily necessities—we have to flush them out every other day to keep them healthy."

"This is pretty impressive but pretty nutty," Reese said.

"I can get used to anything," said Kathy. "They're nice men." She paused just before she closed the door. "I can tell from the way he's humping the bed that he's got a big hard-on," she said. "Turn him on his side, and you'll have a nice present."

She closed the door.

Reese sat next to Nedbody for a moment, looking at the smooth muscular expanse of his back. His arms were flung wide. She smelled his underarms, which though Kathy had washed him had a whiff of man scent. She pulled on the hair, and he shrugged. Then she couldn't stand it—she had to bring out one of her trusty erotic romances. It was *Tastefully Done,* one from the Untamed Wanderer series. She read Nedbody a passage as he slept, gently caressing his perfect bottom as she did and feeling his muscles involuntarily tighten as he dry humped the bed. "Shadow's thighs registered the heat of his haughty stare," she read. "He seized her roughly and lifted the burning torch of her sex to his mouth. 'Shadow, I have craved your salt taste for three long years,' he said, his lips red as embers in the deepening dusk."

"Whoo!" she said. "That's the stuff! Nedbody, baby, do you mind if I kind of help you turn over?" He didn't seem to mind, and she eased her fingers under one of the thick muscles of his upper thigh and pulled gently, feeling like a camel driver. He drew his arms in and turned, and she had her first glance at his cock, which lay like a railroad tie hanging out from his body. It moved with his heartbeat. She watched it for a moment, wondering at its independent spirit.

"It looks like you have something major going on there, Nedbody," she said. She found that she couldn't help herself, and she curled her fingers around the fullness of what remained of his intelligence. "Think with your dick," she whispered, moving her mouth closer. She pulled one knee up and pushed the other away, and he lay sprawled, jutting upward like some travesty of a Michelangelo sculpture, and from him came the dusty, meaty scent of his balls, which she breathed in for a long time and allowed to swirl around in her brain. For she did have a brain as he, poor Nedbody, did not. "You poor brainless man," she said. "I'm going to suck your dick, and you won't even know it. Mmmmmmm."

She encircled the base of his cock and brought it up so that it grazed her lips, and she found that when she did his hips made a little judder, a kind of minithrust, which was precious to her because it was a bit of communication. "That's it," she said, "use those hips, baby." Then she closed her fist on his cock and slid her hand all the way down again until the skin pulled tight on the pistil head of his manjig.

"You don't know this, Nedbody, but I just love sucking dick," she said. "And you've got an unusually fine one, and I'm going to be very, very nice to it." She closed her eyes again and smelled him and stroked him once. His hips moved, sending him toward her. She opened her mouth and felt him push against her tongue. She flattened her tongue out and slathered under his head, and each time she did his pelvis jerked, and that made her happy.

She tried not to look up at his head, because his head wasn't there, and she concentrated on his true self, which was his dick. She was grinding her muffin against the muscle just above his knee, and then she stood for a second because she wanted to be naked. She wondered if he could feel her breasts, and it seemed not too difficult to find out. He was lying with his hands at his sides. She lowered one of her breasts, and when his hand felt her nipple graze the sensitive skin in the middle of his palm his hips made another small jump.

"You got me feeling pussyish, Nedbody," she said, breathily. "Think with your asshole." She grabbed his dick with one hand, and with her left hand she snookered a finger up his ass, and then she held her mouth still and began a slow, deliberate crescendo, jerking him off into her mouth. He raised his arms, and she saw his hands waving in the air in a little twirling dance of pelvis pleasure, and then both his fists clenched suddenly and she felt his asshole crunch. His stomach worked, and his hips rocked, and his legs flumped together, his knees knocking audibly, and she felt a hot jolt of manwater against the back of her throat. Then he trembled and subsided.

"There you are," she said, "you nice headless man. There you go. You stay right there, and I'm going to get my moment now. Wait." She rode his thigh, looking at his spent cock and remembering how it had felt in her mouth, and she twizzled her riddler and moved back and forth on the wet slippery spot on his thigh, and finally she whispered, "Oh, Nedbody, here I come." She clamped her legs around his thigh and came and came and came. Then she flung herself down on the bed next to him and laughed. Nedbody was asleep already, breathing quietly.

Cardell Meets Betsy on the Beach

Cardell knelt to study the footprint in the sand. In the air there was a deep-in-the-nose smell of ocean and seaweed and timeless things that have no name.

The footprint was light and small—the print of a woman. He pressed his own foot into it and tried to imagine her firm footbone. He started following the footsteps, walking in them as much as he could.

The beach curved back into a small bay where the House of Holes condominiums were, and as Cardell turned the corner he saw a distant figure wearing a hat. He increased his pace, still stepping in her footsteps. With each step he took, he learned more about the arch of her foot, the ball of her foot, and her small, strong toes. He was almost loping now.

Finally, he caught up to her. She was wearing a loose, faded dress and a hat, and she held her sandals hooked on her fingers.

Her hat was woven of pale fine straw and made her face glow like a classy tangerine. He recognized her.

"Hi, I bought the pen," he said.

"Oh, good," said Betsy.

"I've been walking in your footsteps," he said. "It was the most intimate experience. Did you feel my feet pressing against your feet?"

"I'm not sure," she said. "Let me try walking in your footsteps, and you can see what you feel."

"Okay."

Cardell walked a few paces ahead and stopped.

"Don't turn around," she said.

He didn't. She walked up to him.

"Did you feel the ball of my foot pressing into your footprint?" she asked.

"Some," he said. "More I felt the arch. But yes, I feel I know you better now."

"And I know you better. We're old friends, in fact."

Cardell paused, full of indecision. "But we're very different."

"That's true. I collect beach glass, and you don't."

"You seem rich."

"I'm not poor. My husband's father was rich. He was supposedly a ruthless businessman, but he was always nice to me." She smiled.

"I'd love to see you come," Cardell said thickly.

She laughed. "Ah, but I'm married, as you know. I don't cheat. Much."

"Does your husband have a friendly sex organ that treats you well?" he asked.

"He does," she said, in a distant voice. "It's got a knobby end that fits me just right. But I suppose that's private information."

Cardell looked out at the ocean. "I wish I had a cold iced tea right now."

Betsy's voice was very small. "I have cold Snapple in my condo, if you want to come back."

So they went back to her condo where there was a tall vase filled with carved canes and a Chinese ceramic pig on a side table, its head resting on a red pillow. There were also many jars of shells and beach glass. Betsy pulled the sliding door half open so that they could still hear the sound of the sea.

"My husband is at his office," she said after a moment. "I—I can call him. Should I?"

"Absolutely, yes, give him a call."

She flipped out her cell phone. "Honey," she said, "I've met a nice-looking young man on the beach who says he wants to watch me come." She paused. "I know. I know. Okay. I know. Okay."

She held the phone away from her ear. Cardell raised his eyebrows questioningly.

"He's kind of angry," she whispered. Then she listened some more to the telephone. "He wants to talk to you."

Cardell took the phone. "Hello, sir?"

There was a strong voice in his ear. "I don't know who you are, but stay away from my wife. Leave the condo immediately."

"I will leave the condo, but I would really like to see her come first, and I know that's a problem for you, but I also know she wants to see my mandingo. I'm just going to shuck my boxers off, and my mandingo will be sticking out, and she'll get a good look at it. She wants to, I know it. Do you say yes?"

"No, you will not bring out any such mandingo!" the husband choked. "You will absolutely do nothing of the sort! You are out of line!" He hung up.

Cardell handed the phone back to Betsy, shaking his head.

"Oh, he's such an old poke-in-the-dough," she said. "Are you disappointed?"

He nodded.

"You poor thing, you wanted to see me come, didn't you?"

He nodded again.

She looked at him appraisingly. "And then you'd come, wouldn't you? You probably have a cock that you'd jerk off bigtime, wouldn't you? I know you just love jerking off that proud nasty cock."

"That I do," he said. "Hard as a ship's biscuit, but fresher."

She had an idea. "I'll tell you what we'll do. Let's go out on the back deck and I'll pretend to have sex with my husband, and I'll tell you all about it, and you'll watch me pretending. Will that work?"

"That sounds like a good fallback," Cardell said.

So they went out to the back deck, and she started with the running commentary.

"Usually I'm in bed first," she said. "He stays up doing the crossword—he's good at it, but it takes him a long time sometimes, and I read a book."

"Like what?"

"Oh, maybe something a little frisky, a little naughty," said Betsy. "And sometimes I just turn my light off and go to sleep, and sometimes I'm still reading when I hear him washing up and sniffing. He hangs up his pants carefully and puts on his pajamas, which are on a hook on the back of the closet door. We have two hooks. Am I boring you?"

Cardell was smiling, watching her tell the story, lying back on a lounge chair and feeling perfectly happy. He shook his head.

"Good. Then he gets in bed, and if I'm awake and I stir he says, 'Good-night, hon,' and I say, 'Good-night, darling.' And often we go to sleep."

"But sometimes you don't."

"Right, sometimes we've made a prior arrangement to do the triple-X dirty nasty."

"I see."

"And we both know that there's the appointment. So I lie there, and he rubs my back for a while." She lay with her eyes closed as she said this, rubbing her hands on her thighs. "Sometimes he teases under my ears, and that makes me shrug, whoo! And then I reach back behind me, and I find his bulgy bits in his pajamas, and I hold them a moment to figure out what's what. Then I reach my hand in and grab a handful, and then usually he shifts and pulls his pajamas down. And then everything begins to make itself known."

She was reaching behind herself as she said this.

"Do you like feeling him get hard?"

"Love feeling him get hard, yes. He says, 'Can I tweak your titties?' And I lift so he can get at them, and he knows just how to play with my nipples so that the two jagged lightning lines go dingalinging straight down. And then I have to turn toward him—" Here she turned in the chaise longue and held her invisible husband. Her hand slid under her blouse. "He kisses me all over me and puddles up one of my tits so that the nipple is aiming straight up. Mmm."

Cardell, watching her tell this, found that his hips had slid forward on the chair and his knees had straightened. "And then he pushes that big cockhead inside you?"

"Yes, he does," she said. "He's quite talkative sometimes when we get going, like if we've been out to dinner at our little Mexican place. There's a nice little Mexican place we go to. And he doesn't know it, nor should he know it, but when he really gets down to fucking me I'm sometimes thinking of sucking off the Mexican busboys. I'm thinking they're tied down on tables after the restaurant closes, and they need me to give them handjobs and blowjobs to relieve all the terrible stresses that come with the job of being a busboy, and I can feel their come boiling up the length of their cocks, and I swallow it all."

"Cocks on the boil, eh?"

"Yes, often I think about jerking off well-knit young men whose dicks are out." Betsy looked pointedly at Cardell when she said this. "But he doesn't know what I'm thinking. Except once I told him and he came so hard afterward. That's why I thought maybe he'd say yes to letting you watch me."

"But he didn't."

"No, he didn't, because he's a poky old thing. But he does know me better than anyone, and I've figured out just how to have a good orgasm with him, which I like."

"I kind of want to bring myself out now for you," Cardell said.

"You want to bring out Mr. Thick Dicky?"

Cardell said, "Mm-hm."

"One sec." Betsy dialed her husband's number again. "Hon, I'm out on the back deck with Cardell, that's his name, and I've been explaining to him how you and I make love. I know. I know, hon. I know. But he's gotten a little aroused, the poor boy, as I have, and I wondered if it would be all right if he took out his dick and played with it, just for a moment or two, in a tasteful way, while I continued to tell him about us and what we do, so I thought I should ask you—"

She listened for a moment.

"Okay, no. I understand. Okay." She clicked the phone off. "He says no. But!" She got a shrewd expression. "He didn't say you couldn't do what you need to do in your bathing suit."

"You mean reach in?"

"Precisely. Reach in. Just don't 'bring it out.'"

Cardell reached in, and as he did she came over. "But I'd like to have a peek," she said. He pulled on his waistband so that she could peer into the depths of his bathing suit. She saw his fist in the green shadows, clutching his swollen packmule.

"Oooh," she said, "I'd like to have a taste of that big hunk of badness. But sadly—it is not to be."

"Why don't you keep telling me how you and he fool around? That was going pretty good."

"Okay, well." She closed her eyes and thought. "Somewhere along the way my panties have been scooted down and kicked off in the bottom of the bed, which means that after we're done I have to hunt around for them for five minutes or give up and get a clean pair and figure I'll find them in the morning."

"Then what?"

"Ah, well, then there comes a point, always, inevitably, where I have to go on my knees and put my ass up. I don't know why it is, but I need to feel the pressure of the bed on my knees and elbows and the high-up feeling of my ass pointing straight up! I can't help it. It simply must go up! Always has."

"Does he like that?"

"Yes, it makes him crazy." She looked at him. "Do you want to see?"

He smiled.

She put her ass up. She was still wearing the light-blue shorts she wore over her bathing suit. She looked entrancingly suggestive, and Cardell began breathing noisily through his nose.

"Does he cram it directly in?"

"Not right away. By the way, does my eye look swollen?"

Cardell leaned and peered at her. "Not too swollen. A little red, maybe, in the corner. Have you been crying?"

"No, just a bug bite this morning. Annoying. Anyway, yes, his cock is knobby, so sometimes he rubs it against my thigh for a second and spanks it against my asscheek, because he likes me to know how big and warm and ass-slappy and hard it is. So hard."

She was lying back on the chaise longue now with her hands in the air. "Then I feel his hands grab my hips, and his woody finds me on its own, and I'm so darn wet and puffy that he can just stab it in one long stroke, right there, that long bone, mmmf."

Floomp, floomp went Cardell's hand in his bathing suit.

She opened her eyes and looked over at him. "You like listening to me tell you about how my husband fucks me?"

Flump flump flump, said Cardell's hand. He was smiling a wanker's smile.

"You love to tug that dirty dick and listen to me chatter, don't you?"

"Yes, I do, and tell me, do you prefer when he's slow and smooth or hard and pounding?"

"I like it when he's been going along slow and then with no warning he just barrels into me at double speed, bam bam bam

205

bam! And I say, 'Fuck me, moneyman, bang me hard, yeah, hard, yeah!' He likes when I call him moneyman." Her arm was up to the wrist in her shorts now. "But he could be anybody, then. In fact, he is anybody. He's not my husband anymore, he's a big bad stranger on a string connected to twelve guys I've seen, some on TV, some in real life. They're cycling around, having at me one by one."

At this Cardell stood wildly and pulled all of his dick out. "Does his dick look like this? Hmmm?" he asked. "Sorry, I can't help it," he added.

She stared at him and blinked. "No, yours is very different— very different in shape and tint and everything—although about the same size. People care so much about size, but size is just the beginning. It's like comparing flavors of apples."

Cardell was slowly working it, leering.

She stared a moment longer and then roused herself. "Put it back now. I'm trying to stay within bounds. Back in the bathing suit, back, back, back, that's right. Do whatever you have to do in the suit."

Cardell started floomp-floomping again, punching from within the bathing suit to make room for his rogue jacquard.

He said, "Tell me about the hardest time you ever came."

She reflected, lightly touching the potted boxwood that was next to her. "In general I come hardest when I put a something in my ass. My husband is away a lot, and I read one of my erotic romance books about bad assfucking vampires, and I start to get a little wild, and I put a screwdriver in a latex glove and put the handle in my ass."

Cardell was silent, surprised, pondering. Then he said, "It would be nice if you could do that for me."

"What, now? Put a screwdriver handle in my ass now? No, I haven't showered. I'd have to shower. I have a whole procedure. Also I'll have to call my husband and ask him if it's okay."

"You know he's going to say no."

"It's worth a try." She blipped out the phone number again. "Hello, hon, I'm still here with this boy. I know, but he's a good listener. I know. You're right, but—I was just telling him about how I read one of my dark urban fantasy books and I play with the screwdriver handle. And he said he wanted me to show him. Yes. In my ass. Yes. It's Cardell." She handed him the phone.

"Cardell, I thought I told you to leave my condo," said the husband in an even voice.

"I will," said Cardell, "but you should know that your wife was telling me all about how you take her like a madman at least once a week, if not oftener, and leave her fully satisfied."

"That's private information!"

"True, but she says you're quite the cocksman. She says you slap your dick on her ass to make her feel its meat. She says she knows just how to come with you inside because your knob is special and fits her perfectly. She seems quite content with you as a husband and a lover."

He sounded relieved. "That's welcome news, at least."

"But look, man, she's clearly a highly sexed woman, and she wants to show me how she takes care of important business when you're out on the road selling the cheese, or whatever."

"I draw the line there."

"You shouldn't draw that line, sir. I'm looking at her, and I can tell you she is nasty for the handle. This is a big, big urge she's got. I think if you don't say yes she may get frustrated and take me as a lover."

"No!" There was real anguish in his voice.

Cardell let the reality sink in for a moment. "How about if she just tells me, briefly, and doesn't show me. Would that work?"

The husband made an explosive sigh. "Did she just go for a walk on that beach?"

"Yes."

"I know she's a beautiful woman and a highly sexed woman. She gets superhorny after she's gone for a beach walk and found a couple of pieces of nice beach glass. Put her back on."

Cardell handed the phone back to Betsy.

"I'll just tell him about it, hon," said Betsy, "I won't show him. Yes, I promise. Okay. Love you, honey. Bye!" She hung up. "I'll pop into the shower, Cardell. Meanwhile, we keep the screwdrivers in a tool belt hanging in the foyer. I like the one with the kelly green handle. Not the huge one with the blue handle—I tried that one once. Troppo big. Feel free to read a magazine. As you can see, my husband's into mountain hiking."

Cardell went and got the screwdriver, and then he sat and read part of an article about crampons. He heard the shower going for a while in the pipes, and then he heard it turn off. Betsy emerged wearing a loose gray cotton dress with her hair turbaned and a different color of lipstick on. She was carrying a tube of something. She walked near him, and he smelled her smell of warm clean wet skin and Kentucky bourbon. He heard a drawer close in the kitchen, and she emerged with one latex glove.

"Now, Card, I gave it some thought in the shower, and here's what I think we might do. You sit in that chair, facing away from me, and I'll sit here on the couch like so. You put the handle of the screwdriver into one finger of this glove and hand it back it to me."

"Right now?"

"Why not? Here's your drink. I'll just take up my usual assplay position on the couch."

"This is where you usually play with your ass?"

"Yes, I like to do it in the living room because it's nastier that way."

"I got it. Here." Cardell handed her the glove with the screwdriver in it. "I figured go with the middle finger."

She smiled. "Ah, the long fuckfinger of the night. Tried and true. Don't turn around, now! You can't look, you horny boy. Now."

He heard sounds. "I just pull up my dress and scooch down, and then I just squirt a whole mess of Push on the screwdriver finger, like so, mmhm, get it all ready, and then some more right around my asshole, mmhm."

"What's 'Push'?"

"It's a kind of organic lubricant. Really thick but really slippery. Magic stuff. Unscented. Ooh, I'm tingly now. And one thing: I'm not a fan of the word 'enema,' but let me just inform you that I'm very clean."

"You mean you squirted a bunch of warm water up your butt and all that?"

"I did, used the syringe and the old red two-quart bottle. It was my grandmother's hot-water bottle. She was a pretty wild lady. Passed it down to me. I used to fill it with hot water and hump it on cold nights. Now, though, mmm. I love to get savage with my ass, but it's got to be squeaky clean. I hate shit, just hate it."

"No, I agree, shit's bad. It's not good."

"So now you want me to fuck myself in the ass while I play with Monsieur Twinklestump?"

"Who's Monsieur Twinklestump? A sex toy?"

"My clit."

"Oh. Yes, if that's what you most want to do, yeah."

"Oh, that's what I want to do, you bet it's what I want to do. See, I get reading these paperbacks about the dark devilish men from New Orleans with their hungry eyes and their long southern python cocks that are always ready to ransack a loving woman's asshole, and while I'm reading I put my feet on the arm of the couch and I just feel that cool air on my cunt's pussyhole, and I put two fingers in there and, slimp, I taste it, and then I kind of pet my clitty with my thumb, like this, ooh. I like to keep everything growling and purring as much as I can. My left hand's for my ass, my right hand's for my cunt and clitty. Separation of powers."

"Phew, I need a rearview mirror."

"Don't you turn, now, Card, you just listen while I devastate my ass for you. Whooo! Oh, it's going to go in slow. Nice and slow. I start to push it in a little and then I stop—not yet, cause I like the push part so much, and I circle it around the outside some where the choirboys sing because it feels so good on the outside and my asshole starts to melt and depuckerize and get all soft and willing and ready for this big hard screwdriver handle that I'm about to—oooooooof, there it goes in. Screwdriver's going in. Awwwll."

"Is it all the way in?"

"No. I can feel the edgy parts, the facets. It's about an inch in. I wish you could see my cunt staring at the ceiling, Card. My cunnyhole is just looking straight up, and I'm holding the metal part of the screwdriver. I can wiggle it a little bit, that feels good. Ooh."

"You're making me nuts!"

"Stand up and slip off that bathing suit. I want to see your ass while I keep pushing and jiggling on this thing."

Cardell's suit dropped to the ground, and he kicked it so that it billowed and landed on a bowl of shells. He flexed his asscheek muscles, trying to look as buff as possible.

She said, "You're a hairy candy-bun boy, aren't you? Can you show me your asshole?"

"What? No."

"Why not?" she asked.

"I'm not into that," said Cardell. "This is about your ass, not mine."

"Nonsense, just show it to me, bun boy, bend over. Give me a good look. Come on."

Finally, Cardell bent and opened his asscheeks for her to have a look.

"Oh, Card, that's one tiny hairy asshole you got. Very discreet. What's the matter, you've never shown anyone your asshole before?"

"This is outside my comfort zone."

"Good, well, good. Now grab your cock and get it in its comfort zone, honey, and do just what you want to do with it. I'm going to screw myself with this screwy fucker, I'm going to—hooo. I'm going to let it go in till my asshole muscle locks on the—almost, almost—handle's—there it is—narrower part. Hoh, it's locked in. Hoo yeah. Fuck. I've got this shiny silver screwdriver pointing straight out my ass, I wish you could see it."

Cardell scanned the room for reflective surfaces. He thought he could almost see some of what was going on behind him in the curve of a glass vase filled with colored sand. "Me, too," he said.

"Well, do the next best thing and jerk your bull cock while I abuse myself with this thing, just jerk and jack and pound it like you love to do every single day and night. And if you can, tighten your buns again so I get something to look at besides your arms and elbow moving, although I must say they're nice arms."

"Okay." He breathed little panting breaths, his hips rocking as he flummoxed his beatstick.

"I'm going to take a moment to check in on my nipples now. Yep, crinkling up nice. And now I'm going to—oh, lord god—pull the handle out, because that empty feeling feels so good, when I feel my ass closing down again, I tighten it on itself, and it's suddenly all, like, empty but concentrating hard on its memories, all the nerves in a huddle, and when it goes tight that always makes me want to work my clit, like right na-ha-ha-how! But then when I do my clitty, that makes me need to feel my ass tingle again, so I'm going to circle it with my fingers and feel it go soft again and oh, god, I need something in my cunt now. I think I'll shove this tube of Push in my cunt, oooh!"

"I'm jacking, Betsy, you've got to know I'm jacking it now."

"Back up toward me, I need to feel those balls when I come. I need a heaping handful of hot hairy balls! Don't turn around."

Cardell backed toward her and stood with his legs parted and felt her hand enclose his balls and tug on them.

"Big warm balls," she said. "You've got a lot of come in these, I can tell."

"I'm close, Betsy!"

"Come all over my coffee table, baby, just shoot it everywhere."

"Betsy, no, I can't come on your coffee table! Those are your husband's hiking magazines."

She spoke in a quiet voice. "You're right. Then close your eyes tight and turn around."

"Okay." He turned, and just before he closed his eyes he saw her with her legs jackknifed back, propped against the arm of the couch, and the screwdriver in one hand and her other hand pincering.

"And now sit on my foot." She held her foot in the air so that Cardell could rest his weight on it, as if he were astride a bicycle seat. "Nestle yourself right down on my foot. Push on my leg. Ooooh, yeah. I like to see your balls squashed and hanging like that around my foot. Can you feel the ball of my foot against your cock root?"

"Oh, god, oh, god, oh, god, yes," said Cardell.

"You like to see me push this in?" She squinted. "It hurts a teensy bit when it goes back in, and then it locks, and it fills my hips so good." She jiggled the screwdriver. "Come for me now. Come very slow now, slow down right on my open cunt. Press your hot butthole against my heel. Oh, that's it, fucking press it and jack it for me. Blow that load!"

He made a strangled shout and put his full weight down on her foot, feeling her heel against his ass. A torrential comeload pitched from his cock and landed on her stomach and thighs. "It's silver," he said, catching his breath.

"I told you. All silver. And now I'm going to put my legs all the way back, all the way, and tickle my ass so it's like an eye staring right at my finger, and I'm going to frig myself now and think about you watching me and coming on me. I'm thinking about the vampire count's cock filling my bowels, oh, my ass, my ass is so freaking hot." She slapped high up on her thighs with a pat pat sound.

"Come for me, you sweet sexy thing," said Cardell.

"I'm almost there, I'm almost there!" She arched. "I'm there, ah, ah, AAAAAH, hoof hoof hoof." She lay splayed, tired, smiling.

"That was fun," said Cardell.

"It was," said Betsy. "Maybe I'll just give my husband a quick call and tell him about it."

"You should," said Cardell.

"Could you put the screwdriver back in the tool belt on your way out?"

Luna Fucks a Penis Tree

Luna woke up in the House of Holes Hotel. She had a great contentment bubbling inside her like the little bubbles that you see when you shake up a bottle of salad dressing.

"So," said Lila to Luna, when Luna wandered into her office after a shower. "What is your plan for joy today?"

"I feel pretty today," said Luna.

"You are pretty," said Lila.

"My breasts feel heavy and flirty. Do you want to see them?"

"Yes, of course, always," said Lila. "But let me call in a man so he can see, too."

"No," said Luna, "just for you."

Luna lifted her clean, pale-blue shirt and scooped her bra up slowly, letting her breasts fall and bobble.

"They do look heavy," said Lila. "And flirty."

"Do you want to feel them?"

"Sure."

Luna walked toward Lila and arched her back and leaned forward. Lila thumb-tweaked both of Luna's nipples at the same time, which made Luna shiver. "As hard as little erasers," Lila said, "erasing all inhibitions."

"Lila," said Luna, "I want to be fucked so many ways right now I don't know where to start. I'm beside myself. In the shower I thought, I want to be fucked by a tree!"

"Well, now," Lila mused, "we do have Jason's Woods. That's where we get the hardwood for our salad bowls and our Dendro line of peckerwood dildos. Have you tried a Dendro dildo?"

"Can't say I have."

"Then you're in for a treat. Anyway, what I've been told is that some of the older pearwood trees have had their branches cut so often that they've developed semihuman traits, and now they are known to exhibit sexual desires of their own. There's a man in there, Jason, who makes the bowls. He'll know the grove of pearwoods I mean. Daggett can buzz you over there in a cart." She pressed a button. "Daggett, we need you, hon."

"Thank you, Lila," said Luna.

"Your pleasure is my pleasure. Where is Daggett? He's a little slower because he misses his cods. Oh, I should say: You're going to have to let Jason hold your breasts, I think. He can't make bowls without inspiration."

"I can live with that."

Daggett drove Luna in silence down a long curving path, past the lake. The wildflowers gave way to lilac and forsythia, and then there was a salt marsh, and then suddenly they were winding through deep silent woods, with mica chips of sunlight sparkling through the leaves. Finally they came to a clearing and a small well-kept shingled house, painted green. "I'll leave you to it," said Daggett with a wink. "Just give Lila a call when you want me to pick you up."

Luna knocked. A tall scruffy man in a leather apron came to the door. His hands were black with stain. His eyes had a crinkly honest look. "I heard you were on your way out here," he said. "Did Lila tell you I make bowls?"

"Yes, and she said I'd probably have to let you fondle my breasts, and I just want you to know I'm okay with that."

"Good. Well then, let's do that first, shall we? You'll have to help me clamp my hands. Can I get you some green tea before we get down to it? Or some home brew?"

"Home brew would be good, thanks."

"Okay, well, why don't you scoot your pants a little ways down for me."

"My pants?"

"I think, yes. I need to experience curving shapes to make my bowls. What lovely hips." He cupped her cameltoe for a moment. "Do you like to eat salad? I do."

Luna nodded, stepping out of her pants.

"Turn around, please, so I can have a look at your—"

"Panties, or no?" She turned.

"Panties are fine. Oh, my. Don't move. Bend forward just a little." Jason walked across his studio and unhooked a very large salad bowl from the wall. He stood behind her and pressed the bowl around her ass. Then he leaned against the bowl, humping at it with his hips. Luna felt well and truly cupped. "Now that's what I call a Cobb salad," he said.

Luna touched the smooth, perfect grain of the bowl. "This is lovely. Who inspired this?"

"Oh, a woman Lila sent me a few months ago. Her name was

Jackie. She tried out some of my dildos, and I made three huge bowls in her honor, and then of course she went on her way. Those were the last dildos I made. I make friends with women, and it's nice, but they just don't want to live out here in the woods with me. They want be in town."

Luna looked around the studio. "Well, you are quite isolated," she said.

"Yes, it helps me concentrate. When I come I can shout as loud as I want. Will you dance for me? Let your breasts roam for a moment—I need to see how they dance."

"Okay." She danced, and as she danced she tried to think of the most delicious salads she could imagine—with artichokes and sundried tomato and blue cheese dressing, and beets, lots of beets.

Jason nodded. "Good, good. I'm beginning to get the gist of them. Now I'll need you to help me clamp both my hands in these vises." He placed his hands, palms up, between two battered, smooth wooden vises. "Just turn the cranks."

"How tight?"

"Uh, not so tight that my hands are crushed, but tight enough so that they are immobilized. I must be immobilized in order to feel your breasts completely. Sorry my fingers are such a mess. I've been staining today." Luna tightened the screws till she reached a point that seemed right. "Good," said Jason. "Will you give me another sip of that brew? And help yourself. And if you could stroke my palms with your fingertips for a moment to sensitize them, that would be very kind of you."

She brushed lightly over his palms with her fingertips. His eyes fluttered, and he began breathing through his mouth as if in a trance.

"Mmm. And now the big event."

"My breasts?"

"Yes. Take them out for me, please. Unfetter them. I want your bosoms naked as jaybirds. Big honking jaybirds." Jason began to sway from side to side, and he looked at her with a look of heavy, slow-blinking lust. "Are you ready?"

"I think so." Luna took off her sweater and her tank top and then, without breaking her gaze, reached back and flicked open her bra and shrugged it off, holding it momentarily like a baby when it landed loose in her hands.

"Let me see. Oh, my, oh, my. Now please lower them, almost to my hands." She reached forward and held his shoulders and leaned, looking down at the hanging outline of her breasts as they came closer to his immobilized hands. She stopped when she was almost there.

"Ah, I can almost feel their warmth. Now very slowly lower. Lower. I want to almost hold them. Just graze the nippletips, graze the nipples, oh, that's it, that's good. I feel the aureole energy. Now give them all to me. Give me those glories!"

"Nope, wait," Luna said, and she lifted her chest and shook her breasts for him.

"Oh, you freaky teaser!" said Jason. "I can't wait any longer for it, right now, please." Strange things were happening under his leather apron.

Luna again descended, as gradually as she could, on the verge of filling his hands with her boobflesh. At first it was just her nipples, then a little bit of the tips of the cones, and then her boobosity began settling in, and they reformed themselves, fattening on the side fill as they gave their titfat to his upturned palms.

"Ohhhhhh, I can feel you forming the bowls for me, Luna, the fullness, the brimmingness of your breasts, there's more of you and more of you, you're so good with your hot boobfat, I can feel the salad bowls in your beautiful knocker-jug-bosom-boobs, that's what I need. Mmmmmm. Thank you, thank you, thank you."

She could feel his hands trying to clench and grasp and pull from her all the knowledge of her palm-smothering abundance. Then he sighed and nodded, indicating that he was done.

"How will you remember them?" she asked.

"I have 'absolute shape'—I never forget any shapes I really care about. Come, unvise me. I'll walk you out to the peckerwood tree."

"Should I put my pants back on?"

"Absolutely not. Never put that bottom away!"

The light snuck in sideways through the trees as they walked, and Luna felt that it was a sexual sneaking in, as if the trees were long legs that could be seen beneath the skirt of the leafy canopy. Then she saw a different angle of trees, and they seemed strong and male. Her underpants, she discovered, were wet.

They stopped. "This is the pearwood penis tree," said Jason. He took off his leather apron. They listened. "Hear the fluids in it, the sap?" he said. "Hear the mushrooms growing at the base?"

She listened. "Yes."

"Good, cause you're going to hug it while I fuck you."

"I thought I was going to fuck the tree."

"After me. That's how we wake the sleeping giant."

He grabbed her ass and pulled her panties down, turning her so that she held the tree. He shoved himself deep into her. It felt sudden and tremendous, and she made a surprised sigh: "Ooof!"

Then she began to hear different sounds—a cracking and a ticking as several small buds of bark appeared on the tree trunk about three feet off the ground. The bark split open, showing a pale, smooth, fleshy branch, and then the branch, thus exposed, began to straighen, while the nodular wooden balls remained covered with a finely wrinkled bark.

Jason was slamming his hips into her. He thumped into her hard, so that she almost lost her grip on the trunk. "Oh, oh, oh, god, Oh, shit! Oh, fuck! Here it comes, baby, oooooooohhhhhhhhhh! Aaaaaaaaah!" Jerk after jerk of Jason's artisanal come filled her rejoicing twathole. "Now quick, hop on this new cockbranch." She grabbed it and held it—it was still warm from its accelerated growing. And then she heard the summer wind begin—a warm wind that made a different kind of rustling in the leaves because the leaves were drier now—and the light that snuck in between the boughs and boles was splaying and scattering, half of it reflected off the water, half direct from the setting sun. "Fuck me deep, tall, strong penis tree," she said.

The cock shape grew longer and pushed into her, and then the whole tree seemed to branch into her core and out her arms and legs and lift her far above the earth. "Hold on!" called Jason, as she was swept up on a high bough impaled on old boreal growth. She looked out from her high-splayed vantage, and she said, "I'm a treefucking woman!" Dappled sunlight shone and emptied itself onto her. She squeezed her Kegeling love muscle around the smooth, thickened branch within, and when the wind came up again all the leaves twittered and shook. The tree itself shuddered: It was having some kind of orgasm. The new growth of penisbranches fell off. Panting and quivering, Luna climbed

221

down. Jason hugged her, then gathered the fallen branches. "I'll polish and stain these tomorrow," he said.

"Dendro dildos?"

"Yes, inspired by you."

"Can I come back and get one?"

"Please do," said Jason. "I'll make a salad for you."

Henriette Goes for a Walk

Henriette decided to take her new extra-big ass on a walk to the noisy quay where the Masturboats docked. She wanted to feed the gulls and see what was up. First she got in the shower to wash herself so that she could be clean all day and the world wouldn't know what a totally freaky, filthy-minded, cocksucking whore of a princess she actually was. She washed her hair and her face and her body, and last of all she washed her pussy and her huge deep asscrack. Her pussy she washed by holding it spread open with her right hand and splashing water up at it a bunch of times, and her asscrack she washed by jamming the cold soap between her pleasantly joggling cheeks and working it around a few times. Washing the asscrack wasn't really that difficult; rinsing was trickier. Soap could burn later if you didn't rinse every bit of it away, Henriette knew from experience—burn like a bastard—and you couldn't just rely on the water that was coursing down your back to do the job.

So Henriette employed what she thought of as the Aswan Dam method. She cupped her left hand in the shape of a C, and then she pressed this C below her anus, but before her pussyhole, in the no-man's-land known as the perineum, which is a word that comes from the Greek word for "pine barrens." She cupped her left hand there and made a seal against her asscheeks so that the water as it coursed down her back would be caught in this temporary well or spillway that she had created. She had in effect dammed her ass temporarily. When her hand was full she began agitating it, still keeping the seal intact—steadily slooshing the water in waves against her anus for ten seconds or so. Then she opened her fingers to let that rinse effluent fall away. Again she made the C-cup with her left hand and let it fill, and again sloshed it vigorously. At last she knew that she had a truly clean, well-rinsed asscrack, ready to greet the day.

She dressed in her new form-fitting ass jeans and went strutting outside. She walked down the Avenue of the Men Who Need to Suck on Twat Every Day and took a left on Upskirt Street. There she heard a voice calling, "Wait, stop, hello, wait!" Ruzty hurried up in his torn jeans, out of breath. His T-shirt was old and red, and it said "Phillies." "I request to squeeze your ass," he said, in his foreign voice. "You will notice that I have the ass-squeezer's license."

"Do you now?" asked Henriette. "Good for you. What else do you have?"

"Basically, that's it," said Ruzty. "Everybody is trying to keep going, but then they turn out to be broke. The size of what they owe is how rich they are. If they can borrow a billion dollars, that makes them rich. Really they have nothing. But never mind, because I have"—he pulled out a folded sheet of paper and patted it—"an ass-squeezer's license, signed. This means I can walk up to a girl like you with a big, beautiful ass and tell her I want to squeeze it, and she has to let me."

"Let's see the license," said Henriette.

Ruzty waved it at her.

"Very well. Where?"

"My hotel."

They went up to his suite at the Portalino Extended Stay Suites.

"How do you want to squeeze it?" Henriette asked.

"I want you up on the bed, as soon as possible."

Henriette took off her roomy denim ass pants and arranged herself bending forward on the bed like a person skiing down a slalom course.

She felt his hands on her, squeezing their way along her backthighs and finding her lower backcheeks and massaging her deeply, with an interest in all her cores and centers. Then she felt his cock pushing strangely at the seams of her underwear. "No, now, Ruzty," she said. "You have an ass-squeezer's license, not a pussy-fucker's license."

"Wait a second, yes, I do, I do, I just forgot to show it," Ruzty said, rummaging in his pockets. He had a slightly desperate sound. He waved another folded piece of paper. "I've been saving it for this moment."

Henriette looked the paper over. "You just typed this yourself and printed it out, didn't you?"

Ruzty looked chagrined. "Yes."

"Is the ass-squeezer's license forged as well?"

"Yes," he said. "Daggett said he couldn't give me a real one because there are too many. I was wrong, I know it now. I went outside the proper channels."

Henriette said, "Ruzty, you very bad boy."

Ruzty said, "I'm sorry."

She looked at his eyes, which traveled to her ass. Then she caught sight of his remarkably solid but curved piece of equipment. She made a tiny hissing sound and said, "Oh, might as well go ahead anyway. Fuck me, horny sailor."

Ruzty's dick bounced with gladness. Henriette gnawed the sheet and waited. She felt his cock helmet finding the sloppy gates. Then impulsively she turned onto her back. "Take me where I can see you," she said.

He sank over her, and she led him inside, forcing his cock to unbend. She gave him the Cook's tour of her innerness. His backbone worked lithely; his bottom, swiveling, rose and fell.

Henriette straightened her knees, so that her feet were up in the air, running. She laughed because it felt so good, and she said, "Ruzty, you are a swervy-dicked master of the fuck! Don't stop! Fill my bitchgroove!"

He squeezed her very hard to him and breathed in her hair and shuddered out everything he had into her. "I give you everything," he said.

Later in the shower, Henriette remembered this and got on her knees and said, "Oh, Ruzty, oh, Ruzty," and came.

Dune Tells Mindy How He Lost His Penis

Mindy, the documentary filmmaker, was standing in her room at the House of Holes Hotel, working on a jigsaw puzzle of marbles in a bowl and listening to "32 Flavors" by Ani DiFranco. There was a knock on her door. She opened it and saw a long-haired, dark-eyed man standing in the hallway, wearing a fringed suede jacket. He was wildly handsome, and he smelled like old cigarettes.

"Hey, I'm Dune," he said. "They took away my penis, and I wonder if you can help me."

"If I can I will," said Mindy. "What happened?"

"Well, they did a switcheroo on me," Dune said. "I've got a vagina now, and it's a hot one, but every day of my life I want my own tackle back. You're Mindy, am I correct?"

"I am," said Mindy. "Would you mind if I set up a video camera and got your story? I'm making a film about this place."

"That's what I heard."

Mindy kicked the tripod mounts out and got her camera running.

"Should I sit here?" Dune sat down heavily. "Hoo, I'm wiped."

"Would you like something to eat? I could make you an omelet."

"I'd love an omelet," said Dune. "I've been flying a pornsucker around Providence, Rhode Island and I ache all over, and frankly I need the attention of a good woman."

Mindy cooked him a three-egg omelet and he ate it. "That was fine food," he said. "What's your secret?"

"Butter and salt."

"So simple. Butter and salt. I'll be fried."

Mindy cleared the plate away and clipped a microphone to Dune's lapel. "So how exactly did you lose your penis?"

Dune told Mindy all about when he lost control on the midway and stuck his pinky into Shandee's pussy.

Mindy, nodding encouragingly, checked the sound levels to be sure she was getting all of it.

"So then I went to Lila and she said, 'Okay for you, Mr. Pussyfinger,' and she called in this woman who said she needed her own penis and a pair of balls—the whole desk set. She got what she wanted, from me." Dune looked down and laughed sadly. "Ah, Mindy, you don't want to hear my problems. I'm just broke, and I don't have money for smokes."

Mindy brightened. "I have a couple of those little Winchester cigars in my purse for emergencies, hold on," she said. "I just quit smoking, that's why I'm doing this jigsaw puzzle."

"Thanks." Dune lit the cigar and took a long squinty drag. "Hm, a nice little Winchester. My dad smoked Winchesters. 'A whole nother smoke.'"

"Dune, do you think you could show me your genitals? I'd like to get that on video."

Dune tapped his cigar. "A week ago if you'd have asked me if I'd bare my crotch for you, I would have said, Sure thing, right away. Now I'm a bit skittish. Everything has its price."

"The price is sometimes steep," said Mindy.

"You got that right, hot goddess. Lila's got us all doing the fucky-fuck and the sucky-suck and the humpy and the squirty and the juicy-Lucy and the ooh, ah, ooh. Everything we do they keep track of, and they know what we want most, and they want to milk us till our money's all gone and our balls ache, if we have balls, which I don't at the present time. Because it's the House of Holes, and is there anything worth paying court to more than a woman with a pretty face and two good titties and one hot switchy ass she wants to shove in your face? Hmm?"

Mindy took that as a rhetorical question. "I'm more into men," she said. "I like men. Sometimes I like smoky men in dirty suede."

"Course you do, Mindy," he said. "You're a lovely lusty woman and you want to be a part of this whole slumber party. You want an 'experience.' And you will have that at the House of Holes, believe me. If you haven't already."

"I already got shrunk down and squirted out of a man's urethra."

"Well, then, there you go." Dune was tiring. "Listen, would you mind if I moved to the couch for a sec?"

"No, go ahead," said Mindy. "Let me just unclip your mike."

"I just need fifteen minutes of downtime. Thanks for dinner, thanks for the smoke." He closed his eyes and was asleep almost immediately.

Mindy watched him sleep. When he sat up an hour later, she had a second Winchester cigar ready for him. She said, "What was she like? The woman you switched with. You mind if I turn the camera back on?"

Dune stretched. "Sure, turn the camera on. Are we rolling? Marcela was her name. She was nice, very friendly. She'd put in a request to do Dick for a Day."

"I've heard of Dick for a Day," said Mindy, with interest.

"Yes, now, Dick for a Day is not that involved because they can morph your clitty out for six, eight hours without too much bother, and it'll go back good as new. But it turned out Marcela wanted something more like Dick for a Couple of Weeks, and that takes a full interplasmic transfer. That's what it's called, a 'cross-crotchal interplasmic transfer.' I'll bet you want to know how they do that."

Mindy nodded that she did.

"Well, you need a tweenella. That's the person who is designated to put her hands on the two crotches that are going to be crossed. She completes the crotchal circuit."

"That sounds like it would be kind of fun," said Mindy.

"Oh, but doing tweenella is hard work, too," said Dune. "You can only do it a few times because the sex plasma travels right through your arms and your chest and your heart. It can actually stop your heart for a moment, to have that much sex plasma traveling through you. They had a piece of hotness named Rianne doing it. They brought in a large stone bowl, and they poured some glowing blue liquid into it—looked like coolant—and Lila told Rianne to soak her hands in the bowl to get them all ready and sensitized for the transfer. She told me to sit in one chair and Marcie in another chair."

"You were naked?"

Dune nodded. "From the waist down, with our feet in stirrups. And then Lila hauls out one of her breasts."

"Uh-oh!"

"They are *not* small, let me tell you. She squirts some of her special magic titty milk on my balls, and she has Marcie hold open her pussy so that she can dribble some right in there, too. Well, that started to work almost immediately, started to burn, like my cock had had a shot of Everclear, and I started to feel that I had this special bond with Marcela. I said, 'Hey, Marcie, are you sure you're okay with the switch? I warn you, my dick can be a handful.' And she said, 'I can handle your dick fine. The real question is whether you can keep up with my cuntatious clit.' So we were having our fun, and then Lila tells Rianne, 'Okay, now take your hands out of the bowl and get to work. Grab their crotches and lean into them hard.' Rianne's sitting cross-legged between us, like a yoga master, and she grabs our crotches, which completes the circuit, and, foong, this ungodly flow of energy comes pouring through her arms, and at first I started to get a huge boner on, and I thought, Well this is nice. Then Rianne's whole body started shaking, her tits are bopping around, but she kept her hands holding our crotches. And then I started to feel Marcie's pussy flowing into me."

"Wow, go on." Mindy checked the viewfinder, making turning gestures in the air to keep him talking.

"I felt my own cock and balls starting to melt and flow, and I felt this channel widening inside me. My boner was still hard as ever, but it was getting smaller and smaller, and Marcie starts going, 'Oh, my word, I feel my clitoris growing like a weed.' And eventually it was all done."

"Transfer accomplished," said Mindy, shifting in her chair.

"Yes, I had Marcie's clit and pussy, and she had my cock. We were all three of us totally wiped afterward—Rianne was exhausted, poor gal—and while we were putting on our clothes I asked Marcela, 'Can I walk you on back to your hotel room?' Lila said she thought that would be a good idea because there's always an adjustment period for the transferees. But Marcela said no, thanks, she wanted to be alone with her new penis. So I went back to my hotel room, and I looked at myself in the mirror, trying to get used to my pussylips, which I kind of liked, and then I took a little nap, and then the phone rang, and it was Marcie."

"What a surprise," said Mindy.

"She said she was having some problems getting the hang of my cock, and could I come down and show her some things. I said, 'Sure, I can visit for a bit.' I went to her room, and she was there posing in front of her mirror, and I asked her how she felt, and she just opened up her bathrobe. And god damn, she was this beautiful naked babe with two big bosoms and my big load of dick just hanging there."

Mindy envisioned it. "Mmm."

"She was a real chick with a real dick, and I'm not going to lie to you, it turned me on to see that cock of mine having found a happy home between her legs."

"Was it hard?" asked Mindy.

"No, not terribly hard—that's what she wanted help with. She said, 'I want a real stiff one, can you help me with that?'"

"I said, 'You want me to play with my own dick? Sure, I can do that. Hell, I've done it a thousand times.' But she said, 'Dune, I want you to suck your dick.' I said, 'Woo, sorry, can't do it. I do draw the line there. But I can give you a handjob because you attract me. I bet you'll look sexy with a stiff dick.' So she sat on the corner of the bed with her knees open, and I sat behind her."

"Can you demonstrate how?" Mindy asked.

Dune took off his pants and his black briefs and sat on the corner of the bed. "I was sitting behind her like this," he said.

"Wait." Mindy adjusted the camera.

"Now you're seeing my pussy, aren't you?" asked Dune. "As requested."

"Yes," said Mindy in a low voice, "thank you."

Dune pulled his pudendum open. "Mindy, let me ask you: Do you want to interview this pussy?"

Mindy nodded.

"Okay, then give me a microphone. Do you have a big microphone? Because what I've learned is that when I play with my cuntpussy, I need something inside or I feel empty."

Mindy brought out a long silver microphone. "I don't think you want to put this piece of equipment inside you," she said. "It's a four-hundred-dollar shotgun mike. A Sennheiser."

"Mindy, that's just how much microphone I need to give you a good in-depth cuntpussy interview."

"Okay," said Mindy.

Dune fished out a condom from his wallet and unrolled it over the end of the microphone. "Now shove it in me and I'll show you something."

Mindy eased the condom-covered microphone into Dune's pussyhole.

"Oooh, that's it, while I whale on this clit," said Dune. "You like the way my clit sticks straight up like a tiny little dick? It's amazing you can get this much feeling out of a little pink bean of a thing, but you can, if you work at it. Now let go of the microphone for a second. I'll show you my muscles. I've been exercising them." Dune clenched himself and said, "Mmm, mmmm, mmmm." The microphone end wigwagged obscenely.

"Nice muscles," said Mindy. "Please go on. What tips did you give Marcela?"

"I said to her, 'Sometimes I pull on the nutsack a little and shake the whole package to make it aware of the fact that it's going to be getting hard soon.' She said, 'Like this?' And she shook my cock, or her cock, whoever's cock it was, and I said, 'Yeah, like that.' Then I said, 'Marcie, while you do that I wonder if you'd mind if I squeezed on your titties.' And she was okay with that, so I squeezed her tits my special way, up from below, and a really amazing thing happened, which was that her dick, my own dick, started to lean out into space, and I realized I was making her dick hard by squeezing her tits, and ooooh, shit, that was some nice madness."

Mindy put one leg on the bed, nodding.

"And then she stood up, and she turned herself around," Dune went on, "and I had a view of her that was like"—he held up his hands. "I looked up at her eyes and her face looking down at me and then these nice heavy, hanging tits and then her big hips and then, look out, there's my heavy cock on her."

"She must have wanted you to jerk her off," said Mindy.

"Yes, she said, 'Now I want you to help me get my dick off.' I said, 'Marcie, it's just as much my dick as it is yours.' And now, Mindy, that's all I'm going to say about this unless you promise me one thing."

"What's that?" said Mindy.

"Promise me that when I get my penis back you'll give some serious thought to fucking me, because you attract me sexually."

Mindy said, "I'll think about it. But right now how about let's jill off together side by side, and you keep telling me what happened, because I can't resist playing with myself, Dune, but I also need to get your story."

"I'm glad to hear it, Mindy, honey—come on and sit next to me," said Dune, scooting himself back on her bed.

Mindy adjusted the camera again and pulled off her shirt. "So what did you and Marcela do?"

"I took both her hands and I said, 'I want to play with your nipples and hold your legs open while you do your cock,' and I gently put her hands on the cock bundle. She took it, and she began moving her hand up and down, and it was amazing how quickly she got a feel for it. That dick got harder on her than it had been on me in a long time. I said, 'That's the business, honey. You get that dick to do what's right for you.' She was getting hot, and she said, 'It feels so good to jack on it, and I'll tell you what I want to do, I want to fuck you with it.'"

Mindy had eased her hand into her sweatpants as she listened. "Really?"

"So I said what the hell," said Dune. "I flung myself back on the bed like a bride on her wedding day and I said, 'Go on ahead, Marcie, fuck me like you know how.' She said, 'Guide me in you, baby—you know where you want it to go.' So I circled around my cunny to get the head all juiced and ready and then I said, 'Shove it on inside, Marcie, I'm ready for a dick pounding.'"

Mindy's eyes were closed and her hand was moving as she imagined the scene. "How did it feel?" she asked.

"Well, it was a good feeling, Mindy, a good full feeling. I was a virgin, and Marcie was considerate. She said, 'I'm going to go slow, Dune,' and I put my hands on her wonderful full, smooth ass and felt her long, long, deep push, and she started really fucking me in and out, ung, ung, and I said, 'Oh, lord help my naked soul, I've never been fucked by own cock before.' She said, 'You're getting it now.' I said, 'Marcie, fuck me, I'm so confused and I love it, fuck me harder, tear up my virgin pussy!" Dune looked over at Mindy. "Mm, twat yourself, Mindy, bat your bug, that's the way."

Mindy's head was back, and she was biting her tongue. "Don't stop," she said.

"Then Marcie lay down on her back and I saw my cock sticking straight up on her, and she pulled on it, and I said, 'What do you want, baby?' She said, 'I want you to sit right down and rock on this big thick piece of rhubarb.' So I straddled her, and I let myself sink down, and oh, shoot, was that nice. I started bouncing up and down on it, and it nailed me so good. She said, 'Now tickle your clit, and you will come.' So I found my clit, which was, as I say, a tiny little thing but quite sensitive, and I started rubbing and nubbing and scrubbing on it, and meanwhile I was bouncing up and down like a horse thief."

"Mmm," said Mindy, dipping a finger deep and then circling.

"And I think all the nerve connections were still being sketched in because I had something that I think was a very teeny orgasm, and then another little one, but bigger. And I thought, Shit, that's it? That's all? That's a woman's pussy orgasm? And then, whoa, my clit screamed out, and this incredible shaky feeling tore like a wrecking ball through my whole body."

"Was it mainly in your vagina or your clit?"

"I don't know, clit, vagina—it was all over the county, and I held her tits and looked up at her pretty face and let everything just flow through me, huhhh, huhhh."

Mindy's breathing got fast and she said, "I'm going to come, Dune, mercy, I'm going to come!"

Dune shuttled his finger over his clit, spanking it once, and he lifted himself up and he went, "Ahhhh, errrrrr, aaaahhh!" He frigged himself with the microphone and then he started hip-jouncing on the bed, and after he came he laughed and swore.

He said, "This is just plain daffy, Mindy. I need my old dick back. Marcela's going to want her pussy back soon, I know it. Will you go with me to Lila and dip your hands in the blue bowl and be the go-between?"

"Sure," said Mindy, "if I can get it on film."

Rhumpa Visits the Pornmonster

A keeper named Harry, who wore short pants and had a little goatee, took Rhumpa to see the pornmonster. They went into the first airlock, and after the pressure equalized there they went into a second. It was darker there. The air was close, if not fetid. The hatch made a sucking sound and opened. They stood on the shore of a large underground lake, now the repository of the distilled contents of all the House of Holes's pornsucker missions.

Harry and Rhumpa went up a set of stairs hewn into the rock and stood on a balcony overlooking the lurid water, which glowed and glopped and slopped around the edges of the cavern.

"It's not terribly nice in here, is it?" said Rhumpa.

Harry shook his head despairingly. "The more porn we've sucked out of the world, the larger the monster has grown," he said. "This wasn't in our forecasts. We thought there might be small anomalies of spontaneous generation, of course. But this— this is a personification of polymorphousness unlike anything the world of human suck-fuckery has ever known. I used to work as a trainer at Ocean Playground. The squid show there was nothing compared to this."

At that moment an enormous arm reached out of the oily liquid, and a huge hand grasped at nothing in the air. Five penises hung dangling off the forearm—it looked like a bizarre bagpipe. The hand was made up of half a dozen clustered vaginas.

"That's gross," said Rhumpa.

Harry made a little fatalistic laugh. "They're pumping so much porn in here that it's just feeding and feeding, and it grows a new appendage every few days. It's got about ten arms. One's really long, but a lot of them are smaller."

"I can see that it's not pretty," Rhumpa said. "But is it good or is it evil?"

"Nobody knows," said Harry. "Nobody knows its language."

"I'm going to try to talk to it," said Rhumpa. She put her hands to her mouth. "Hey, longdog!" she called with loud authority. "Jizm! Weeperhole!"

The pornhand paused for a moment, ceased groping, then subsided under the vermilion waves of mingling smut imagery.

"You really know languages," said Harry, impressed.

Rhumpa knew she could talk to the pornmonster given enough time and quiet. "I can't engage with it here," she said. "Do you have a side chamber where we can go?"

"Sure," said Harry. "The sluice gate has an overflow tank, and sometimes the monster goes in there to rest."

Suddenly, several fountains of what looked like sperm, but orchid and navel orange in color, jetted up from the froth.

Rhumpa looked at Harry questioningly. "It masturbates constantly," Harry said. "You'll have to put on a wetsuit."

Rhumpa nodded. They went to the room off the overflow tank. Rhumpa shucked off her shirt and pants and stepped into the suit.

"Be careful," said Harry. "Our containment system is only as good as its weakest link."

"Do you think it can feel love?" asked Rhumpa.

"I doubt it," said Harry. "I was reading Hawking's book about the first seconds of the universe. I think our monster is as close as I'll ever come to knowing what that's like." Harry hesitated. He looked a little green around the gills. "I'm going to have to leave you on your own here. I'll be watching on the monitor. Men can't take pornfumes for very long without fainting. We need breathing equipment. Women seem more immune." Harry withdrew.

Rhumpa walked out onto the tiled edge of the ancillary holding tank. She called out, "Hey, pornmonster! Cuntcall! Here it is!" She cupped her crotch through the wetsuit.

There was a burbling and a different feeling in the air. Rhumpa sensed that the pornmonster had slid into the ancillary tank. She waited.

"If you're here," she called, nervously, "let me see your biggest hand."

There was a powerful odor of sexual fluids, and a huge mottled hand appeared. Rhumpa was shocked by how large it was, how freshly formed and strong. It reached and found the bars that separated her from the pornslurry.

"If you understand my cuntlips talking to you, and if you understand how I like to frig myself silly every morning before I go to work, please hold up your middle finger."

The pornmonster flung up his middle finger, and a splash of iridescence surged over Rhumpa in a wave.

She called on the walkie-talkie back to Harry at the control console. "Harry, unlock the electric gate. I need to go mano a mano."

"Can't do it, for insurance reasons."

"Pish-posh," said Rhumpa. "He needs a friend. He's been in these tanks too long."

Harry made a doubtful sound. "Okay," he said. The gate clicked open, and Rhumpa stepped out, unprotected—a set of jiggy curves in a wetsuit. She knelt and put her rubber-gloved hand in the liquid. She could feel the energy of warm spiffle juice going up her arm. Under the liquid she flipped out her middle finger. "I'm here to talk about hot, hard holefucking," she said. "Come on over, you big sexy vulgarian, climb out where I can see you naked."

Almost before she'd finished there was a sudden volcanic swirling of the waters. An amalgamation of body parts heaved itself up on the widest part of the ledge and stood dripping. There must have been a hundred penises—some pale pink, some coffee colored—along with breasts and eyes and clits and an enormous mouth at the center. It stood on a mass of arms and legs.

"There you are," Rhumpa said, more appalled than she let on. "Take a moment to relax. May I touch you?"

Seventeen penises nodded yes.

"Where's your head?" she asked.

The hands and feet shook: none.

"No head? Why not?"

Then ten hands grabbed ten semi-erect cocks and began

stroking them. Another ten hands circled tiny clitlike buttons of flesh in folds of skin.

"Must you do that right now in front of me?" Rhumpa asked.

Suddenly a very large hand came thrusting out of the central fleshball and scooped her up.

"I'm lurid and loveless and lost," the monster seemed to say. "I need a real person. I'm growing out of control. I'm propagating without guidance."

"You need a head," she said. "If I dance for you, will you develop a head?"

All the legs and hands said no. No way. No head today. And the big hand gave her a squeeze to say, "Never mind my head, dance for me anyway."

"Let go of me, and I'll dance," Rhumpa said.

The hand put her down and smacked the water hard. Another drench of sexual splatterment went over her. It made her tingle everywhere. She felt she was in touch with a giant collaborative moan.

Climbing the five steps of a metal ladder, she stood on a tall platform that technicians used when they needed to open or close a hydraulic valve that led to a smaller treatment tank. She began singing the Benassi Brothers, swinging her ass: "I love men, money, power, and I love my sex." She could see the monster turning on its legs, trying clumsily to keep time. On an impulse, she unclamped and unsealed the front of her wetsuit and danced with her breasts on display, her nipples high and pointy in unpuzzled skyward erections. Almost immediately, many monster hands took hold of many penises, and there was a general convulsion of orgasmic fluid release. The monster sat in a puddle of its own secretions.

Then it revived. Rhumpa spoke: "I will give you good loving if you grow a head."

There was silence, and then a bulb formed at the top of the fleshy confusion. There was a huge sucking sound, and a head popped into place. It was a normal head, male, with a mouth and a nose and two eyes, and it blinked at her.

"Can you hear me now?" she voiced.

Out of the mouth came a strange amphibious croak: "Aaaa-oooowwwawaooo."

"Take a moment to organize your thoughts," she said. "You are built from other people's orgasms, and yet you seem to have a soul."

"Not much of a soul, but it's there," said the pornmonster.

"And do you wish to be freed from the tank?"

"Yes, I do."

"Do you think you would live a normal life if you were free?"

"No, not normal," said the pornmonster. "I have way too many sex organs for that. But I could lead a better life. I would like to help in some way. My name is Friggley."

In the control room, Harry watched and took notes, squeezing his crotch from time to time. The creature looked like a hedge ball with frondy things hanging off it. It moved rapidly but shufflingly forward, a tumorousness of overstimulated desire. Harry observed as it surrounded Rhumpa and slid her wetsuit completely off. One after another of the penises found and sounded her cervix. Rhumpa seemed, oddly, to be enjoying it—it was a gangbang from a single source. When the fleshly storm had passed, she leapt onto its back and grabbed hold of what looked like two scrotums.

"Harry, open the main hatch, I've got my new friend Friggley by the balls, and I'm going to take him to the Handjob Festival."

Harry, in awe, opened the main gate of the tank enclosure, and Friggley shuffled down the road. Then, in a sudden flurry, more drama. The Pearloiner leapt out from a bush with a cackle and tried to snatch away several of Friggley's clitorises and hide them in her freezing jar. A small tussle ensued, which Friggley easily won by clasping the Pearloiner in several of its wank-strong arms. "Don't let her go!" said Rhumpa. She seized the precious clitty jar, remounted Friggley, and the curious trio lurched toward Lila's office.

The Pearloiner Says She's Sorry

The Pearloiner was sitting on the couch, staring forward remorsefully. She'd been crying. The icy jar of clits was on a side table, shedding a soft gray mist. Zilka and Cheyenne stood on the open pussyrug, stripped down to their bras. Friggley was tied by the balls outside.

"It was a misguided passion," the Pearloiner was saying. "There are better things to collect. I see that now. I'm truly sorry for my compulsive thieving." She fished in the jar, finding the plastic bags with Zilka's and Cheyenne's clits in them.

"Thank you, Madame Pearloiner," said Lila. "Zilka and Cheyenne will fix your hair and dress you for the Sherry Cobbler and Farewell Handjob Festival. As a first step, we must forgive."

The two lovely almost-naked women washed and blow-dried the Pearloiner's hair and dressed her in a white shirt and a flattering navy-blue linen jacket. They left her naked down below.

"Now, Madame, you know what you must do," said Lila. She put the clitorises in the Pearloiner's open palms. "Cup their pussies and reinstate their joys. Only you can give back what you took away."

The Pearloiner cupped the women's crotches and jiggled her hands rapidly, saying, "By the power and the authority of the federal Transportation Security Administration, Eastern Region, HQ, I hereby give you back your clits and humbly ask your forgiveness for being so greedy to possess them."

"Oh, ooochie," moaned Zilka, feeling her tender stem reconnecting. Moments after, Cheyenne's clitoris went live. Her face cleared, and she beamed. "Finally!" she said.

"Now down on the pussyrug, you two," said Lila. "You must fix the repairs in place by gently grinding your gorgeous twats against each other."

Zilka and Cheyenne scissored themselves together and humped and ground, clit to blissfully reanimated clit.

"Sealing it with a crimson pussy kiss," said the Pearloiner, visibly moved.

Lila opened a drawer and pulled out a large smooth wooden dildo, which she handed to the Pearloiner. "Madame, put this handmade Dendro wherever you would like it to go," she said.

The Pearloiner threw her strong tanned legs open and steered the dildo deep into her fur. She shook her head. "It's good, but it's not what I need," she said. "I need live dick."

Lila pondered, then smiled. "Zilka, Cheyenne, take Madame P. to the pussywall and strap her so that her pussy and fanny are exposed for all to see. The last batch of Deprivos are arriving. They'll take care of her hungry twitchet."

"Oh!" said the Pearloiner, feeling ripples of arousal.

Shandee Goes to the Festival

Shandee got up late and wasn't sure what to do with herself. She walked through the Cockstorm Room blindfolded and held about seventy stiff and semi-stiff cocks. Then she washed her hands and sat for a while in a darkroom talking to a nice couple who ran a vegetarian restaurant. She went outside and had a sherry cobbler at the Sherry Cobbler and Farewell Festival. It was a fine end-of-summer day; the Garden of the Wholesome Delightful Fuckers was crowded with celebrants, and many brightly painted pedal-powered Masturboats were out on the White Lake. Luna and Chuck churned by, circling each other. There were screams and splashes from the pussysurfers.

As Shandee came closer to the dock and the tent, she heard Lila's loudspeakered voice announcing the handjob cumshot contest. She paused to watch a little of the proceedings. The contestants stood on a raised dais dressed in crotchless tuxedos, their arms tied at the wrists behind their backs, while Lila, pacing with her cordless microphone and her wild hair, urged on the strokers, who knelt in position beside or behind the cocks they stroked. Women who wanted to be jizz-splashed stood in the shallows of the lake wearing waders with blue butterflies painted on them, holding their mouths open, making beckoning gestures. "Okay, we're in the final ejaculatory launch window," Lila was saying to the cheering audience. "Our contestants must shoot hot sauce within the next ninety seconds. Lift your tops and show them your titties, my friends, floof out your hair, stick out your tongues, and let's get some nice moneyshots out of these bad beautiful cocks and these gorgeous sexy hardworking cockstrokers. Because, boy, are they at it! That's it, my lovely strokers, jack the big dicks off, work them, bring that cream to market, don't hold back, jack them harder, that's it, Trix, honey, jack Pendle off, come on, Jessica, closer, closer, really fast now, that's it, *wank those hunky spunk pipes!*" There were male groans of amplified pleasure. "And here goes Pendle first, oooh, lovingly stroked by the delightful Trix—well climaxed, you two, and let's hear it for the Heftyshot bathing suit that's down around Pendle's ankles!" Applause, followed by another moan and more airborne come-drops flying through the air. "And now our Kathy's got Ned launching—there it goes! And Hax, oh, my goodness, three big squirting jizz bombs from Hax, our tattoo master, smoothly cockstroked by Jessica—thank you, Hax and Jessica, with your beautiful smiles! And now comes Wade and Crackers, what a team—look at her fist fly on that eye-popping pink dick—ah, out it tosses!" More applause and cheering, and several women who'd been splashed jumped up and down flashing peace signs. Then there was a trumpeting noise. "And, oh dear, there goes Friggley, our pornmonster. Yeek, I don't even know what that was, pumped off by Rhumpa, the Pearloiner, Donna, and Polly, all together. Very good effort, women—not at all disgusting. Let's hear it for these resourceful jerkoff artists!" Lila turned and held a hand out. "And now—ah!—a tremendous sideways splash of semen from handsome Ruzty's banana dick. Has he, yes, he's taken the lead with a long arching slider. Ruzty's ahead now. But now, last but never least, here's Marcela, our dazzling heavy-dicked ladyboy, stroked by Dune. She's new to having a penis, and it's a biggie, and she has obviously taken to it in a major way. But she's almost out of time. Will she get there? Will she shoot? She's working her hips, she's almost—now"— suddenly an enormous "Graaaawh!" was ripped from Marcela's throat—"blowing a—whoa, shit!—a glorious spunkbomb of Elmer's goo from that prodigious transplasmic dick of hers! My gravy! Stroked by Dune, like the master cockjerking bad boy you are, Dune. Mwah, blow you both a kiss. An absolutely amazing cumshot by Marcela and Dune!" Zilka gave Lila a piece of paper with some numbers on it. "And the official results are in: I declare Marcela and Dune the winners of the Sherry Cobbler Handjob and Massive Cumshot Contest. But all you jizzblasters deserve a prize." More cheering, whistles.

Shandee applauded briefly and turned back toward her hotel. Sad about Ruzty, she thought. Maybe if she'd been stroking him he would have won. She got in bed and turned on a house-fix-up show and watched a man repair a screen door. She got Dave's arm out and fed him and changed his liquid wastes, and they lay together and looked at the ceiling fan. Dave's arm tweaked her nipple solicitously. She reached a moment of decision. "Come on, honey, let's go," she said.

Dave Gets His Old Cock Back

Shandee went to Dave's room, number 434, and knocked. There was no answer. "Probably out carousing," she said to Dave's arm. "Would you feel comfortable writing him a note?" Dave's hand took her pen and wrote this:

> Hey Dave, I'm not feeling too good. Shandee has been taking care of me and showing me some of her kind and loving ways, but I miss being attached to you and doing all the fun things we could do together. I want back on. Shandee will be in her room, 676, tonight after seven. Do not miss this opportunity. Signed, Your Arm.

Shandee folded the note and held Dave's arm as he slipped it under the door. They went back and took a nap together. At 7:15 there was a knock on the door.

Shandee straightened her skirt and checked her lipstick before she answered.

"Hi, I'm Dave," said Dave.

"Oh, hi, Dave," said Shandee, as nonchalantly as she could. "I've got your arm for you. I found it in a quarry." She kissed Dave's arm softly on the knuckles and handed him over, and as she did she took a slow second to look Dave up and down. He was wearing a soft nubbly greeny-gray shirt with the sleeves rolled up, and he needed a haircut. She saw his stump, which ended smoothly and tastefully just below his elbow, and she felt tender stirrings in her nethers.

Dave greeted his arm. "Hey there, dude," he said. "I'm sorry I left you in the lurch." He looked up at Shandee. "Thanks for taking care of him."

"I'm going to miss him a lot," said Shandee. "He's been nice to me—very caring, very responsible. Very sensual in the bedroom, may I add. A little jealous, which isn't a bad thing."

"No, I guess not," said Dave.

Shandee waved at the couch. "You want to sit down? I feel I know a lot about you. You look the way I thought you'd look, except you're taller."

"Well, you are quite stunningly, incredibly—damn!" Dave blushed at his enthusiasm.

"I would have gotten in touch before now," said Shandee, "but Lila said you were not ready to be reunited because then you'd have to say good-bye to your huge dick. I thought I'd see you onstage today at the festival."

Dave shrugged. "I kind of decided that being jacked off in front of hundreds of people wasn't my style."

"I understand," said Shandee.

They were quiet for a moment.

"I hope you've had some fun times here," said Dave.

"Oh, definitely. You?"

"I snuck off the reservation, did some crazy stuff. Spent more time in the old Porndecahedron than I care to admit." He breathed. "And now here we are."

"Here we are." Shandee smiled at him, loving his rueful intelligent eyes. Her vagina—or maybe it was her heart?—felt as if it weighed about eight pounds.

Dave's arm snapped its fingers impatiently.

"So," said Dave, "how do we do this?"

"Lila told me how," said Shandee. "I've been sleeping every night with the cloth of Ka-Chiang tucked in my pussyhole, so my juices have special healing powers."

"Oh, nice."

"Now all you have to do is, ah"—she lay back on her bed and pulled up her little denim skirt—"press your stump right here on my cunny." She pulled her panties to one side and pointed.

"I can do that," said Dave. "But could we maybe kiss a little bit first?"

Shandee nodded, and Dave knelt by the bed. She felt the full-on murflement of his enveloping kiss. Their tongues made friends; they'd known each other forever, it seemed. Shandee let her hand fall as if casually till it found the cocky thickness under his pants. She smoothed it over, feeling it swell, and he made a happy sound. Then he pushed his sleeve up higher and aimed his stump so it touched her gently between her legs—too gently.

"You can go ahead and grind it in," she said.

He ground it in. "Like that?"

"No, harder. You have to get it all wet. In other words, fuck me with your stump."

He pushed harder. "How about that?"

"Oh, god, aaah, whoa, fuck, that's far enough. Now tighten your biceps muscle so I can feel it jerk. Aaah! Good." She sat up and straightened her hair. "That should do it, yes, you're all moistened up now."

"Feels strange, a little like burning," said Dave.

"Now, quickly," said Shandee. Dave held out his glistening stump, and Shandee peeled off the cap on Dave's arm. She pushed the two ends together, and they joined, making a juicy sloomping sound. Dave was whole again.

He fell on the bed, clutching his elbow. "Eee, eee, eee!" he said. "Pins and needles, and thorns and burrs and shrapnel—ow! I can feel the bone knitting back together." Then, after the pain passed, he smiled, flexing his hand. "My arm is sending me up some vivid memories of touching your face," he said. "May I touch your face?"

"Mmm," said Shandee. She moved toward him and opened her mouth to be kissed again. But just at that moment there was a knock on the door. Zilka strode in, followed by Jason the bowl man, who held an enormous wooden bowl of his own fashioning, and Glenn the Australian wilderness photographer, and Betsy the beachgoer, and Lanasha the masseuse, and Daggett. Lanasha had a spray tank strapped to her back, and Daggett was carrying his bag of bras.

"We're the field unit for crotchal transfers," said Daggett.

"That was awfully fast, guys," said Dave. "You must have been waiting in the hall." He waved. "Hi, Glenn. I've enjoyed your dick very much."

Glenn, dressed in a blue button-down shirt and stone-colored chinos, looked pleased. "I've enjoyed yours," he said.

Daggett, his days as a Deprivo over, took charge. "Now everyone take off your clothes—let's just right off get crazy batshit naked, okay? If you women want a special bra, feel free. And I hope you will admire my new balls." They all admired Daggett's balls as they shucked off their clothing, and then Lanasha sprayed Glenn's genitals with the special plasmic transfer liquid from the tank on her back.

Daggett had more commands. "Shandee, if you would sit down in the bowl and make yourself comfortable, we can wash your pussy with the magic blue fluids. Jason, you could help by holding Shandee's legs apart. Spread her wide so Lanasha can spray all of her. Good. And Betsy, could you please suck on Glenn's cock till he's good and stiff?"

"I'll have to call my husband," said Betsy, dialing. "Hi, honey, I'm here with some important people, and they need me to prepare a cock for transfer. Is that okay with you? Probably have to suck on it a little. Well, it's sort of big, not quite as big as yours is. Great. Thanks, honey, I'll call you later, bye."

Betsy went to work. When Glenn's cock was good and stiff, he lay on the floor on his back. Dave, still in his pants, sat spread-eagled on a chair directly over Glenn's head. Shandee, her pussy ring-dinging like mad, got astride Glenn, and Betsy held Glenn's cock at the right angle.

"That pussy spray makes me sick horny," said Shandee. "When do I sit down on Glenn?"

"Right now, Shandee, fuck his pole. Betsy will help you guide it in. Soon you'll feel the plasmic cockmeat puree begin to move right through your body."

Shandee spiraled slowly down on Glenn's cock. "Ohhh, that feels so nice," she said.

"Thank you," said Glenn.

"And it's actually my cock down there, so thank you from me, as well," said Dave.

"Now Lanasha," said Daggett, "haul out Dave's current cock and give it a spray of the blue fluid and a good sprinkle of Bohu's beardwater, too."

Everyone politely suppressed a gasp at the massive rude cockitude of Dave's equipment as Lanasha unfolded it and shook it free from the confines of Dave's pants.

Shandee was mesmerized. She and Lanasha together worked their fists up and down on its length, and as their hands rose and fell, pulling the cockskin, Dave's mobile balls hopped up and down in their hairy handbag.

"Oh, my god, I've got so much dick going on here!" said Shandee.

"Keep fucking Glenn and meanwhile always suck and jack on Dave," said Daggett. "Keep the flow going."

Everyone went quiet, watching Shandee do her strenuous double service. She pulled up on and then slumped down on Glenn's rigid stonker, and she gave simultaneous attention to Dave's jaw-dropping mouthful of dickstick.

"Both genitals are going plasmic—they're about to flow," Daggett announced, wrapping a bra strap tightly around his balls. "Are you ready for the transfer? It'll happen fast."

Shandee nodded yes as her ass rose and fell, and then she involuntarily grunted as a huge molten mass of shifting sexmeat crissed and crossed through her body. She grabbed Dave's hips to steady herself and felt the enormity of the testosterodick travel from her mouth down through her middlemost uterine self and into Glenn's rapidly growing loinstem.

Dave's cock was still hard, but it was shrinking in girth and length. Shandee popped her head off of it for an instant, working it with her hands instead. "More and more of the dick is going down through me, oh, my god!" she said. She chewed one side of her cheek. "It's growing huge in my vagina! Oh, there's so much hot, bad ball-hopping dick in me now! Oh, this feels so good, oh, Dave, this dick! This dick! This dick! How can you possibly give up this massive dick, it feels so fucking full in my cunt canal, aaaaaaaaaaaaah, shit, shit, oh, shit, Glenn, unbelievable!"

She caught her breath for a moment and looked around the room. Daggett, balls a-waggle, was slamming himself into Lanasha, and Jason was doing Zilka. Betsy had her legs hooched and the beardwater sprayer-wand up her ass and was jiggling it lasciviously.

Suddenly, Glenn's orgasm slammed into gear, and he threw the first hot clot of a busted nutload of jizzling twizzlering sperm up inside her. Shandee let out a ragged joyous screamy cry of pure consummated cockfuckedfulness. Then she said to Dave, "Dave, I'm ready to tug you off onto my lips. Come on these lips, these Terranova lips that will always be true to you." She saw his eyes meet hers and felt both his hands—the one she knew and the one she didn't—hold her head. She said, "I'm going to jack off your beautiful real Dave cock onto my face now—oh, my god, it's never been this good." And suddenly Dave bucked in her hands, and she felt a Tuileries Garden of manly Dave-jizm leap onto her forehead and then again on her cheek and her neck. She was dripping with one perfect man's cockjuice, and she loved it so much that when Glenn touched her clit with his thumb she wonked down full force on his restored dickitude, and that was enough to start the Atlas-shrug shudderation of arrival that made her shiver her way through the seven, eight, nine, twelve seconds of worldwide interplanetary flux of orgasmic strobing happy unmatched tired coughing ebbing thrilled spent ecstasy.

Lila Says It's Almost Time to Go

Lila stood on the dais, her arms raised. "Thank you all for coming," she said. "I hope you'll be back next year." A deep foaming whirlpool had formed in the middle of the White Lake. Some of the guests were beginning to paddle their boats toward it. It was the group exit portal, and it made a distant roaring sound.

"One last event, though," Lila said. "Cardell, are you here? Will you please come up?"

Cardell leapt the three steps up to the stage.

"Is that an egg in your pocket, hon?"

"Yes, it is, as a matter of fact," Cardell said. "A silver egg. From my friend Jackie." He handed it to Lila, who set it down on a folded washcloth.

"Now let's let it hatch," said Lila. "The egg of love, ladies and gentlemen. Farewell."

The Silver Egg Hatches

Gallanos woke up curled in what he later found out was a small egg made of silver. Around him was a woman. Their heads were sometimes at opposite ends of the egg, and sometimes they stared at each other, blinking their silver luminous eyes. They floated in a shadowy fluid. They drank it, they breathed it. Their bodies were dull silver.

Gallanos seemed to have forgotten how to talk. He remembered that he'd had a former life—that there was a space for him somewhere that wasn't a silver person sharing an egg, but he had no details. He couldn't recollect what had happened.

The first time that she smiled was when they were both feeling especially cramped. Either the egg was getting smaller, or they were getting a little larger. They fell asleep, and when Gallanos woke his hand was cupping the silver chalice of her breast. He pulled it away, horrified that he'd been so forward, and bumped his elbow on the slippery curving wall of their enclosure.

And then she smiled and shrugged: Oh well, it can't be helped.

Gallanos opened his mouth and tried to make a sound. Nothing came out. They slept, and they breathed the glutinous liquid that gave them sustenance, and they slept some more, and sometimes they smiled and nodded and shrugged, and then gradually they developed a sort of language of gestures. They tapped to say "I'm going to sleep now, good night." And when they woke up they tapped and waved to say good morning.

Mellinnas was very concerned about her hair, which was marvelous fine silvery angel hair stuff that she moved and sometimes adroitly twisted into a small bun. He tapped her shoulder when she had arranged her hair especially well. They were never not touching. They lived inches away from each other, but they couldn't smell each other, and they couldn't talk.

And then one day they discovered kissing. Their lips found each other and smooched and lipped over each other and centered, and Gallanos couldn't believe how much Mellinnas was giving him with her soft metallic shiny perfect lips.

After a long day of kissing, Gallanos told her that he was going to go to sleep, and she bade him with her taps and looks that she was going to sleep, too. But that night he dreamed that she was wearing clothes and wasn't silver and that they were both in a bedroom, and she was unbuttoning her clothes and then she pulled his head down so that he could listen to her heart beating. He could smell her skin and hear her talking and telling him interesting facts using sound waves, and suddenly he felt an incredibly pleasurable dollop of liquid happiness traveling in his transmission bump. Then he woke and looked down and saw that his silver cock was much larger than normal and that it was sticking out at an angle from his body, though subsiding. He was alarmed, and he looked over at her, but her eyes were closed, and she was sleeping. Soon the stiffness went away, and he went back to sleep.

Then one day they were jostled greatly and thrown into confusion. They looked at each other with alarm; it was clear that their enclosure was being tossed around on some ocean or tumbled down some steep incline. There was a sudden sharp concussion and an inrush of blinding searing light, which poured in as their fluid suspension slowly leaked away. They lay cupped and sprawling in one half of a silver egg that had cracked apart. After a moment, they stood. Their hands found each other. They were a couple, newly hatched.

Loud sounds blossomed from enormous fleshy flushed faces, and Gallanos and Mellinnas were frightened. Moreover, their silver skin began to dry, and as it did they felt an almost unbearable warmth. They held on to each other tightly for protection but also because it soothed the burning of their acclimatizing skin. Gallanos's penis was swollen and hot, and it seemed almost without their knowing it to slide inside Mellinnas. Then they were tightly embraced, a writhing ball of silver. The huge faces came closer to watch, and the silver couple could hear enormous booming noises, which they later understood were speech. But all they could do was move together to try to adjust to the shock of being exposed to air.

Gallanos lay down on the surface of something hard and smooth, with a grain to it—the wooden tabletop—and his eggmate squashed herself to him and moved with amazing flexibility around and around on his molten twig. She opened her mouth, and he opened his, and then as feelings they hardly remembered gushed through them they pushed against the muteness of their throats until finally a series of small cries came out, strange uncertain sounds that increased in volume and pace until, as they reached the final throes of their lovemaking, they became groans of joy. The faces, watching, blinked and smiled. Gallanos and Mellinnas crawled onto a folded washcloth and fell asleep.